Anonymous

The British novelist

Virtue and vice in miniature

Anonymous

The British novelist
Virtue and vice in miniature

ISBN/EAN: 9783337126377

Printed in Europe, USA, Canada, Australia, Japan

Cover: Foto ©Andreas Hilbeck / pixelio.de

More available books at **www.hansebooks.com**

THE

BRITISH NOVELIST:

O R,

VIRTUE AND VICE

I N

MINIATURE;

· Confifting of a

VALUABLE COLLECTION

OF THE

BEST ENGLISH NOVELS,

Carefully felected from the WORKS of

Mrs. BEHN,	Mr. S. RICHARDSON,
GRIFFITHS,	Dr. SMOLLET,
LENOX,	Dr. CROXALL,
Mifs FIELDING,	Dr. JOHNSON,
Signior CERVANTES,	Mr. BROOKE,
Monf. LE SAGE,	Dr. GOLDSMITH, &c.
HENRY FIELDING, Efq.	&c. &c.

A N D

Other WRITERS, whofe NOVELS have been origi-
nally printed in or deemed worth tranflating into
the ENGLISH Language.

Faithfully abridged, fo as to contain all the SPIRIT
of the ORIGINALS.

The Whole forming a Complete LIBRARY of
NOVELS.

VOLUME the THIRD,

Containing the HISTORY of PAMELA, or VIRTUE RE-
WARDED; The HISTORY and ADVENTURES of PE-
REGRINE PICKLE; and The HISTORY of AMELIA.

LONDON:

Printed for J. FRENCH, No. 28, in the *Poultry.*

1774.

P A M E L A,

O R

VIRTUE REWARDED.

THIS novel is the firſt production of the late ingenious Mr. Samuel Richardſon, and is in every ſenſe of the word an original. But here it is neceſſary to conſider the leading ſentiments of the author, becauſe many others have written on a plan diametrically oppoſite. Novel-writing has but two things in view, namely, either to repreſent human nature as it is, or as it ſhould be. The laſt was what Mr. Richardſon had in view, when he wrote this as well as the reſt of his celebrated novels, that have made ſuch a diſtinguiſhing figure in the republic of letters, and have been tranſlated into moſt of the European languages. His opinion was that vice ſhould be repreſented as a deformed thing, but

B virtue

virtue as a free voluntary act of the mind. That the firft fhould appear embarraffed with that conftraint which natural confequence lays on the mind, but that the fecond fhould, in all its operations, flow fpontaneoufly from an unadulterated mind, and terminate in happinefs. We have here an inftance of a young woman born of mean parents, whofe circumftances were fuch that they could not afford to keep her any longer at home than fhe was fit for fervice. Accordingly they prevailed upon a lady of fincerity and benevolence to take her into her fervice in the moft humble ftation, where fhe behaved with fo much modefty that fhe was in confequence thereof married to the lady's fon, and fo became a woman of quality.

PAMELA ANDREWS was the daughter of John and Elizabeth Andrews, (or at leaft reputed fo) who lived in a fmall village in the Weft of England, and who, by pinching themfelves more than they were already by the narrownefs of their circumftances, got her taught to read and write. When fhe was grown up to the age of fixteen, a lady who lived in the fame neighbourhood, and to whom the manor belonged, took her into her fervice, and granted her all thofe little indulgencies that are fo agreeable to youthful minds.

Pamela did every thing to render herfelf worthy of fuch indulgences, but before fhe had been long in her fervice the lady died and left a fmall legacy. This was extremely agreeable to Pamela,

mela, who tied the money up in a bag ; but
when fhe began to reflect that fhe would be
obliged to return to her parents, who were not
able to fupport her, her mind was filled with
gref, and fhe wifhed ftill for fome ftate of fervi-
tude. While fhe was writing the letter to her
parents, with an account of the death of her
good lady, her young mafter, the 'fquire, came
in, and wanting to fee it, told her fhe could
write and fpeak very well, which put her fo
much to the blufh that fhe was unable to make
any anfwer, but went out of the room.

Her parents, in feveral letters that they had
fent to her, warned her to be on her guard, and
not liften to the moft alluring or lavifh promifes
that would tend towards promoting her ruin. In
the fame houfe with Pamela was an aged woman,
who had long ferved the family, and had acquired a large fhare of prudence. Her name
was Mrs. Jarvis, and fhe took every opportunity
of inftructing Pamela, not only in domeftic duties, but alfo in every thing that could be of fervice to her in the world. Her young mafter
made her a prefent of a great number of rich
clothes belonging to his deceafed mother, both
filks and laces, with a promife that he would
fee that fome perfon fhould be paid for altering
them ; but when fhe fent an account of thefe
things to her parents, they cautioned her againft
pride, or being too forward in receiving prefents.
She had fome thoughts of leaving her mafter
and going to live with Lady Davers, his fifter,
but no fooner had fhe fignified her refolution
for that purpofe, than the young gentleman
difcovered the true fentiments of his mind. He

told

told her, if she would confent to live with him as his miftrefs, he would make her fortune, and then he proceeded to fome indecencies. The girl flung away from him, and good Mrs. Jarvis who had heard the danger she was in, took her to lay along with her.

Next day the young gentleman renewed his attacks on her virtue, but she repulfed them all, and told her friend Mrs. Jarvis that she had refolved to go away from the houfe. But nothing could fet bounds to his paffions, for he infifted that she should not go away, and even threatened poor Mrs. Jarvis for being fo very affidious in taking her part. Mrs. Jarvis, however, was not in the leaft intimidated, but told him, that as she was an innocent young creature, fo it would be the greateft fin in the world to do her any injury.

Thefe freedoms taken by the mafter did not pafs unnoticed by the reft of the fervants, and fome of them began to whifper that she was either his miftrefs, or that he intended to marry her. This gave her fo much uneafinefs that she told Mrs. Jarvis, who anfwered that it was not impoffible but her mafter might intend to make her his wife, but ftill cautioned her to be on her guard. Pamela, who was all virtue, began to fee her danger, and refolving not to expofe herfelf any longer, bought fome plain ftuff of a farmer's wife, and having got fome decent linen, she made it up into fmocks: she then bought fome plain caps, with a neat round ftraw hat, all which she intended to make ufe of in order to depart from the houfe in the moft private manner.

Next

Next day fome gentlemen and ladies came to dine at the houfe, and fome of them took notice that Pamela was too handfome to live in the fame houfe with her mafter. They knew his amorous difpofition; and this made the poor girl more unhappy than ever. Dinner being over fhe went up ftairs to try on her new drefs, which pleafed her fo much that fhe went down ftairs to fhew it to Mrs. Jarvis. While fhe was with the good old woman, her mafter came in, and fo charmed was he with her innocent appearance that he could not refrain from kiffing her. At laft fhe got away from him, but next morning when fhe came into Mrs. Jarvis's apartment, he had unknown to the good old woman, concealed himfelf behind a fkreen. Putting off her fhoes fhe fat down on the bed, and entered into a long converfation with Mrs. Jarvis, but before fhe had time to finifh it, her mafter rufhed from behind the fkreen, and fhe was fo much frightened that fhe fell into fits. Mrs. Jarvis took proper care of her, and put her to bed, where fhe remained till next morning, when fhe got up and was again met by her mafter, who promifed that he would never give her any offence for the future. This, however, did not fatisfy her, for fhe fpoke to one of the neighbouring fervants to affift her in making her efcape. Mrs. Jarvis, who was afraid that fome mifchief would happen, propofed going along with her, but her mafter told her fhe had been fo long in the family that he could not part with her.

In the mean time the gentleman attacked the amiable Pamela in a more tender manner than ever, but with as little fuccefs. He knew that

her

her parents were poor, that she loved them dear-ly, and .constantly sent them what money she could spare; he therefore told her that if she would be a good girl, and stay with him, he would provide for all her family. She trembled at the proposal, and well knowing that if she consented it must be at the expence of her virtue, she leant a deaf ear to all his promises and entreaties. He then told her that the chariot should be ready to carry her home next day, but he had no such intentions, for having resolved to seduce her one way or other, he employed his coachman, who, under pretence of carrying her home to her parents was to take her to an estate that he had in Lincolnshire. Accordingly the perfidious coachman carried her five miles on the road leading to her father's, but then turning out of the road with which she was but little acquainted, he drove on till he came to the mansion-house in Lincolnshire. The person whom he she had employed to carry her letters to her father had been bribed by her master, so that her poor parents knew nothing of all this.

It was necessary that the gentleman should make some apology for his conduct in the best manner he could, so he wrote a letter to the father of Pamela, telling him that his daughter was such an intriguing girl that he had sent her out of the way, in order to prevent her from asperfing his character. It is impossible to express what the poor old man felt when he read this letter, he burst into tears, and next day he set out on foot for the house of the 'squire. When he arrived at the place, some of the servants knew him, and told him that his daughter was gone

home ;

home; for indeed they did not know any thing to the contrary. As he had some reason to doubt, the truth of what they said, he desired to speak with Mrs. Jarvis, who received him in a proper manner, and could not help shedding tears when she read the 'squire's letter. She told him that she was utterly ignorant of any design that he had in taking her away; upon which he desired to be admitted to the 'squire. He asked him, in the most earnest manner, with tears flowing from his eyes, what had become of his daughter; but all the answer that he received was, that she was safe, and waiting on the lady of a bishop, who would take proper care of her. He then ordered Mrs. Jarvis to give him two guineas to bear his expences home, upon which, that good woman asked him to dine with her in her own apartment.

The poor old man gave some ease to his mind in tears, and, taking leave of Mrs. Jarvis, returned home, with a heavy disconsolate heart. In the mean time an unknown servant brought a letter from Pamela, to Mrs. Jarvis, informing her, that the coachman had betrayed her, by taking her to a strange place, where she had never been before. Mrs. Jarvis, as well as the rest of the servants, made all the enquiry they could in order to find out what was become of the lovely girl, but all to no purpose, the more they enquired the more they were in darkness. The poor father returned home to his disconsolate wife, whom he found drowned in tears. But, alas! he could not give her any consolation. He had done all he could to recover his

lost

loft child, but to no purpofe, fo that he could only fympathize with his diftreffed fpoufe. They both put their truft in Divine Providence, and prayed. that God would be gracioufly pleafed to' preferve her from every injury. The fervants were equally concerned for her fafety, and even thofe who envied her before, began to look upon her as an object of pity ; fo different are we in our common apprehenfion of things, and fo contradictory to what we too often profefs to be our leading fentiments. We are apt to find fault with thofe whom we look on as favourites to perfons in high life, but no fooner do we fee them in diftrefs, than our hearts relent, and we forgive all thofe trifles that before gave us offence.

Her mafter, who had plotted this artful fcheme, ordered the wife and daughter of a farmer, to attend her, and in the mean time wrote to her a letter, wherein he affured her, that he was fo mad with love, that he could not help acting in the manner he did, but that if fhe would comply with his defires, he would make her fortune for ever. He wrote to the farmer at the fame time, telling him that Pamela was a young lady, who was deeply engaged in love affairs, and that he had fent her there to prevent her being ruined. The farmer believed the whole ftory, and next morning the chariot came and conveyed her to a public inn on the road, where fhe was met by Mrs. Jewkes, an infamous woman, who lived by being a procurefs for the fquire. Pamela, who had heard the character of this woman, was much frightened, when fhe made her appearance, and being obliged to get into the chariot with her, they arrived in the evening at an old caftle belonging .

longing to the fquire. As the poor young creature was now convinced that her ruin was intended, fhe refolved to put her truft in divine
providence. She turned to the coachman, and
told him that he had now done his part, and as
for Mrs. Jewkes, fhe might do her's. Mrs.
Jewkes nettled to think that a young girl fhould
lecture her in that manner, told her that fhe did
not know what fhe meant, but for her own part
fhe would ferve the fquire as far as fhe could.
In this difconfolate manner, Pamela continued
till Sunday, when fhe afked leave to go to church,
but that favour was denied her, though Mr. Williams, the curate pleaded hard in her favour.
She would have gone by force, but the fervants
were called in, and ordered to pull off her fhoes.
On the evening of the fame day, the footman,
who had betrayed her by concealing her letters
from her parents, arrived at the hall, and before
he departed, took care to write an acknowledg-
ment of his guilt, which he dropped at the door
of Pamela's apartment. She was fhocked when
fhe faw the letter, at the depravity of human
nature, and could fcarce believe that fhe had been
fo long impofed on. Mr. Williams, the curate,
was admitted to vifit Pamela, and one day as they
were walking in the garden, fhe propofed that as
two tiles happened to lay on a bed of flowers, fo
they might correfpond together, by putting loofe
papers under them. Mr. Williams agreed to the
propofal, for he had a key that let him in at any
time, by a back door near where the flower-bed
was. In the mean time, the artful Mrs. Jewkes
came up to them, which put an end to their converfation for that time.

For the future, one of the servant maids was ordered to attend her, when she went to the garden ; but one day, having wrote a letter for Mr. Williams, she purposely dropped her pocket-book, and when she came to the place where the letter was to be left, she told the girl to bring it to her. In the mean time she slipped the letter under the tile, without being so much as perceived. As she doubted not but Mr. Williams would write her an answer, she attempted to get down by herself into the garden, but the artful Mrs. Jewkes followed her, and a smart dialogue ensued between them. Pamela, who was now convinced that her ruin was determined on, called Mrs. Jewkes, Jezebel, which exasperated her so much, that she struck her a violent blow on the shoulder, and then hurried her into the house. There she was locked up during the whole of the night, but next morning a little more indulgence being allowed her, Mrs. Jewkes consented to walk with her into the garden. As they were walking along, Pamela told Mrs. Jewkes, that she wanted a cucumber, and the other stepping forward a little to call the gardner, Pamela snapped up the letter from Mr. Williams, without being noticed. When she had got home to her closet, she read the letter, and found that the good gentleman sympathized with her. He told her that he would come regularly to the place for her letters, but advised her to be extremely cautious. In answer, she returned him a thousand thanks, but had much difficulty in delivering her letters. She and Mrs. Jewkes went out to angle in the fish-pond, and Pamela caught a carp, but immediately gave it its liberty, declaring that its case was

similar

similar to her own. Mrs. Jewkes was surprised, and taking the rod in her hand, Pamela embraced that opportunity of depositing her letter under the tile, covered with a handful of horse-beans. Pamela had about six pounds in money in her pocket, with which she intended to make her escape, and Mrs. Jewkes having some suspicion of her intention, told her that she had a bill to pay to a tradesman, amounting to eight pounds, and Pamela not imagining her craft, lent her the money. When she complained, the wicked woman only laughted at her, and told her that her money was safe, and that she had taken it from her, in order to prevent her making a bad use of it. This was done, in consequence of a letter she had received from the squire, accompanied with another to Pamela, wherein he declared that he would not wait on her without her permission. This made her more afflicted than ever, especially as the very next day, she received a note from Mr. Williams, informing her that their correspondence began to be suspected, or at least that he imagined so. He had spoken in her favour to a lady who wanted a servant, but the proposal did not succeed. In the mean time, Mrs. Jewkes watched her so closely, that she could not converse with any one, but an old clergyman, whose living had been promised to Mr. Williams, happening to die, Mrs Jewkes sent for him, to congratulate him on his good fortune. The truth is, Mr. Williams was really in love with Pamela, and Mrs. Jewkes could not help taking notice of it, but that did not put an end to their correspondence. Nay, even Mrs. Jewkes herself, in consequence of instructions
from

from her mafter, pretended to give every encouragement to Mr. Williams, telling him that fhe
would procure him Pamela for a wife. A report
had been induftriously fpread, that Mr. Williams
had been robbed, and otherwife fo ill ufed, that
his life was in danger, which affected Pamela fo
much, that fhe gave herfelf up to melancholy.
Mrs. Jewkes, in order to carry on her fcheme
with the greateft facility, pretended to be much
concerned for Mr. Williams, and going on a vifit
to him, returned, and told Pamela that he was
not in any danger, for he had only received a few
fcratches on his face. This, however, was no
more than an artifice, in order to conceal her real
defign, but that was impoffible, for the next time
that Mr. Williams came to the houfe, fhe behaved to him with great referve, upon which he
afked her, whether he had ever given her any
offence. He did not, however, receive any other
anfwer, but that fhe had her reafons, which he
would know in proper time. The poor clergyman was obliged to retire, and foon after he was
gone, Pamela happened to go into Mrs. Jewkes's
apartments, where fhe found fome letters from
her mafter, which left her no reafon to doubt
what were his real intentions. The poor girl
gave herfelf up to defpair, nor was it poffible to
comfort her, although Mrs. Jewkes brought in a
vagabond Frenchman for that purpofe, and to
complete her misfortune, fhe heard next day
that Mr. Williams was arrefted, and taken to
Stamford gaol. This fcheme had been contrived
by Mrs. Jewkes, and the Frenchman, in order
to feize the papers of Mr. Williams, to difcover
the nature of the correfpondence that had been
carried on between him and Pamela. As no time

was

was to be loft, she got up one night juft as the clock ftruck twelve, and having with much difficulty made her way through a fmall window, let herfelf down upon the leads, and from thence into the garden. Her defign was to have let herfelf out at the garden door, for which purpofe she had got the key from Mr. Williams, but when she came there, she found that the lock had been altered. She then attempted to get over the wall, but juft as she had laid hold of the upper part, the bricks gave way, and she once more found her whole fcheme fruftrated. Self-murder now feemed the only means that she could ufe, in order to put an end to her miferies, but the fear of offending God got the better of her refolution, fo that she fpent the remainder of the night, under the moft agonizing tortures of mind.

In the morning Mrs. Jewkes arofe, and going into Pamela's apartment, found her gone, fo that the whole of the fervants were alarmed. It was not doubted but she had made her efcape, and each went different ways in purfuit of her, till at laft she was found in the wood-houfe by one of the maids. The girl run to inform her fellow fervants, who coming to the place, carried Pamela home to the houfe, and lodged her in her own apartment, where she flept till the clock ftruck twelve, and then got up, in order to get fome refrefhment. For feveral days she continued in a violent fever, but that having at laft fubfided, Mrs. Jewkes indulged her with a ride in the coach, telling her that her mafter would be there in a few days, and make every thing eafy to her. At laft, her mafter arrived, and fent up word, that he would fup with her; but fcarce
had

had he entered her room, than she fainted away, and lay for some time motionless on the floor. When she had recovered a little, her master told her that she was a wicked girl to put him to so much trouble, after he had relieved her parents, and was willing to provide for her. He proposed written articles to her upon what footing she was to be his kept mistress, but she rejected them with disdain, and told him rather than comply with his request, she would lose her life. She represented to him the great sin he was attempting to commit, and at the same time asked him, whether it would redound to his honour to ruin a poor innocent girl. To all this he made no answer, but suffered her to retire, upon which she told Mrs. Jewkes that she would not that night go to bed. Next day her master went to dine at the house of a neighbouring gentleman, so that she had some little respite, only that the odious Mrs. Jewkes still continued to teaze her. That no imputation might lay upon her character, she repeated to Mrs. Jewkes all the particulars of her life, concluding, by telling her, that she had lived in a state of innocence sixteen years, and that she would not now change her conduct.

For that night she was suffered to go to bed, but in the morning her master, attended by Mrs. Jewkes, came into her apartment, in order to complete the horrid scheme they had projected. The 'Squire was dressed in woman's cloaths, but no sooner did he come up to Pamela's bed, than he began to use such indecent freedom, that she soon discovered what he was. The distress in which Pamela was, made her use every expression to induce him to withdraw, upon which he uttered

tered feveral bitter imprecations upon himfelf that he had never intended her the leaft injury. Another attempt was made on her, but fhe was fo much overpowered that fhe was obliged to be put to bed, where fhe remained feveral days in a violent fever. The goodnefs of her conftitution at laft got the better of her diforder, and then the fame practices were renewed, and pufhed on with greater vigour than ever. No appearance of redrefs now prefented itfelf, and Pamela gave herfelf up for loft. She had no other refource but in her conftant reliance on Divine Providence. She knew that her caufe was good, that fhe was expofed to the arts of a defigning man, and therefore whatever fhould happen to her, fhe was determined to lofe her life, rather than do any thing inconfiftent with her virtue.

The 'fquire, under pretence of going to Stamford, ordered Pamela to be more clofely confined than ever, and fuch of the fervants as were fufpected of favouring her efcape, were turned away. Soon after breakfaft, a gypfey came up to the gate, and offered to tell all their fortunes, and although Pamela did not much like fuch fort of perfons, yet fhe confented, having fome hopes that the woman was bringing a letter. The gypfey told Mrs. Jewkes that fhe would be married foon to a hufband younger than herfelf, but Nan, one of the fervants who attended, was to be drowned. As for Pamela, the gypfey looking at her hand, faid it was too fair for her to fee the lines, fo that fhe rubbed it with grafs. She then told her that fhe would never be married, but fhe would die of her firft child, upon which Pamela faid, fhe had now had enough of fortune-telling.

telling. The gipſey upon that returned, and Mrs. Jewkes ſeeing a man lurking about, called down ſome of the ſervants to demand what was his buſineſs. This circumſtance afforded Pamela an opportunity of examining the grafs where the gypſey ſtood, and there ſhe found a flip of paper, which ſhe put into her boſom, and went to her cloſet to read it. It was written in an unknown hand, cautioning her to be on her guard, for a fellow who had been once an attorney, was to perſonate a miniſter, in order to marry her and the 'ſquire. The writer deſcribed this fellow ſo exactly, that there was not the leaſt fear of her miſtaking him. The 'ſquire, who had not been at Stamford, but only at the houſe of an ac-quaintance, returned the ſame day towards even-ing, and Mrs. Jewkes having ſeized all Pamela's papers, carried them to her maſter. It was then that he diſcovered that ſhe correſponded with Mr. Williams, and interrogated her very ſeverely on that ſubject. All the anſwer ſhe made him was, that ſhe had no thoughts of marriage, and that ſhe only deſired to be at home with her parents. Her maſter ſpoke in the ſevereſt terms of poor Mr. Williams, and from ſeveral of his expref-ſions, it appeared that he intended his ruin. Pa-mela was ordered to tell if ſhe had any other papers, and being weary of her cloſe confinement, ſhe anſwered, that ſhe would deliver up all ſhe had. Accordingly, ſhe went up ſtairs to undreſs herſelf, and taking the concealed letters out of the lining of an old petticoat, tied them up, and then ſat down to write a letter to her maſter. She informed him, that her confinement was become ſo miſerable to her, that ſhe could not bear it any longer,

longer, and begged in the moſt ſerious manner, that he would releaſe her. She put him in mind of his duty to God, and begged that he would not add one ſin to another.

The next ſcheme was to take her to a ſmall village, under a ſecond pretence of carrying her home to her father's, but in reality with another deſign. The chariot ſet off from the village next morning, at which time Pamela received a letter from her maſter, telling her that every thing belonging to her, ſhould be ſent home to her father's, adding, that he would ever regard her in the moſt affectionate manner. About noon they ſtopped at an inn, kept by Mrs. Jewkes's ſiſter, where they had ſcarce dined, when one of the ſervants came up on horſeback with another letter from his maſter to Pamela, telling her that if ſhe would return to his houſe in a voluntary manner, no injury ſhould be done her, but if not, ſhe might continue on her journey to her father's. This had ſo much effect on her mind, that ſhe complied with his requeſt, and towards evening, they arrived within twelve miles of the 'ſquire's houſe. There the coachman propoſed ſtaying all night, but as Pamela did not chuſe to lodge on the road, if ſhe could poſſibly avoid it, told the coachman that he might continue on his journey, and about one in the morning they arrived at the houſe. She found herſelf very much fatigued, and her maſter had been all day confined to his bed with a ſlight indiſpoſition. Next morning ſhe went to pay her dutiful reſpects to her maſter, who received her with great kindneſs, and to'd her that he had ordered Mr. Williams to be ſet at liberty, and that he was then keeping his ſchool as ufual, but at the fame time defired her not to fee him. Lady Davers, fifter to the 'fquire, fent her brother a letter, telling him that fhe had been informed that he had ran away with a common fervant wench, to the utter difgrace of his family. This letter the 'fquire gave to Pamela, who carried it to her chamber, and having read it, could not help reflecting on the vanity of thofe poor worms of pride, who have nothing to recommend them befides their titles, fome of which had been purchafed with the wages of iniquity, and others ftained with the moft aggravated crimes. Next day the 'fquire being a little better, propofed taking an airing in the coach, and took Pamela along with him. He was all kindnefs, and pretended that he had never given Mrs. Jewkes orders to ufe her with cruelty, and that as he was determined to part with that wicked woman, he would employ our young heroine to fuperintend the affairs of his family. In anfwer to this, fhe told him that nothing would give her greater pleafure than to obey his orders in every thing, confiftent with her duty, but at the fame time fhe added, that fhe muft never be fo far engaged, as to neglect attending on the worfhip of God, either private or public.

Her mafter was, or at leaft pretended to be, charmed with her good fenfe and the judicious remarks that fhe made on every circumftance, and fhe being encouraged by his behaviour, fhewed him the letter that had been fent her wherein the account of the fham marriage was mentioned. He was fo artful that he told her he had actually formed fuch a fcheme, but he had fince relented, and would never for the future think of any thing

thing of that kind. About two in the afternoon the chariot came up to the gate, and the
fquire having conducted Pamela into the parlour,
he fent for Mrs. Jewkes, and told her that Pamela muft not be ufed for the future in the manner fhe had too long been. Mrs. Jewkes pretended to afk pardon, and Pamela who could not
bear to harbour refentment, told her that fhe
freely forgave her. The next morning the fquire
came to her apartment and propofed marriage to
Pamela, and at the fame time told her that it
would be beft to have the ceremony performed
in private. Pamela anfwered, that as it was a
holy ceremony, fo it ought to be performed in a
holy place. He then told her that he had an
old chapel that had been built by his great grand-
father, and that as it had been ufed feveral years
for a lumber room he would have it cleaned out
for that purpofe. This, however, was what fhe
refufed to comply with, and in the mean time
a fervant arrived from her parents and told her
that they were almoft dead with grief on her account. This difconcerted the fquire's fcheme,
and therefore he was obliged to have recourfe
to new inventions. He pretended to have fome
bufinefs to tranfact, and going out in the chariot
returned in the evening and told Pamela that he
had feen Mr. Williams, and had had feveral
hours converfation with him. He added, that
Mr. Williams had faid every thing in her favour, and being determined not to delay his
happinefs any longer, he had given orders for
every thing to be got ready for the nuptials. In
the mean time he fent invitations to fome perfons to come and vifit him, but their behaviour
was

was fo fhocking to Pamela that fhe began to
doubt they were very different from what they
pretended; for the fquire had reprefented them
as perfons of the higheft rank. When dinner
was over, the ladies invited Pamela to the garden to walk with them, but ftill fhe had not
much pleafure in their company. The fquire
whifpering, told her that Mr. Williams was
waiting to fpeak with her, but how great was
her furprize when inftead of Mr. Williams fhe
met with her aged father, who had at laft difcovered the place of her confinement.

The fquire treated the old man with fo much
refpect that he was overpowered with joy, and
fcarce knew what to do or fay. He told him
that he was going to make Pamela his wife, and
that one day next week was fixed for the nuptials. The next morning the good old man got
up betimes to walk in the garden, where he was
foon joined by Pamela, and in lefs than an hour
afterwards by the fquire. After walking fometime and converfing on indifferent fubjects they
went home to breakfaft, and it being a fine day
the fquire propofed that they fhould all take an
airing in the coach. The old man would have
excufed himfelf on account of the meannefs of
his apparel, but nothing would fatisfy the fquire,
who ftill infifted on his company although he
knew that he would be laughed at. After the
coach had drove about two miles from the houfe,
they met Mr. Williams riding by the fide of a
brook, for nothing is fo pleafing to a virtuous
mind as folitude. Pamela could not help wifhing
to fpeak with him whom fhe looked upon as
an honour to the chriftian religion, and her requeft

queft was permitted by the 'fquire. After the mutual compliments were over fhe told her father that Mr. Williams was the clergyman who had treated her with fo much civility, upon which tears of joy ran down from the old man's eyes. The 'fquire treated Mr. Williams with fo much feeming kindnefs that the poor young divine began to imagine that all his fears were over, and beftowed a thoufand bleffings on his generous benefactor. The 'fquire took them to fee his little chapel, upon which after Mr. Williams had furveyed it in the moft attentive manner, he told him he would go home and prepare a difcourfe to preach next day. This requeft was granted, and next day being Sunday, the father of Pamela was dreffed in fine cloaths, and the gentry who had been there at the time when he arrived, were all ready to meet the company at the chapel. Mr. Williams preached a moft excellent difcourfe on liberality, and the public devotions of the church were performed with folemn decency fuitable to the majefty of that God to whom they were addreffed. In the afternoon they had only prayers, for the 'fquire faid that one fermon was enough in a day. Service being over they retired home to tea, after which they went to walk in the garden, and nothing but good humour was to be feen among them, for the 'fquire and his company contrived every thing to pleafe Pamela and her father.

The Frenchman whom we have already mentioned, arrived on Monday with a licence, and the 'fquire propofed that they fhould be married the next day, but Pamela would not confent that it fhould be any fooner than Thurfday. The

'fquire

'fquire was a good-deal difpleafed, but not chufing to lofe the favourite object, he diffembled his refentment, and went out for the day with one of his fervants. In the evening he returned, and being in feeming good humour, told Pamela that he did not chufe Mr. Williams fhould marry them, left he fhould be too much fhocked; to all which the lovely maid confented. But at laft, the ceremony was performed in the moft private manner by Mr. Williams, contrary to expectation, and next day fhe wrote to her parents that no perfon could be more indulgent to her than her hufband. It is in a manner impoffible to exprefs the kindnefs he fhewed her for feveral days, and having invited the fame gentry who formerly vifited at the houfe, the ladies began to whifper to each other, that there had been a ftolen match. Pamela blufhed, upon which the ladies wifhed her much joy, and fhe not fufpecting any mifchief, retired for that night to reft. In the morning the 'fquire got up, under pretence of his being obliged to vifit a gentleman, who was lying fick, and as he did not return foon enough in the evening, Mrs. Jewkes offered to lay with Pamela. To this fhe objected, telling her fhe would rather lay alone. In the morning, no news arriving concerning the 'fquire, Pamela went to breakfaft with Mrs. Jewkes, and foon after fhe received a letter from him, dated to her in her maiden name, telling her that his friend was fo bad, that he could not come for a few days. This was very uncomfortable news to one who loved fo tenderly as Pamela, but fhe was foon mortified in a more fenfible manner. Lady Davers, with her fon, a young giddy coxcomb, who had heard of the

the whole affair, came to the houfe about noon, and ordered the wench Pamela to come into her prefence. Pamela, though fhe expeƈted to be called by another name, yet confented, and as foon as fhe came into the parlour, the lady treated her with the utmoſt contempt. She told her fhe was a young faucy ſlut, whom her brother kept as a miſtrefs,. but fhe would take care that fhe fhould be fent home to her parents. Pamela could not help burfting into tears, but at the fame time told the lady that fhe had not been criminal, for fhe was married by a licence according to the fervice of the church. This was received with a loud laugh, and Pamela was given to underſtand that fhe had been impofed on.

Innocence always fpeaks in defence of itfelf, or rather it has no reafon for vindication. Pamela told the lady, that fhe was to dine at the houſe of a neighbouring gentleman, and ordering the chariot to be got ready, fet out and arrived juſt as the company were fitting down to dinner; they all made her extremely welcome, and juft at that inſtant the 'fquire came in. He embraced Pamela, and told her he was forry that he could not come fooner, but when fhe told him in what manner his fifter had ufed her, he feemed very much difpleafed, wifhing he had been then at home. At fupper, Pamela being obliged to repeat every thing that happened between her and Lady Davers, the whole company declared that fhe had been ufed extremely ill, and the 'fquire faid that his fifter had always been an infolent woman, but he would make her acknowledge her fault. When fupper was over, the 'fquire and Pamela got into the chariot and returned home about twelve at night,

night, when they were informed that Lady Davers was gone to bed an hour before. The 'fquire afked feveral queftions of Mrs. Jewkes, who fcarce knew what anfwer to make, and at laft they retired to bed. In the morning they were both awaked by a violent rapping at the door, and the 'fquire getting up found it was his fifter. Lady Davers flew into a violent paffion, and calling in her fervants, told them to take notice that the young harlot was in bed. The 'fquire pretending to be vexed, took her up in his arms, carried her to her own chamber, after which he returned to Pamela, and told her not to make herfelf in the leaft uneafy, for his fifter had always been a woman of a moft unhappy temper. At noon, the 'fquire returned, and told her to come down to dinner, adding, that fhe muft not mind his fifter, upon which fhe complied, and having dreffed herfelf, came down to the parlour. She had fcarce taken her feat, when fhe heard a violent difpute between the 'fquire and Lady Davers, and as fhe was afraid fome mifchief would happen, fhe went out, and begged that the lady might be forgiven for any expreffions that fhe had ufed to her difadvantage. This put the lady into a moft violent paffion, fhe could not fet any bounds to her rage, and turning to Pamela, called her infolent creature. She added, that fhe did not defire to employ fuch advocates as her to plead in vindication of her conduct, as fhe was no more than a common ftrumpet, whom her brother kept in the houfe. She concluded, by telling her brother that fhe would expofe him to all his relations, nor would fhe ever reft till

fhe

she had seen the insolent creature driven away from the family, to which she was a disgrace.

Pamela, who could not bear to see the lady in such a rage, retired to the parlour, and listened to hear what they were saying. The lady insisted to know if they were married, and being answered in the affirmative, declared she would not believe him, unless he swore. He told her he would humour her for once, and then swearing a most solemn oath, declared they were married. He added, that they were married in his own chapel by Mr. Williams, upon which she burst into a flood of tears, and told him that he had brought a dishonour on his family. The 'squire endeavoured to convince her of the propriety of his conduct, by mentioning several instances, wherein many persons of the highest rank had married women merely on account of their merit. He concluded, by telling her that the burial service would level all distinctions, and then no difference would be known. Nothing, however, could pacify the lady, for she declared that she would that moment call her coach, and set out. It was with the utmost difficulty that she could be prevailed upon to stay dinner, but during the whole time that she sat at table, she was so much out of temper, that she scarce knew by what names to call poor Pamela. She called her brother a murderer, upon which he told Pamela, that while he was at college, he had an affair of honour, but now he sincerely repented of his folly. After some conversation, Lady Davers was brought into seeming good humour, and condescended to speak with Pamela, as her sister, upon which the latter said all she could to

reconcile

reconcile her to the 'fquire. This feemed, however, to give fome offence to the 'fquire, who
told Pamela that fhe demeaned herfelf, by taking
the part of his fifter, and at the fame time propofed fetting out for his feat in Bedfordfhire,
leaving her behind till his return. In the mean
time he took his fifter out on an airing in the
coach, and about ten in the evening returned in
the beft humour imaginable. Lady Davers told
Pamela that fhe was quite reconciled to the match,
and after treating her with the utmoft civility,
retired for that night to her apartmentt. The
'fquire took the opportunity of her abfence to
make Pamela acquainted with the methods he had
ufed, in order to bring her over to the voice of
reafon, and he was happy that his endeavours had
been attended with the defired fuccefs. He then
told Pamela, that he was of a ftrange temper, but
fhe muft endeavour to bear with it on all occafions, and humour him, fo as to make him
happy.

In the morning Pamela got up at her ufual
time, and went to vifit Lady Davers, who received her in the moft complaifant manner, and
afked her a thoufand queftions with refpect to her
marriage. Pamela anfwered her in the moft
fimple manner, not imagining that any mifchief
was hatching againft her, and concluded, by
telling her that her brother had given her a lift of
rules to be obferved in her conduct, which although hard, fhe fhould obey them rather than
put him to one moment's uneafinefs. It was
then propofed that Lady Davers fhould accompany them to the houfe in Bedfordfhire, which
fhe confented to do, and next day the coach
brought

brought them to the place. Pamela was over-joyed to find Mrs. Jarvis and all the old fervants at the houfe, and clafping the good woman in her arms, told her that fhe had had a happy reverfe of fortune, for now all her troubles were over. All the fervants in the houfe came to pay their refpects to her, and to each of them fhe gave a prefent, as is ufual, on fuch occafions. New cloaths were ordered to be got ready for Pamela, and all the fervants appeared in rich liveries. The neighbouring gentry fent feveral invitations to them to come and vifit them, but in all thefe excurfions Pamela was ftill teazed with queftions concerning the validity of her marriage. To all thefe queftions fhe made no other anfwers but what were confiftent with modefty, for the 'fquire had defired her not to be too forward in declaring her marriage. One Sunday they went to church together, a place that Pamela always loved to frequent, and heard a moft excellent fermon, after which they returned home, and next morning he fignified his intentions, that fhe fhould fend for her parents, he being willing to fee them. No news could be more agreeable to Pamela, fhe longed to fee her dear parents, and as her parents were ever-dear to her, fhe waited with the utmoft impatience to fee them. She beftowed a thoufand bleffings on her hufband for his noble generofity, and calling one of the fervants, wrote a letter to her father, defiring him and her mother to come to her as foon as poffible. The man obeyed his orders, and fet out immediately for the place, where the aged couple refided, while Pamela, with her fpoufe, fpent their time in all the innocent amufements of a country life. The 'fquire pluming himfelf on

his

his own ingenuity, and the poor Pamila repofing herfelf in that innocence that had hitherto mark- ed her character.

When every thing was fettled at the country- feat, Pamela fent her parents an account of the happy life fhe enjoyed, and how the 'fquire had propofed providing for all her relations. To this propofal fhe had no further objection than what was reafonable, and which fhewed that fhe was endowed with a large fhare of real good fenfe. She obferved that to relieve the indigent fhould be the principal work of her life, for this reafon, that we are injoined to do all the good we can for each other; and in particular for thofe who are nearly connected with us by the ties of nature. But for her to folicit her hufband in favour of all her near rela- tions would be to lay an unneceffary burthen upon him, by which his own relations might be difguifed, and his affections alienated. In an- fwer to this, her father told her, he would take care to manage a fmall eftate her hufband had given him with fuch care that he would have it in his power to do a great deal of good for his relations, and therefore begged that fhe would not abufe her hufband's good nature by making any further requeft, unlefs in cafes of the utmoft neceffity, which he hoped would not occur.

Lady Davers pretended to be reconciled to Pamela, and wrote to her, defiring to hear the reft of her ftory. She added, fhe would not call her fifter till fhe had complied with her requeft, for fhe ftill looked on the marriage as no better than an intrigue, which her brother had carried on, in order to feduce her and deceive his own re- lations. Pamela in anfwer told her, that fhe did not

chufe

chufe to relate any more of her ftory than fhe already knew; for as all her fears were over fhe looked on her happinefs as complete, and therefore trifling incidents were not worthy of being remembered. This anfwer, however, did not fatisfy Lady Davers, who could not be brought to confider Pamela as her fifter, but ftill confidered, or rather wifhed, that fhe might turn out to be the kept miftrefs of her brother. She told her of feveral of her brother's gallantries, which were all confiftent with the character of a true libertine, particularly with an affair he had with a young lady whom he had feduced, and who had born him a child. Her name was Mifs Godfrey, and fhe was the daughter of a gentleman of great fortune who died before fhe arrived at years of maturity. This ftory, however, Pamela was no ftranger to, and therefore fhe told the lady that fhe was under no apprehenfions on that head, having already received the ftrongeft proofs of her hufband's love.

As Pamela devoted the greateft part of her time to actions of benevolence, fo new objects daily prefented themfelves, for there is no end of human wants; and where fhould the wretched go but to thofe who are poffeffed of affluence? Mrs. Jewkes, whom we have already mentioned, was in many refpects a bad woman; but for all all that fhe had done fome good actions. Two children of hers had been very extravagant, and had contracted debts which their mother had engaged to pay. This had kept her extremely poor, and Pamela, in order to extricate her out of all her difficulties, not only paid her debts but alfo provided for two poor orphans, her grand children. This generous action made a

lafting

lasting impression on the mind of a woman who had been too long engaged in vicious practices, but Pamela was one of those who bestowed her favours consistent with the rules laid down by our Divine Lord, namely, not to let the one hand know what the other did.

Mrs. Jarvis was the next whose wants attracted her notice, and she treated her as a mother rather than one who was under any obligations to her. Such was the manner in which this amiable young woman began housekeeping, and new objects of distress daily presented themselves. Sir Simon Dunford, a gentleman with whom the 'squire, husband of Pamela, was very intimate, had a daughter, a vain girl, and it was proposed, that in order to improve her mind Pamela and she should enter into a correspondence, but this gave great offence to the old gentleman, who could not bear the thoughts of stooping so low. He wrote his sentiments to the 'squire, complaining of the conduct of his wife, but the answer he received justified all she had done.

This brought on a correspondence between our heroine and Miss Dunford, which was continued for some time; for such was the natural disposition of Pamela, that nothing came amiss to her that could promote any beneficial purpose. She had learned to write that she might be able to do good to her fellow creatures, well knowing that all those talents which God has bestowed upon us will either turn out a blessing or a curse, according to the use that we make of them. The subject matter of the letters that passed between them were on things of the utmost importance. Pamela had learned to consider

der

der human nature, not as reprefented by fome gloomy writers, but merely as it difcovers itfelf in the affairs of human life. She had drawn her obfervations from the fountain-head without copying thofe rules which had never exifted any where but in the brains of their authors.

During the time they were carrying on this correfpondence, Mr. Williams, the good clergy-man, was prefented to a valuable living, and he came to pay his refpects to the 'fquire, his ge-nerous benefactor. His converfation was chear-ful and inftructive, confiftent with the nature of his facred prcfeffion for every duty he performed was a tranfcript of his real life. He had learn-ed that a clergyman fhould teach as much by precept as example, and therefore every exhor-tation that dropped from his mouth was what he had previoufly conformed to without hefitation. In a word he was one of thofe divines who leave nothing undone to revive the true fpirit of real genuine chriftianity, which has been fo much obfcured by the inventions and paffions of men. He had fet the example of his Bleffed Mafter before him as a pattern to be copied after in all his labours, and to do honour as far as was confiftent with human nature to that holy religion he profeffed.

While he remained at the hall Mifs Dun-ford prevailed on her father to let her accom-pany Pamela to London, for fhe was now by her obliging behaviour become fo engaging, that fhe knew not what to do without her ad--vice. So true are thefe words of the poet:

C 4   A good

A good repute, a virtuous name,
   (As moralifts fet forth)
Is the unerring road to fame,
   If fame confifts in worth.
This jewel, rarely to be found,
   Sets merit full in view;
A moral glory fhines around
   Whate'r the virtuous do,
The precious ointment gently fhed,
   O'er mental ills prevails,
And when the fragrant med'cine's fpead,
   It animates and heals.

Pamela then gave Mifs Dunford an account
of the arrival of two country 'fquires, who were
profeffed libertines, and who had the affurance
to enter into an argument with her againft the
truth of both natural and revealed religion. The
virtuous education which Pamela had received,
enabled her to baffle all they advanced, for fhe
made it appear that religion was a thing of fo
univerfal a nature, that no man had a right to
look for the benefits of this life, who either defpifed it's doctrines, or neglected it's duties.
She enumerated the feveral virtues as taught in
the facred volume, and pointed out how far
they were fuited to the ftate of our nature, as
a revelation worthy of God to beftow, and fuch
as fhould be received by us, with the utmoft humility and gratitude.

It is perhaps impoffible that in the marriage
ftate difputes will not arife, and although the
caufes may be trifling, yet the tendernefs of the
paffions often winds them up to a great height.
The 'fquire who had hitherto treated his wife,
                                 who

who was far advanced in her pregnancy, with every mark of refpect, yet could not on feveral occafions refrain from fhewing his fuperiority, or, in other words, claiming that privilege which the law allows to hufbands to command their wives. The love of power is predominant in the human mind, and let our ftation be either high or low, we are fond of exercifing it.

Pamela, in one of her letters to Mifs Dunford, told that young lady, that fhe had many infirmitfes that her hufband had hitherto born with ; and fome of thefe letters falling into his hands, gave him no fmall degree of uneafinefs. He accufed her of having revealed what paffed between them ; and one day finding her writing defired to fee her letter. This fhe refufed to comply with, becaufe Mifs Dunford had injoined her fecrecy, which feemed to vex him a good deal, but inftead of giving way to his refentment he modeftly withdrew.

Next day the 'fquire went out to ride, and did not arrive till towards the evening, which made Pamela extremely unhappy. At laft fhe heard his fteps on the ftairs, and as fhe was writing, the joy of his arrival made her drop her pen. He approached her with more formality than ufual, which fhe could not help taking notice of, for fhe was more afraid of lofing his affections than all the world, had it been laid at her feet.

She expoftulated with him upon it in fo engaging a manner, that all his refentment feemed changed to love, and the reft of the evening was fpent in the moft harmonious manner. Next morning, when breakfaft was over, he ordered the chariot to be got ready, and taking her into it, gave her an airing in the park, from whence

C 5

they

they proceeded to fome of the neigbouring vil-
lages, where new objects of compaffion ftill prefented themfelves to their view.

The 'fquire took notice of fome pretty young
children, who were playing in the moft innocent
manner, and having commanded the chariot to
ftop, he made enquiry into their particular circumftances, and among the reft found two of the
name of Goodwin, who feemed more engaging
than the others. He beftowed upon them valuable prefents, and having ordered the coachman
to drive home, he told his dear Pamela, that as
he was about fetting out for London along with
her, fhe muft fignify that particular to her friend
Mifs Dunford.

When they arrived in town, Pamela was fo
far advanced in her pregnancy, that the 'fquire,
her hufband, took her out in the chariot every
day, and was charmed to hear what fine remarks
fhe made on all the public buildings. She
thought the expence in decorating them had been
too great, and that the money might have been
laid out to much better purpofes, in alleviating
the diftreffes of the poor, and removing the burden from the widow and orphans.

As the time of her delivery drew nigh, a difpute arofe between her and her hufband concerning the obligation binding on every woman to
nurfe her own children, but as fhe had not thoroughly confidered the fubject, fhe wrote to her
parents defiring to know what was their opinion
of the matter. In anfwer to her letter, her parents told her, that certainly nothing could be
more natural than for mothers to nurfe their
own children, and they lamented that her hufband

band fhould, on fuch an important point, have
thought different from her. They faid it was the
order of God, who had provided mothers with
milk for that purpofe, and nothing but the
luxury of modern times could ever have brought
it into difrepute. Pamela fhewed the letter to
her hufband, who was fo condefcending that he
promifed to grant her requeft, but could not
help obferving that it would appear very roman-
tic for a lady to nurfe her child, for although
fuch things might have taken place in antient
times, yet they were in a manner become as it
were antiquated now. On the other hand Pamela faid all fhe could to convince him that
nothing could fet afide the order of nature,
for that which is once right muft be fo for
ever.

Lady Davers, who had now furmounted all
her fcruples concerning her brother's marriage,
for the firft time wrote to Pamela under the apel-
lation of fifter, and along with her letter fent
her a valuable prefent of fuch things as were neceffary for one in her circumftances, all which
Pamela received with fuch marks of gratitude as
can only flow from a virtuous mind. She fent a
long letter to lady Davers containing fome very
curious remarks on the tragedy of The Diftreffed
Mother, from which the lady was fo well convinced of her good fenfe, that fhe wrote to her
in language of the higheft approbation. One
day while fhe was folding up one of her letters
to lady Davers, the 'fquire, her hufband, came
up ftairs, and afked her what fhe had been writing? fhe told him, and a curious dialogue enfued between them, on the different manners of
ancient

ancient and modern times, but Pamela maintained her former propofition, that what was once right was always fo.

In order to make her time as agreeable as pofſible, her husband took her to a mafquerade, but that afforded her no real pleafure, for in a letter fhe fent to lady Davers, fhe told her that her thoughts were engaged on more important objects. Her mind was filled with the confideration of that trial fhe had to go through within child-bearing, and fhe implored the Divine Being to give her his powerful affiſtance. Soon after this fhe was delivered of a fine boy, and being perfectly recovered, propofed to fet out for the country, which fhe always efteemed in preference to London.

In confequence of that refolution, fhe fet out with her hufband, and having arrived at Bedford, in their way to the country houfe, fhe wrote a letter to Lady Davers, telling her how happy fhe was, and that in order to improve her mind, her hufband had given her Locke's Effay on Education to perufe. Lady Davers in anfwer faid many kind things, but Pamela, in her next letter could not help taking notice that her hufband was not fo cordial in his refpects to her as formely; for fhe had without making any enquiry, found, or at leaft been informed, that he was engaged in fome intrigue. Lady Davers, endeavoured to make her as eafy as pofſible, and at the fame time promifed to come and vifit her, but this Pamela, who was all innocence, would not confent to. Her hufband brought fome perfon to dinner, and fhe taking notice of the vifible change in his behaviour, could

could not refrain from the moſt uneaſy thoughts. To increaſe her unhappineſs, ſome perſons ſent her letters, telling her, that her husband was engaged in intrigues with ſeveral ladies, which made her ſo uneaſy that ſhe went to the door of his cloſet, whether he had retired when the company was gone, and begged to know what ſhe had done to offend him. He made her ſit down, and told her that ſhe had given him no occaſion to be offended with her, for the whole of her conduct had been free from blame. In the mean time he begged that ſhe would not afflict herſelf, but ſhe was ſo much overpowered with grief that ſhe ſent an account of the whole affair to lady Davers, who, in anſwer, ſpoke in the higheſt terms of reſentment againſt her brother. She told her that the ladies whom ſhe ſuſpected were both widows of very looſe characters, whoſe buſineſs it was to to be continually engaged in intrigues, and that they had ruined the peace of m..ny families, Her brother, ſhe ſaid, was one who could not refrain from intrigues, that he had ſeduced many young women, and as he had now met with ladies agreeable to his own inclination, there was no doubt but he would purſue what he conſidered as his advantage till he had brought it to the utmoſt.

Things, however, begun to take a more favourable turn, for the ſquire gave Pamela the moſt convincing proofs that ſhe was as dear to him as ever. It ſeems he had taken ſome liberties at the maſquerade with a lady, who appeared in the character of a nun, and this circumſtance had been exaggerated to the higheſt pitch. Pamela

mela was now eafy in her mind ; but no fooner
was the ftorm blown over, when her pretty little
boy was feized with the fmall-pox, during the
time that his father was gone to vifit one of his
eftates in the country.

At firft it was thought that the diforder was
what is called malignant, but it turned out
otherwife, and the dear boy, contrary to expectation recovered. Pamela, with all the tendernefs of a real mother, though fhe had never had
the fmall-pox, attended him all the time he lay
ill, and at laft caught the infection, but it pleafed
God that fhe recovered, to the great joy of all
thofe with whom fhe was connected.

As foon as fhe was perfectly recovered, fhe
fent an account thereof to Lady Davers, and
defired her to join with her in praifing God for
the many mercies fhe had received. In the conclufion fhe added that her husband had treated
her with fo much kindnefs, that fhe was forry
fhe had ever harboured fufpicious notions of his
fidelity, and refolved, for the future, to keep a
more ftrict watch over her natural difpofition.
The truth is, fhe was not naturally of a fufpicious temper, but the falfe infinuations that had
been thrown out were fufficient to have difcompofed the mind of the moft experienced perfon
in the world.

In her next letter to Lady Davers, fhe told
her, that fhe had thoroughly confidered Mr.
Locke's Treatife on Education, and was entirely
of the fame opinion with that learned author.
It is neceffary here to obferve that Mr. Locke
prefers a private to a public education, on condition that parents will take care not to admit
any

any perfons into their fervice but fuch as are ftrictly virtuous, and make it a point of confcience to perform every religious duty. To this it was objected by her husband, in a converfation that they had together, that the emulation that takes place among boys in a public fchool, ferved to ftimulate them on to make the utmoft proficiency in literature, whereas when they were brought up in private, their fpirits were apt to become dejected, and all the beauties of learning were confidered by them as reftraints on their natural inclinations, calculated for no other purpofe than to make them melancholy, and extirpate from their minds the love of learning.

In anfwer to this Pamela told him, that there was nothing more wanting to make Mr. Locke's fcheme preferable than by attending to his rules, which was the duty of every mafter of a family to do; for how could a man admit a fervant into his houfe, unlefs he believed that he was one who would not corrupt the morals of his children. She then went over the whole plan of education laid down by the celebrated Mr. Locke, and concluded by telling her husband that nothing in her opinion could be more natural or rational, for every branch of fcience was put in its proper place, fo that the pupil would rife gradually to comprehend the moft abftruce parts of learning, without trudging through all the formal rules, by which it has been fo long degraded. The 'fquire was fo well convinced of the principles of what his wife advanced in her argument, that he declared himfelf to be of the fame opinion with her, and all
the

the family relations were fo obliging as to ac-
quiefe with him.

The 'fquire from this time forward lived in
the moft regular manner, and Pamela who was
the happy mother of many lovely children, fpent
her whole time in fuperintending their education. The gentry in the neighbourhood declared that they had never feen a family kept under
fuch ftrict regulations, and fome of them began
to imitate the example that had been fet before
them.

Poor Mrs. Jewks died a fincere penitent, and
in her laft moments acknowledged her former
crimes, fo that humanity looked upon her as an
object of compaffion. Good Mrs. Jarvis funk
under the decay of nature, and yielded up the
ghoft, lamented by all that knew her.

Mr. Williams, the worthy clergyman, was
raifed from one degree of preferment to another,
till at laft he became an eminent dignitary of the
church, and then his benevolence diffufed itfelf
among all thofe that knew him, fo far as his
circumftances would permit. Mifs Dunford
was honourably married, and the old fervants
were provided for in the moft decent manner.

Pamela and her hufband enjoyed all thofe plea-
fures that flow from virtuous love: they were
beloved by their tenants, who confidered them in
the fame light as a child does a parent, and
having fpent their days in the practice of every
religious duty, they died, and left a progeny behind them that has been an honour to the nation. From this let every perfon learn that virtue is the foundation of happinefs, and that none
can be truly great who are not truly good.

There

There were few women, efpecially young ones, who could ever write fuch fine fentiments as the amiable Pamela; for let the fubject be what it would, fhe turned it in fuch a manner as to point out a moral duty. All her hours of retirement were fpent in writing to her friends and relations, and that young people in general, particularly women, may learn how to make a proper ufe of thofe faculties heaven has beftowed upon them, the reader is here prefented with fome of her own words.

" *My dear Lady* G.

" I will chearfully caufe to be tranfcribed for you the converfation you defire, between myfelf, Mrs. Towers, and Lady Arthur, and the three young ladies their relations, in prefence of the dean and his daughter, and Mrs. Brooks; and glad I fhall be, if it may be of ufe to the two thoughtlefs mifles your neighbours; who, you are pleafed to tell me, are great admirers of my ftory, and my example; and will therefore, as you fay, pay greater attention to what I write, than to the more paffionate and interefted leffons of their mamma.

" I am only forry, that you fhould have been under any concern about the fuppofed trouble you give me, by having miflaid my former relation of it. For, befides obliging my dear Lady G. the hope that I may be able to do fervice by it to a family fo worthy, in a cafe fo nearly affecting his honour, as to make two headftrong young ladies recollect what belongs to their fex and their cha-
raders,

racters, and what their filial duties require of them, affords me high pleasure ; and if it shall be attended with the wish'd effects, it will be an addition to my happiness.

" I said, cause to be transcribed ; because I hope to answer a double end by it ; for, after I had re-confidered it, I set Miss Goodwin to transcribe it,' who writes a very pretty hand, and is not a little fond of the task, nor, indeed, of any task I set her ; and will be more affected as she performs it, than she could be by reading it only ; although she is a very good girl at present, and gives me hopes, that she will continue to be so.

" As soon as it is done, I will inclose it, that it may be read to the parties without this introduction, if you think fit. And you will forgive me for having added a few obfervations to this transcription, with a view to the cases of your inconsiderate young ladies, and for having corrected the former narrative in several places."

" *My dear Lady* G.

" The papers you have mislaid, relating to the conversation between me and the young ladies, relations of Mrs. Towers, and Lady Anne Arthur, in presence of these two last-named ladies, Mrs. Brooks, and the worthy dean, and Miss L. (of which, in order to perfect your kind collection of my communications, you request another copy) contained as follows :

" I first began with apprising you, that I had seen these three ladies twice or thrice before, as visitors, at their kinswomen's houses ; so that
they

they and I were not altogether ſtrangers to one
another : and my two neighbours acquainted me
with their reſpective taſtes and diſpoſitions, and
gave me their hiſtories, preparatory to this viſit,
to the following effect :

" That Miſs Stapylton is over-run with the
love of poetry and romance, and delights much
in flowery language, and metaphorical flouriſhes :
is about eighteen, wants not either ſenſe or po-
liteneſs ; and has read herſelf into a vein, that is
more amorous (that was Mrs. Towers's word)
than diſcreet. Has extraordinary notions of a
firſt-ſight love ; and gives herſelf greater liberties, with a pair of fine eyes, (in hopes to make
ſudden conqueſts in purſuance of that notion)
that is pretty in her ſex and age ; which makes
thoſe who know her not, conclude her bold and
forward ; and is more than ſuſpected, with a
mind thus prepared for inſtantaneous impreſſions,
to have experienced the argument to her own diſ-
advantage, and to be ſtruck by (before ſhe has
ſtricken) a gentleman, whom her friends think
not at all worthy of her, and to whom ſhe was
making ſome indiſcreet advances, under the name
of PHILOCLEA to PHILOXENUS, in a letter which
ſhe intruſted to a ſervant of the family, who,
diſcovering her deſign, prevented her indiſcretion
for that time.

" That, in other reſpects, ſhe has no mean
accompliſhments, will have a fine fortune, is
genteel in her perſon, though with ſome viſible
affectation, dances well, ſings well, and plays
prettily on ſeveral inſtruments; is fond of reading,
but affects the action and air, and attitude, of a
tragedian ; and is too apt to give an emphaſis in
the

the wrong place, in order to make an author mean more fignificantly than it is neceflary he fhould, even where the occafion is common, and in a mere hiflorical fact, that requires as much fimplicity in the reader's accent, as in the writer's ftyle. No wonder then, that when fhe reads a play, fhe will put herfelf into a fweat, as Mrs. Towers fays; diftorting very agreeable features, and making a multitude of wry mouths, with one very pretty one, in order to convince her hearers, what a near neighbour her heart is to her lips.

"Mifs Cope is a young lady of nineteen, lovely in her perfon, with a handfome fortune in poffeffion, and great profpects. Has a foft and gentle turn of mind, which difpofes her to be eafily impofed upon. Is addreffed by a libertine of quality, whofe courtfhip, while permitted, was imperioufnefs; and whofe tendernefs, infult; having found the young lady too fufceptible of impreffion, open and unreferved, and even valuing him the more, as it feemed, for treating her with ungenerous contempt; for that fhe was always making excufes for flights, ill-manners, and even rudenefs, which no other young lady would forgive.

"That this facility on her fide, and this infolence on his, and an over-free, and even indecent degree of ramping, as it is called, with her, which once her mamma furprifed them in, made her papa forbid his vifits, and her receiving them.

"That this, however, was fo much to Mifs Cope's regret, that fhe was detected in a defign to elope to him out of the private garden-door; which, had fhe effected, in all probability, the indelicate

indelicate and dishonourable peer would have triumphed over her innocence; having given out since, that he intended to revenge himself on the daughter, for the disgrace he had received from the parents.

"That though she was convinced of this, it was feared she still loved him, and would throw herself in his way the first convenient opportunity; urging, that his rash expressions were the effect only of his passion; for that she knows he loves her too well, to be dishonourable to her: and by the same degree of favourable prepossession, she will have it, that his brutal roughness, is the manliness of his nature; that his most shocking expressions, are sincerity of heart; that his boasts of his former lewdness, are but instances that he knows the world; that his freedoms with her person, are but excess of love, and innocent gaiety of temper; that his resenting the prohibition he has met with, and his threats, are other instances of his love and his courage: and peers of the realm ought not to be bound down by little narrow rules, like the vulgar; for, truly, their honour, which is regarded in the greatest cases, as equal with the oath of a common gentleman, is a security that a lady may trust to, if he is not a profligate indeed; and that Lord P. cannot be.

"That excepting these weaknesses, Miss has many good qualities; is charitable, pious, humane, humble; sings sweetly, plays on the spinnet charmingly; is meek, fearful, and never was resolute or courageous enough to step out of the regular path, till her too flexible heart became touched with a passion, that is said to polish the most brutal temper; and therefore her rough peer
has

has none of it; and to animate the dove, of which Miss Cope has too much.

"That Miss Sutton, a young lady of the like age with the two former, has too lively and airy a turn of mind; affects to be thought well read in the histories of kingdoms, as well as in polite literature. Speaks French fluently, talks much upon all subjects; and has a great deal of that flippant wit, which makes more enemies than friends. However, is innocent, and unsuspectedly virtuous hitherto; but makes herself cheap and accessible to fops and rakes, and has not the worse opinion of a man for being such. Listens eagerly to stories told to the disadvantage of individuals of her own sex; though affecting to be a greater stickler for the honour of the sex in general: will unpityingly propagate such stories: thinks (without considering to what the imprudence of her own conduct may subject her) the woman, that slips, inexcusable; and the man who seduces her, much less faulty: and by this means encourages the one sex in their vileness, and gives up the other for their weakness, in a kind of silly affectation, to shew her security in her own virtue; at the very time, that she is dancing upon the edge of a precipice, presumptuously inattentive to her own danger."

"I had been writing, (you must know, Lady G.) for the sake of suiting Miss Stapylton's flighty vein, a little sketch of the style she is so fond of; and hoped for some such opportunity as this question gave me, to bring it on the carpet; for my only fear, with her and Miss Cope, and Miss Sutton, was, that they would deem me too grave; and so what should fall in the course of converfation, would make the lefs impreffion upon them. For even the beft inftructions in the world, you know, will be ineffectual, if the method of conveying them is not adapted to the tafte and temper of the perfon you would wifh to influence. And, moreover, I had a view in it, to make this little fketch the introduction to a future occafion for fome obfervations on the ftiff and affected ftyle of romances, which might put Mifs Stapylton out of conceit with them and make her turn the courfe of her ftudies anou..er way ; as I fhall mention in its place.

I anfwered, that I had been meditating upon the misfortune of a fine young lady, who had been feduced and betrayed by a gentleman fhe loved ; and who, notwithftanding, had the grace to ftop fhort, (indeed, later than were to be wifhed) and to abandon friends, country, lover, in order to avoid any further intercourfe with him ; and that God had blefled her penitence and refolution, and fhe was now very happy in a neighbouring dominion.

" A fine fubject, faid Mifs Stapylton !—was the gentleman a man of wit, madam ? was the lady a woman of tafte ?

" The gentleman, madam, was all that was defirable in man, had he been virtuous : the lady all that was excellent in woman, had fhe been more circumfpect. But it was a firft love on both fides ; and little did fhe think he could have taken advantage of her innocence and her affection for him.

" A fad, fad ftory ! faid Mifs Cope : but, pray, madam, did their friends approve of their vifits ? for danger fometimes, as I have heard,
arifes

arifes from the cruelty of friends, who force lovers upon private and clandeftine meetings; when, perhaps there can be no material objection, why the gentleman and lady may not come together.

"Well obferved, Mifs Cope, thought I! how we are for making every cafe applicable to our own, when our hearts are fixed upon a point?

"It cannot be called cruelty in friends, madam, faid I, when their cautions, or even prohibitions, are fo well juftified by the event, as in this cafe——and, generally, by the wicked arts and practices of feducers. And how happy is it for a lady, when fhe fuffers herfelf to be convinced, that thofe who have lived forty years in the world, may know twice as much, at leaft, of that world, as fhe can poffibly know at twenty, ten of which moreover are almoft a blank! If they do not, the one muft be fuppofed very ignorant; the other, very knowing.

"But, madam, the lady, whofe hard cafe I was confidering, hoped too much, and feared too little; that was her fault; which made her give opportunities to the gentleman, which neither liberty nor reftraint could juftify in her. She had not the difcretion, poor lady! in this one great point of all, that the ladies I have in my eye, I dare fay, would have had in her cafe.

"I beg pardon, faid Mifs Cope and blufhed. I know not the cafe, and ought to have been filent.

"Ay, thought I, fo you would, had not you thought yourfelf more affected by it, than it were to be wifhed you were.

"I think

"I think, said Mifs Sutton, the Lady was the lefs to be pitied, as fhe muft know what her character required of her; and that men will generally deceive when they are trufted. There are very few of them, who pretend to be virtuous; and it is allowed to be their privilege to afk, as it is the lady's to deny.

"So madam, replied I, you are fuppofing a continual ftate of warfare between the two fexes; one offenfive, the other defenfive: and, indeed, I think the notion not altogether amifs; for a lady will affuredly be lefs in danger, where fhe rather fears an enemy in the acquaintance fhe has of that fex, than hopes a friend; efpecially as fo much depends upon the iffue, either of her doubt, or of her confidence.

"I do not know neither, madam, returned Mifs Sutton, very brifkly, whether the men fhould be fet out to us as fuch bugbears, as our mothers generally reprefent them. It is making them too confiderable; and is a kind of reflection upon the difcretion and virtue of our fex, and fuppofes us weak indeed.

"The late Czar, I have read, continued fhe, took a better method with the Swedes, who had often beat him; when, after a great victory, he made his captives march in proceffion, through the ftreets of his principal city, to familiarize them to the Ruffes, and fhew them they were but men.

"Very well obferved, replied I: but then, did you not fay, that this was thought neceffary to be done, becaufe the Ruffes had been often defeated by the Swedes, and thought too highly of them; and when the Swedes, taking advantage

D of

of that prepoſſeſſion, had the greater contempt of
the Ruſſes?

"She looked a little diſconcerted; and being
ſilent, I proceeded:

"I am very far, madam, from thinking the ge-
nerality of men very formidable, if our ſex do
juſtice to themſelves, and to what their characters
require of them. Nevertheleſs, give me leave to
ſay, that the men I thought contemptible, I would
not think worthy of my company, nor give it to
them, when I could avoid it. And as for thoſe,
who are more to be regarded, I am afraid, that
when they can be aſſured, that a lady allows it to
be their privilege to ſue for favours, it will certainly embolden them to ſolicit, and to think
themſelves acting in character when they put the
lady upon hers, to refuſe them. And yet I am
humbly of opinion with the poet:

"*He comes* too near, *who comes to be* denied."

"For theſe reaſons, madam, I was pleaſed
with your notion, that it would be beſt to look
upon that ſex, eſpecially if we allow them the
privilege you ſpeak of, in an hoſtile light.

"But permit me to obſerve, with regard to the
moſt contemptible of the ſpecies, fops, coxcombs,
and pretty fellows, that many a good general has
been defeated, when, truſting to his great ſtrength
and ſkill, he has deſpiſed a truly weak enemy.

"I believe, madam, returned ſhe, your obſer-
vation is very juſt. I have read of ſuch inſtances.
But, dear madam, permit me to aſk, whether we
ſpeak not too generally, when we condemn every
man

man who dreſſes well, and is not a ſloven, as a
ſop or a coxcomb?

" No doubt, we do, when this is the caſe.
But permit me to obſerve, that you hardly ever
in your life, ſaw a man who was very nice about
his perſon and dreſs, that had any thing he
thought of greater conſequence to himſelf to regard. It is natural it ſhould be ſo; for ſhould
not the man of body take the greateſt care to
ſet out and adorn the part for which he thinks
himſelf moſt valuable? And will not the man of
mind beſtow his principal care in improving that
mind? perhaps, to the neglect of dreſs and outward appearance, which is a fault, but ſurely,
madam, there is a middle-way to be obſerved in
theſe, as in moſt other caſes; for a man need not
be a ſloven any more than a fop. He need not
ſhew an utter diſregard to dreſs, nor yet think it
his firſt and chief concern; be ready to quarrel
with the wind for diſcompoſing his peruke, or
fear to put on his hat, leſt he ſhould depreſs his
foretop; more diſlike a ſpot upon his clothes,
than in his reputation: be a ſelf-admirer, and
always at the glaſs, which he would perhaps
never look into, could it ſhew the deformity of
his mind, as well as the finery of his perſon:
who has a taylor for his tutor, and a milliner
for his ſchool-miſtreſs: who laughs at men of
ſenſe (excuſably enough, perhaps in revenge becauſe they laugh at him): who calls learning pe-
dantry: and looks upon the knowledge of the
faſhions, as the only uſeful ſcience to a fine gentleman.

" Pardon me, ladies: I could proceed with
the character of this ſpecies of men; but I need

not;

not ; becaufe every lady prefent, I am fure, would defpife fuch a one, as much as I do, were he to fall in her way : and the rather, becaufe it is certain, that he who admires himfelf, will never admire his lady as he ought ; and if he maintains his nicenefs after marriage, it will be with a preference to his own perfon : if not, will fink, very probably into the worft of flovens. For whoever is capable of one extreme, (take almoft all the cafes in human life through) when he recedes from that, if he be not a man of prudence, will go over into the other.

" But to return to the former fubject, (for the general attention encouraged me to proceed) permit me, Mifs Sutton, to add, that a lady muft run great rifques to her reputation, if not to her virtue, who will admit into her company any gentleman, who fhall be of opinion, and know it to be hers, that it is his province to ask a favour, which it will be her duty to deny.

" I believe, madam, I fpoke thefe words a little too carelefly : but I meant honourable queftions, to be fure.

" There can be but one honourable queftion, replied I ; and that is feldom afked but when the affair is brought near a conclufion, and there is a probability of its being granted ; and which a fingle lady, while fhe has parents or guardians, fhould never thing of permitting to be put to herfelf, much lefs of approving, nor, perhaps, as the cafe may be, of denying. But I make no doubt, madam, that you meant honourable queftions. A young lady of Mifs Sutton's good fenfe and worthy character, could not mean otherwife. And I have faid, perhaps, more than I
needed

needed to fay, upon this fubject, becaufe we all know how ready the prefuming of the other fex are, right or wrong, to conftrue the moft innocent meanings in favour of their own views.

" Very true, faid fhe ; but appeared to be under an agreeable confufion, every lady, by her eye, feeming to think fhe had met with a deferved rebuke ; and which not feeming to expect, it abated her livelinefs all the time after.

" Mrs Towers feafonably relieved us both from a fubject too applicable, if I may fo exprefs it. faying, but, dear Mifs B. will you favour us with the refult of your meditation, if you have committed it to writing, on the unhappy cafe you mentioned ?

" I was rather, madam, exercifing my fancy than my judgment, fuch as it is, upon the occafion. I was aiming at a kind of allegorical or metaphorical ftyle, I know not which to call it ; and it is not fit to be read before fuch judges, I doubt.

" O pray, dear madam, faid Mifs Stapylton, favour us with it to chufe ; for I am a great admirer of that ftyle.

" I have a great curiofity, faid lady Arthur, both from the fubject and the ftyle, to hear what you have written ; and I beg you will oblige us all.

" It is fhort and unfinifhed. It was written for the fake of a friend, who is fond of fuch a ftyle ; and what I fhall add to it, will be principally fome flight obfervations upon this way of writing. But, let it be ever fo cenfurable, I fhould be more fo, if I made any difficulties after

fuch

fuch an unanimous requeft. So taking it out of my letter-cafe, I read as follows :

" While the banks of difcretion keep the proud waves of paffion with their natural channel, all calm and ferene, glides along the filver current, enlivening the adjacent meadows, as it paffes, with a brighter and more flowery verdure. But if the torrents of fenfual love are permitted to de-fcend from the hills of credulous hope, they may fo fwell the gentle ftream, as to make it difficult, if not impoffible, to be retained betwixt its ufual bounds. What then will be the confequence? —why, the trees of refolution, and the fhrubs of cautious fear, which grew upon the frail mound, and whofe intertwining roots had contributed to fupport it, being loofened from their hold, they, and all that would fwim of the bank itfelf, will be feen floating on the furface of the triumphant waters.

" But here, a dear lady, having unhappily failed, is enabled to fet her foot in the new made breach, while yet it is poffible to ftop it, and to fay, with little variation, in the language of that power, which only could enable her to fay it, ' Hither, ye proud waves of diffolute love, al-though you have come, yet no further fhall ye come ;' is fuch an inftance of magnanimous refolution and felf-conqueft, as is very rarely to be met with."

" I beg then, madam, faid Mifs Stapylton, you will open the caufe, be the fubject what it will. And I could almoft wifh, that we had as many gentlemen here as ladies, who would have
reafon

reafon to be afhamed of the liberties they take in cenfuring the converfations of the tea-table ; fince the pulpit, as the worthy dean gives us reafon to hope, may be beholden to that of Mrs. B.

" Nor is it much wonder, replied I, when the dean himfelf is with us, and it is graced by fo diftinguifhed a circle.

" If many of our young gentlemen were here, faid Mrs. Towers, they might improve themfelves in all the graces of polite and fincere complaifance. But, compared to this, I have generally heard fuch trite and coarfe ftuff from our race of would-be-wits, that what they fay, may be compared to the fawnings and falutations of the afs in the fable, who emulating the lap-dog, merited a cudgel rather than encouragement.

" But, Mrs. B. continued fhe, begin, I pray you, to open and proceed in the caufe ; for there will be no counfel employed but you, I can tell you.

" Then give me a fubject, that will fuit me, ladies, and you fhall fee how my obedience to your commands will make me run on.

" Will you, madam, faid Mifs Stapylton, give us a few cautions and inftructions on a theme of your own, that a young lady fhould rather fear too much, than hope too much ? A neceffary doctrine perhaps ; but a difficult one to be practifed by one who has begun to love, and who fuppofes all truth and honour in the object of her favour.

" Hope, madam, faid I, in my opinion, fhould never be unaccompanied by fear ; and the more reafon will a lady ever have to fear, and to fufpect herfelf, and doubt her lover, when fhe once

begins

begins to find in her own breaft an inclination to
him. For then her danger is doubled, fince fhe
has herfelf (perhaps, the more dangerous enemy
of the two) to guard againft, as well as him.

" She may fecretly wifh the beft indeed ; but
what has been the fate of others, may be her
own ; and though fhe thinks it not probable,
from fuch a faithful protefter, as he appears to
her to be, yet while it is poffible, fhe fhould
never be off her guard : nor will a prudent
woman truft to his mercy or honour, but to her
own difcretion ; and the rather, becaufe, if he
mean well, he himfelf will value her the more
for her caution, fince every man defires to have
a virtuous and prudent wife ; if not well, fhe
will detect him the fooner ; and fo, by her
prudence, fruftrate all his bafe defigns.

" The ladies feeming, by their filence, to approve what I faid, I proceeded.

" But let me, my dear ladies, afk, what that
paffion is, which generally we dignify by the
name of love ; and which, when fo dignified,
puts us upon a thoufand extravagancies ? I
believe, if it were to be examined into, it would
be found too generally to owe its original to ungoverned fancy ; and were we to judge of it by
the confequences that ufually attend it, it ought
rather to be called rafhnefs, inconfideration,
weaknefs ; any thing but love ; for, very feldom,
I doubt, is the folid judgment fo much concerned
in it, as the airy fancy. But when once we dignify the wild mifleader with the name of love, all
the abfurdities, which we read in novels and romances, take place, and we are induced to follow
examples that feldom end happily but in them.

But

" But, permit me further to obferve, that love, as we call it, operates differently in the two fexes, as to its effects. For in woman it is a creeping thing, in man an incroacher; and this ought, in my humble opinion, to be very ferioufly attended to. Mifs Sutton intimated thus much, when fhe obferved that it was the man's province to afk, the lady's to deny :—Excufe me, madam, the obfervation was juft, as to the men's notions; although, methinks, I would not have a lady allow of it, except in cafes of caution to them-felves.

" The doubt, therefore, proceeded I, which a lady has of her lover's honour, is needful to pre-ferve her own, and his too. And if fhe does him wrong, and he fhould be too juft to deceive her, fhe can make him amends, by inftances of greater confidence, when fhe pleafes. But if fhe has been accuftomed to grant him little favours, can fhe eafily recall them? and will not the incroacher grow upon her indulgence, pleading for a favour to-day, which was not refufed him yefterday, and reproaching her want of confidence, as a want of efteem; till the poor lady, who, perhaps, has given way to this creeping, infinuating paffion, and has avowed her efteem for him, puts herfelf too much in his power, in order to manifeft, as fhe thinks, the generofity of her affection; and fo, by degrees, is carried faither than fhe intend-ed, or nice honour ought to have permitted; and all becaufe, to keep up to my theme, fhe hopes too much, and doubts too little? And, permit me, ladies, to add, that there have been cafes, where a man himfelf, purfuing the dictates of his in-croaching paffion, and finding a lady too con-

D 5   ceding,

ceding, has taken advantages, of which probably, at firſt, he did not preſume to think.

" Miſs Stapylton ſaid, that virtue itſelf ſpoke when I ſpoke ; and ſhe was reſolved, when ſhe came home, to recollect as much of this conver-ſation as ſhe could, and write it down in her common-place book, where it would make a better figure than any thing ſhe had there.

" I ſuppoſe, Miſs, ſaid Mrs. Towers, your chief collections are flowers of rhetoric, picked up from the French and Engliſh poets, and novel-writers. I would give ſomething for the pleaſure of having it two hours in my poſſeſſion.

" Fie, madam, replied ſhe, a little abaſhed, how can you expoſe your kinſwoman thus, be-fore the dean and Mrs. B ?

" Mrs. Towers, madam, ſaid I, only ſays this to provoke you to ſhew your collections. I wiſh I had the pleaſure of ſeeing them. I doubt not but your common-place book is a ſtore-houſe of wiſdom.

" There is nothing bad in it, I hope, replied ſhe ; but I would not, that Mrs. B. ſhould ſee it, for the world. But, let me tell you, madam, (to Mrs. Towers) there are many beautiful things, and good inſtructions, to be collected from novels, and plays, and romances ; and from the poetical writers particularly, light as you are pleaſed to make of them. Pray, madam, (to me) have you ever been at all con-verſant in ſuch writers ?

" Not a great deal in the former ; there were very few novels and romances, that my lady would permit me to read ; and thoſe I did, gave me no great pleaſure ; for either they dealt ſo

much

much in the marvellous and improbable, or were fo unnaturally inflaming to the paffions, and fo full of love and intrigue, that hardly any of them but feemed calculated to fire the imagination, rather than to inform the judgment. Tilts and tournaments, breaking of fpears in honour of my miftrefs, fwimming over rivers, engaging with monfters, rambling in fearch of adventures, making unnatural difficulties, in order to fhew the knight-errant's prowefs in overcoming them, is all that is required to conftitute the hero in fuch pieces. And what principally diftinguifhes the character of the heroine, is, when fhe is taught to confider her father's houfe as an inchanted caftle, and her lover as the hero who is to diffolve the charm, and to fet her at liberty from one confinement, in order to put her into another, and, too probably, a worfe : to inftruct her how to climb walls, drop from windows, leap precipices, and do twenty other extravagant things, in order to fhew the mad ftrength of a paffion fhe ought to be afhamed of : to make parents and guardians pafs for tyrants, and the voice of reafon to be drowned in that of indifcreet love, which exalts the other fex, and debafes her own. And what is the inftruction, that can be gathered from fuch pieces, for the conduct of common life ?

" Then have I been ready to quarrel with thefe writers for another reafon ; and that is, the dangerous notion which they hardly ever fail to propagate, of a firft-fight love. For there is fuch a fufceptibility fuppofed on both fides, (which, however it may pafs in a man, very little becomes the female delicacy) that they are fmitten with a glance ;

glance ; the fictitious blind god is made a real
Divity : and too often prudence and difcretion
are the firft offerings at his fhrine.

" I believe, madam, faid Mifs Stapylton,
blufhing, and playing with her fan, there have
been many inftances of peoples loving at firft
fight, which have ended very happily.

" No doubt of it, replied I. But there are
three chances to one, that fo precipitate a liking
does not. For where can be the room for caution, for inquiry, for the difplay of merit, and
fincerity, and even the affurance of a grateful
return, to a lady, who thus fuffers herfelf to be
prepoffefled ? Is it not a random fhot ? Is it
not a proof of weaknefs ? Is it not giving up
the negative voice, which belongs to the fex,
even while fhe is not fure of meeting with the
affirmative one from him whofe affection fhe
wifhes to engage ?

" Indeed, ladies, continued I, I cannot help concluding, (and I am the lefs afraid of fpeaking my
mind, becaufe of the opinion I have of the prudence of every .lady that hears me) that where
this weaknefs is found, it is no ways favourable to
a lady's character, and to that difcretion which
ought to diftinguifh it. It looks to me, as if
a lady's heart were too much in the power of
her eye, and that fhe had permitted her fancy to
be much more bufy than her judgment.

" Mifs Stapylton blufhed, and looked around
her.

" But I have generally obferved Mrs. B. faid
Lady Towers, that whenever you cenfure any
indifcretion, you feldom fail to give cautions how
to avoid it. And pray let us know what is to
be

be done in this cafe? That is to fay, how a young lady ought to guard againft and overcome the firft favourable impreffions?

"What I imagine, replied I, a young lady ought to do, on any the leaft favourable impreffions of this kind, is immedialely to withdraw into herfelf, as one may fay; to reflect upon what fhe owes to her parents, to her family, to her character, and to her fex; and to refolve to check fuch a prepoffeffion, which may much more probably, as I hinted, make her a prey to the undeferving than otherwife, as there are fo many of that character to one man of real merit.

"The moft I apprehend a firft fight favour can do, is to infpire a liking; and a liking is conquerable, if the perfon will not brood over it till fhe hatches it into love. Then every man and woman has a black and a white fide; and it is eafy to fet the imperfections of the perfon againft the fuppofed perfections, while it is only liking. But if the bufy fancy be permitted to work as it pleafes, unchecked, uncontrould, then it is very likely, were fhe but to keep herfelf in countenance for her firft impreffions, fhe will fee perfections in the object which no living foul can fee but herfelf. And it will hardly be expected, but that, as a confequence of her firft indifcretion, fhe will confirm, as an act of her judgment, what her wild and ungoverned fancy had mifled her to think of with fo much partial favour. And too late, as it may too probably happen, fhe will fee and lament her fatal, and, perhaps, undutiful error.

We

" We are talking of the ladies only, added I, (for I faw Mifs Stapylton was become very grave): but I believe the cafe of firft-fight love often operates alike in both fexes, and the fame inconveniencies may arife to both, from a rafhnefs of this kind : And where it is fo, it will be very lucky, fhall I fay ? if either gentleman or lady find reafon, on cool reflection, to approve a choice, which they were fo ready to make without thought.

" It is allowed, my dear Mrs. B. faid Lady Towers, that rafh and precipitate love may operate pretty much alike in the rafh and precipitate of both fexes ; and which-foever loves, generally exalts the perfon beloved, above his or her merits : but I am defirous, for the fake of us maiden ladies, fince it is a fcience in which you are fo great an adept, to have your advice, how we fhould watch and guard againft its firft incroachments, and that you will tell us what you apprehend gives the men moft advantage over us.

" Nay, now, Lady Towers, you rally my prefumption indeed !

" I admire you, madam, replied fhe, and every thing you fay and do ; and I won't forgive you to call what I fo ferioufly fay and think, raillery. For my own part, continued fhe, I never was in love yet, nor, I believe, were any of thefe young ladies—(Mifs Cope looked a little filly upon this) And who can better inftruct us to guard our hearts, than a lady who has fo well defended her own ?

" Why then, madam, if I muft fpeak, I think, what gives the other fex the greateft advantage, over even many of the moft deferving of ours,

is

is, that dangerous foible, the love of praise, and the desire to be flattered and admired : a passion that I have often observed predominant, more or less, from sixteen to sixty, in most of our sex. We are too generally delighted with the company of those who extol our graces of person or mind ; for will not a grateful lady study hard to return a few compliments to a gentleman, who makes her so many ? She is concerned to prove him a man of distinguishing sense, or a polite man, at least, in regard to what she thinks of herself ; and so the flatterer shall be preferred to such of the sincere and worthy, as cannot say what they do not think. And by this means many an excellent lady has fallen a prey to some sordid designer.

" Then, I think, nothing gives gentlemen so much advantage over our sex, as to see how readily a virtuous lady can forgive the capital faults of the most abandoned of the other ; and that sad, sad notion, That a reformed rake makes the best husband ; a notion that has done more hurt and discredit too, to our sex, (as it has given more encouragement to the profligates of the other. and more discouragement to the sober gentlemen) than can be easily imagined. A fine thing indeed ! as if the wretch, who had run through a course of iniquity to the endangering of soul and body, was to be deemed the best companion for life, to an innocent and virtuous young lady, who is to owe the kindness of his treatment of her, to his having never before accompanied with a modest woman ; nor, till his interest on one hand, (to which his extravagance,
perhaps,

perhaps, compels him to attend) and his impaired conſtitution on the other, oblige him to wiſh it,
wiſhed to accompany with one ; and who always
made a jeſt of the married ſtate, and, perhaps, of
every thing ſacred and juſt !

" You obſerve very well, my dear Mrs. B.
ſaid Lady Towers ; but people will be apt to
think, that you have leſs reaſon than any of our
ſex, to be ſevere againſt the notion you ſpeak of ;
for who was a greater rake than a certain gentleman, and who a better husband ?

" Madam, replied I, the gentleman you mean
never was a common town-rake : he is a gentleman of ſenſe, and fine underſtanding ; and his reformation, ſecondarily, as I may ſay, has been
the natural effect of thoſe extraordinary qualities.
But beſides, madam, I will preſume to ſay, that
that gentleman, as he has nor many equals in
the nobleneſs of his nature, ſo it is not likely, I
doubt, to have many followers, in a reformation
begun in the bloom of youth, upon ſelf-convic-
tion, and altogether, humanly ſpeaking, ſponta-
neous !—Thoſe young ladies, who would plead
his example, in ſupport of this pernicious notion, ſhould find out the ſame generous qualities
in the gentleman, before they truſt to it ; and it
will then do leſs harm : though even then I
could not wiſh it to be generally propagated.

" It is really unaccountable, ſaid Lady Towers, after all, as Mrs. B. I remember, once formerly ſaid, that our ſex ſhould not as much in-
ſiſt upon virtue and ſobriety, in the character of
a gentleman, be he ever ſuch a rake, does in that
of a lady. And it is certainly a great encouragement to libertiniſm, that a worn-out debauchee

ſhall

shall think himself at any time good enough for a husband, and have the confidence to imagine, that a modest lady will accept of his address with a preference.

" I can account for it but one way, said the Dean ; and that is, that a modest lady is apt to be diffident of herself, and she thinks this diffidence an imperfection. A rake never is: so he has in perfection a quality she thinks she wants ; and, knowing too little of the world, imagines she mends the matter by accepting one who knows too much.

" That's well observed, Mr. Dean, said lady Towers : but there is another fault in our sex, which Mrs. B. has not touched upon ; and that is, the foolish pride some ladies take in taming a wild fellow ; and that they have been able to do more than many of their sex before them could do: a pride that often costs them dear enough ; and as I know in more than one instance.

" Another weakness, said I, might be produced against some of our sex ; and that is, in joining too readily to droll upon, and sneer at, the misfortune of any poor young creature, who has shewn too little regard for her honour : and that (instead of speaking of it with concern, and thinking themselves happy, it was not their own case, and inveighing against the seducer) they will too highly sport with the unhappy creature's fall, propagate the knowledge of it—(I would not look upon Miss Sutton, while I spoke this) —and avoid her as an infection ; yet, after a while, not scruple to admit into their company the vile aggressor, and even smile with him at his
barbarous

barbarous jeſts upon the poor ſufferer of their own ſex.

" I have known three or four inſtances of this in my time, ſaid lady Towers, that Miſs Sutton might not take it to herſelf ; for ſhe looked down, and was a little ſerious.

" This, rejoined I, puts me in mind of a little humorous copy of verſes, written, as I believe, by Mr. B. and which to the very purpoſe we are ſpeaking of, he calls

Benefit of making other misfortunes our own.

Thou'ſt heard it, or read it, a million of times,
That men are made up of falſhoods and crimes:
Search all the old authors, and ranſack the new,
Thou'lt find in love-ſtories, ſcarce one mortal
    true.
Then why this complaining ? And why this wry
    Face ?
Is it 'cauſe thou'rt affected moſt, with thy own
    caſe ?
Hadſt thou ſooner made others misfortunes thy
    own,
Thou never, thyſelf, this diſaſter hadſt known ;
Thy compaſſionate caution had kept the from
    evil,
And thou might'ſt have defy'd mankind and the
    Devil.

" The ladies were pleaſed with the lines ; but Lady Towers wanted to know, ſhe ſaid, at what time of Mr. B.'s life they could be written. Be-cauſe, added ſhe, I never ſuſpected before, that the good gentleman ever took pains to write cau-

tions or exhortations to our fex, to avoid the de-
lufions of his own.

" Thefe verfes, and this facetious, but fevere
remark of Lady Towers, made every young lady
look up with a chearful countenance ; becaufe it
pufhed the ball from felf : and the dean faid to
his daughter, fo, my dear, you that have been
fo attentive, muft let us know what ufeful in-
ferences you can draw from what Mrs. B. and
the other ladies have fo excellently faid ? .

" I obferve, fir, faid mifs, from the faults the
ladies have fo juftly imputed to fome of our fex,
that the advantage the gentlemen chiefly have
over us, is from our own weaknefs ; and that it
behoves a prudent lady to guard againft firft impreffions of favour, fince fhe will think herfelf
obliged, in compliment to her own judgment,
to find reafons, if poffible, to confirm them.

" But I would be glad to know, ladies, added
mifs, if there be any way, that a lady can judge,
whether a gentleman means honourably or not,
in his addrefs to her ?

" Mrs. B. can beft inform you of that, Mifs
L. faid Lady Towers : What fay you, Mrs. B ?

" There are a few figns, anfwered I, eafy to
be known, and, I think, almoft infallible.

" Pray let's have them, faid Lady Arthur ; and
they all were very attentive.

" Thefe are they, replied I : I lay it down
as an undoubted truth, that true love is one
of the moft refpectable things in the world.
It ftrikes with awe and reverence the mind of
the gentleman, who boafts its impreffion. It
is chafte and pure in word and deed, and can-

not

not bear to have the leaſt indecency mingle with it.

" If therefore a gentleman, be his birth or quality what it will, the higher the worſe, preſume to wound a lady's ears with indecent words: If he endeavour, in his expreſſions or ſentiments, to convey groſs or impure ideas to her minds : if he is continually preſſing for her confidence in his honour : if he requeſts favours, which a lady ought to refuſe : if he can be regardleſs of his conduct or behaviour to her : if he can uſe boiſterous or rude freedoms, either to her perſon or dreſs—(Here poor Miſs Cope, by her bluſhes, bore witneſs to her caſe—) If he avoids ſpeaking of marriage, when he has a fair opportunity of doing it (—Here Miſs L. looked down, and bluſhed—) or leaves it once to a lady to wonder that he does not :—

" In any, or in all theſe caſes, he is to be ſuſpected, and a lady can have little hope of ſuch a perſon, nor, as I humbly apprehend, conſiſtent with honour and diſcretion, encourage his addreſs.

" The ladies were ſo kind as to applaud all I ſaid, and ſo did the Dean. Miſs Stapylton, Miſs Cope, and Miſs L. were to try to recollect it when they came home, and to write down what they could remember of the converſation: and our noble gueſts coming in ſoon after, with Mr. B. the ladies would have departed, but he prevailed upon them, with ſome difficulty, to paſs the evening; and Miſs L. who has an admirable finger on the ſpinnet, as I have heretofore told you, obliged us with two or three tunes. Each of the ladies did the like, and prevailed upon me to play a tune

or

or two : but Mifs Cope, as well as Mifs L. fur-
pafied me much.   We all fung too in turns, and
Mr, B. took the violin, in which he excels.
Lord Davers obliged us on the harpficord : Mr.
H. played on the flute, and fung us a fop's fong,
and performed it in character.   So that we had
an exceeding gay evening, and parted with great
fatisfaction on all fides, and high delight on the
young ladies ; for this put them all into good
fpirits, enlivening the former fcene, which otherwife might have clofed, perhaps, more gravely
than efficacioufly.

" The diftance of time fince this converfation paffed, enables me to add what I could
not do, when I wrote the account of it, which
you have miflaid : and which take briefly, as
follows :

" Mifs Stapylton, upon her return home, was
as good as her word, and wrote down all fhe
could recollect of the converfation ; and fuffered
it to have fuch an effect upon her, as to turn
the courfe of her reading and ftudies, to
weightier and more folid fubjects ; and avoiding
the gentleman fhe had began to favour, gave
way to her parents recommendation ; and is happily married to Sir Jonathan Barnes.

" Mifs Cope came to me a week after this,
with the leave of both her parents, and tarried
with me three days ; in which time fhe opened
all her worthy heart to me ; and returned in
fuch a difpofition, and with fuch refolutions,
that fhe never would fee her peer again ; nor
receive letters from him, which fhe owned to
me fhe had done clandeftinely before : and fhe
is

is now the happy lady of Sir Michael Beaumont, who makes her the beſt of husbands, and permits her to follow her charitable inclinations, according to a ſcheme, which ſhe prevailed upon me to give her.

" Miſs L. by the dean's indulgent prudence and diſcretion, has eſcaped her rake ; and, upon the diſcovery of an intrigue he was carrying on with another, conceived a juſt abhorrence of him ; and is ſince married to Dr. Jenkins, as you know, with whom ſhe lives very happily.

" Miſs Sutton is not quite ſo well off as the three former; though not altogether unhappy neither, in her way. She could not, indeed conquer her love of dreſs and tinſel ; and ſo became the lady of Col. Wilſon : and they are thus far eaſy in the marriage-ſtate, that, being ſeldom together, in all probability they ſave a multitude of miſunderſtandings ; for the Col. loves gaming, in which he is generally a winner ; and ſo paſſes his time moſtly in town. His lady has her pleaſures, neither laudable nor criminal ones, which ſhe purſues in the country. And now and then a letter paſſes on both ſides, by the inſcription and ſubſcription of which, they remind one another, that they have been once in their lives at one church together.

" And what now, my dear Lady G. have I to add to this tedious account (for letter I can hardly call it) but that I am, with great affection,

Your true friend and ſervant,

P. B.

My

" *My dear Lady* G.

" You defire me to fend you a little fpecimen of my nurfery tales and ftories, with which, as Mifs Fenwick told you, on her return to Lincolnfhire, I entertain my Mifs Goodwin and my little boys. But you make me too high a compliment, when you tell me, it is for your own inftruction and example. Yet you know, my dear Lady G. be your motives what they will, I muft obey you, although, were others to fee it, I might expofe myfelf to the fmiles and contempt of judges lefs prejudiced in my favour. So I will begin without any further apology; and, as near as I can, give you thofe very ftories with which Mifs Fenwick was fo pleafed, and of which fhe has made fo favourable a report.

" Let me acquaint you then, that my method is, to give characters of perfons I have known in one part or other of my life, in feigned names, whofe conduct may ferve for imitation or warning to my dear attentive Mifs; and fometimes I give inftances of good boys and naughty boys, for the fake of my Billy, and my Davers; and they are continually coming about me, dear madam, a pretty ftory now, cries Mifs: and, dear mamma, tell me of good boys, and of naughty boys, cries Billy.

" Mifs is a furprizing child, for her age, and is very familiar with many of the beft characters in the Spectators; and having a fmattering of Latin, and more than a fmattering of Italian, and being a perfect miftrefs of French, is feldom at a lofs for the derivation of fuch words, as are not of Englifh original. And fo I fhall give you a

ftory

ſtory in feigned names, with which ſhe is ſo delighted, that ſhe has written it down. But I
will firſt treſpaſs on your patience with one of
my childiſh tales.

" Every day, once or twice, if I am not hin-
dered, I cauſe Miſs Goodwin, who plays and ſings
very prettily, to give a tune or two to me and my
Billy and my Davers, who, as well as my Pamela, love and learn to touch the keys, young
as the latter is ; and ſhe will have a ſweet finger,
I can obſerve that ; and a charming ear ; and her
voice is muſic itſelf !—O the fond, fond mother !
I know you will ſay, on reading this.

" Then, madam, we all proceed hand in hand
together to the nurſery, to my Charley and Jemmy : and in this happy retirement, ſo much my
delight in the abſence of my beſt beloved, imagine you ſee me ſeated, ſurrounded with the joy
and the hope of my future proſpects, as well as
my preſent comforts.

" Miſs Goodwin imagine you ſee, on my right
hand, ſitting on a velvet ſtool, becauſe ſhe is
eldeſt, and a miſs : Billy on my left, in a little
cane elbow chair, becauſe he is eldeſt, and a
good boy : my Davers, and my ſparkling-eyed
Pamela, with my Charley between them, on little
ſilken cuſhions at my feet, hand in hand, their
pleaſed eyes looking up to my more delighted
ones, and my ſweet-natured promiſing Jemmy
in my lap ; the nurſes and the cradle juſt behind
us, and the nurſery maids delightfully purſuing
ſome uſeful needle-work, for the dear charmers of
my heart—all as huſh and as ſtill, as ſilence
itſelf, as the pretty creatures generally are, when
their little watchful eyes ſee my lips beginning to
open :

open : for they take great notice already, of my rule of two ears to one tongue, infomuch that if Billy or Davers are either of them for breaking the mum, as they call it, they are immediately hufh, at any time, if I put my finger to my lip, or if Mifs points hers to her ear, even to the breaking of a word in two, as it were : and yet all my boys are as lively as fo many birds ; while my Pamela is chearful, eafy, foft, gentle, always fmiling, but modeft and harmlefs as a dove.

" I began with a ftory of two little boys, and two little girls, the children of a fine gentleman and a fine lady, who loved them dearly : that they were all fo good, and loved one another fo well, that every body who faw them, admired them, and talked of them far and near : that they would part with any thing to one another : loved the poor : fpoke kindly to the fervants : did every thing they were bid to do ; were not proud ; and knew no ftrife, but who fhould learn their books beft, and be the prettieft fcholar : that the fervants loved them, and would do any thing they defired ; that they were not proud of fine cloaths; let not their heads run upon their play-things, when they fhould mind their books ; faid grace before they eat ; their prayers before they went to bed, and as foon as they rofe ; were always clean and neat ; would not tell a fib for the world, and were above doing any thing that required one : that God bleffed them more and more, and bleffed their papa and mamma, and their uncles and aunts, and coufins, for their fakes. And there was a happy family, my dear loves !—No one idle ; all prettily employed ; the mafters at their books ; the miffes at their books

E too,

too, or their needles; except at their play-hours, when they were never rude, nor noisy, nor mischievous, nor quarrelsome: and no such word was ever heard from their mouths, as, why may'nt I have this or that, as well as Billy or Bobby?—or, why should Sally have this or that, any more than I?—But it was, as my mamma pleases; my mamma knows best; and a bow and a smile; and no surliness, or scouling brow to be seen, if they were denied any thing; for well did they know, that their pappa and mamma loved them so dearly, that they would refuse them nothing that was for their good; and they were sure when they were refused, they asked for something that would have done them hurt, had it been granted. Never was such good boys and girls as these! and they grew up, and the masters became fine scholars, and fine gentlemen, and every body honoured them; and the misses became fine ladies, and fine housewives; and this gentleman, when they grew to be women, sought to marry one of the misses, and that gentleman the other; and happy was he that could be admitted into their companies! so that they had nothing to do but to pick and chuse out of the best gentlemen in the county: while the greatest ladies for birth, and the most remarkable for virtue, (which, my dears, is better than either birth or fortune) thought themselves honoured by the addresses of the two brothers. And they married, and made good papas and mammas, and were so many blessings to the age in which they lived. There, my dear loves, were happy sons and daughters! for good masters seldom fail to make good gentlemen; and good misses, good
ladies;

ladies ; and God bleffes them with as good children as they were to their parents ; and fo the bleffing goes round !—Who would not but be good ?

" Well, but, mamma, we will all be good : won't we, Mafter Davers, cries my Billy ? Yes, brother Billy. Then they kifs one another, and if they have play-things, or any thing they like, exchange with each other, to fhew the effect my leffons have upon them. But what will become of the naughty boys ? tell us, mamma, about the naughty boys !

" Why, there was a poor, poor widow wo- man, who had three naughty fons, and one naughty daughter ; and they would do nothing that their mamma bid them do ; were always quarrelling, fcratching, and fighting ; would not fay their prayers ; would not learn their book ; fo that the little boys ufed to laugh at them, and point at them, as they went along, for block- heads ; and nobody loved them, or took notice of them, except to beat and thump them about, for their naughty ways, and their undutifulnefs to their poor mother, who worked hard to maintain them. As they grew up, they grew worfe and worfe, and more and more ftupid and ignorant, fo that they impoverifhed their poor mother, and at laft broke her heart, poor, poor widow wo- man !—and her neighbours joined together to bury the poor widow woman ; for thefe fad un- gracious children made away with what little fhe had left, while fhe was ill, before her heart was quite broken : and this helped to break it the fooner ; for had fhe lived, fhe faw fhe muft have

E 2 wanted

wanted bread, and had no comfort from such wicked children.

" Poor, poor widow woman ; said my Billy, with tears ; and my little dove fhed tears too, and Davers was moved, and Mifs wiped her fine eyes.

" But what became of the naughty boys, and the naughty girl, mamma !—Became of them ! why one fon was forced to go to fea, and there he was drowned : another turned thief, (for he would not work) and he came to an untimely end : the third was idle, and ignorant, and no-body, who knew how he had ufed his poor mother, would employ him ; and fo he was forced to go into a far country, and beg his bread. And the naughty girl, having never loved work, pined away in floth and filthinefs, and at laft broke her arm, and died of a fever, lamenting too late, that fhe had been fo wicked a daughter to fo good a mother !—And fo there was a fad end of all the four ungracious children, who never would mind what their poor mother faid to them ; and God punifhed their naughtinefs as you fee ! —while the good children I mentioned before, were the glory of their family, and the delight of every body that knew them.

" Who would not be good ! was the inference: and the repetition from Billy, with his hands clapt together, poor, poor widow woman ! gave me much pleafure."

" In your maiden ftate, think yourfelf above the gentlemen, and they'll think you fo too, and addrefs you with reverence and refpect, if they fee there be neither pride nor arrogance in your behaviour, but a confcioufnefs of merit, a true dignity,

dignity, fuch as becomes virgin modefty, and untainted purity of mind and manners, like that of an angel among men; for fo young ladies fhould look upon themfelves to be, and will then be treated as fuch by the other fex.

" In your married ftate, which is a kind of ftate of humiliation for a lady, you muft think yourfelf fubordinate to your hufband ; for fo it has pleafed God to make the wife. You muft have no will of your own, in petty things : and if you marry a gentleman of fenfe and honour, fuch a one as your uncle, he will look upon you as his equal ; and will exalt you the more, for your abafing yourfelf.—In fhort, my dear, he will act by you, juft as your dear uncle does by me : and then, what a happy creature will you be !

" So I fhall, madam ! to be fure I fhall !—but I know I fhall be happy whenever I marry, be-caufe I have fuch wife directors, and fuch an ex-ample before me : and if it pleafe God, I will never think of any man, (in purfuance of your conftant advice to young ladies at the tea-table) who is not a man of fenfe, and a virtuous gentle-man. But now, dear madam, for your next character. There are two more yet to come, that's my pleafure ! I wifh there were ten !

" Why the next was Profufiana, you remem-ber, my dear love. Profufiana took another courfe to her ruin. She fell into fome of Co-quetilla's foibles, but purfued them for another end, and in another manner. Struck with the grandeur and magnificence of what weak people call the upper life, fhe gave herfelf up to the Cir-cus, to balls, to operas, to mafquerades and affem-

E 3   blies;

blies ; affects to shine at the head of all company, at Tunbridge, at Bath, and every place of public refort, plays high, is always receiving and paying visits, giving balls, and making treats and entertainments ; and is so much above the conduct which mostly recommends a young lady to the esteem of the deserving of the other sex, that no gentleman, who prefers solid happiness, can think of addressing her, though she is a fine person, and has many outward graces of behaviour. She becomes the favourite toast of the places she frequents, is proud of that diftinction ; gives the fashion, and delights in the pride, that she can make apes in imitation, whenever she pleases. But yet, endeavouring to avoid being thought proud, makes herself cheap, and is the subject of the atttempts of every coxcomb of eminence ; and without much ado, preserves her virtue, though not her character.

" What, all this while, is poor Profusiana doing ? She would be glad, perhaps of a suitable proposal, and would, it may be, give up some of her gaieties and extravagancies ; for Profusiana has wit, and is not totally deftitute of reason, when she suffers herself to think. But her conduct procures her not one solid friendship, and she has not in a twelvemonth, among a thousand professions of service, one devoir that she can attend to, or a friend that she can depend upon. All the women she sees, if she excels them, hate her ; the gay part of the men, with whom she accompanies most, are all in a plot against her honour. Even the gentlemen, whose conduct in the general, is governed by principles of virtue,

come

come down to thefe public places to partake of the innocent freedoms allowed there, and oftentimes give themfelves airs of gallantry, and never have it in their thoughts to commence a treaty of marriage, with an acquaintance begun upon that gay fpot. What folid friendfhips and fatisfactions then is Profufiana excluded from?

"Her name indeed is written in every public window, and proftituted, as I may call it, at the pleafure of every profligate, or fot, who wears a diamond to engrave it: and that, it may be, with moft vile and barbarous imputations and freedoms of words, added by rakes, who very probably never exchanged a fyllable with her. The wounded trees are perhaps taught alfo to wear the initials of her, name, linked, not unlikely, and widening as they grow, with thofe of a fcoundrel. But all this while, fhe makes not the leaft impreffion upon one noble heart: and at laft, perhaps, having run on to the end of an uninterrupted race of follies, fhe is cheated into the arms of fome vile fortune-hunter; who quickly lavifhes away the remains of that fortune which her extravagance had left; and then, after the worft ufage, abandoning her with contempt, fhe finks into an obfcurity, that cuts fhort the thread of her life, and leaves no remembrance but on the brittle glafs, and more faithful bark, that ever fhe had a being.

"Alas! alas! what a butterfly of a day, faid Mifs, (an expreffion fhe remembered of Lady Towers's) was poor Profufiana!—What a fad thing to be fo dazzled by worldly grandeur, and to have fo many admirers, and not one real friend!

E 4

"Very

" Very true, my dear, and how carefully ought a perfon of a gay and lively temper to watch over it ! and what a rock may public places be to a lady's reputation, if fhe be not doubly vigilant in her conduct, when fhe is expofed to the cenfures and obfervations of malignant crouds of people ; many of the worft of whom fpare the leaft, thofe who are moft unlike themfelves !

" But then, madam, faid Mifs, would Profufiana venture to play at public places ? will ladies game, madam ? I have heard you fay, that lords, and fharpers but juft out of liveries, in gaming, are upon a foot in every thing, fave that one has nothing to lofe, and the other much, befides his reputation : and will ladies fo difgrace their characters, and their fex, as to purfue this pernicious diverfion in public ?

" Yes, my dear, they will, too often, the more's the pity ? and do not you remember, when we were at Bath, in what a hurry I once paffed by fome knots of genteel people, and you afked, what thofe were doing ? I told you, whifperingly, they were gaming ; and loth I was, that my Mifs Goodwin fhould ftop to fee fome fights, to which, till fhe arrived at years of difcretion, it was not proper to familiarize her eye ; in fome fort acting like the antient Romans, who would not affign punifhments to certain atrocious crimes, becaufe they had fuch an idea of human nature, as to fuppofe it incapable of committing them : So I was not for having you, while a little girl, fee thofe things, which I knew would give no credit to our fex, and which I thought, when you grew older, fhould be new and fhocking to you :

you : but now you are fo much a woman in difcretion, I may tell you any thing.

" She kiffed my hand, and made me a fine
courtefy—and told me, that now fhe longed to
hear of Prudentia's conduct. Her name, madam,
faid fhe, promifes better things, than thofe of her
three companions; and fo it had need : For how
fad is it to think, that out of four ladies of
diftinction, three of them fhould be naughty, and
of courfe, my dear, faid I, were very prettily put
in : let me kifs you for them : fince every one
that is naughty, firft or laft, muft be certainly
unhappy.

" Far otherwife than what I have related, was
it with the amiable Prudentia. Like the in-
duftrious bee, fhe makes up her honey-hoard from
every flower, bitter as well as fweet; for every
character is of ufe to her, by which fhe can improve her own. She had the happinefs of an
aunt, who loved her, as I do you; and of an
uncle, who doted on her, as yours does : for,
alas ! poor Prudentia loft her papa and mamma
almoft in her infancy, in one week : but was fo
happy in her uncle and aunt's care, as not to
mifs them in her education, and but juft to remember their perfons. By reading, by obfervation, and by attention, fhe daily added new
advantages to thofe which her education gave her.
She faw, and pitied, the fluttering freedoms, and
dangerous flights, of Coquetilla. The fullen
pride, the affectation, and ftiff referves, which
Prudiana affumed, fhe penetrated, and made it
her ftudy to avoid. And the gay, hazardous
conduct, extravagant temper, and love of tin-
felled grandeur, which were the blemifhes of

E 5.   Profufiana's

Profuſiana's character, ſhe dreaded and ſhunned. She fortifies herſelf with the excellent examples of the paſt and preſent ages, and knows how to avoid the faults of the faulty, and to imitate the graces of the moſt perfect. She takes into her ſcheme of that future happineſs, which ſhe hopes to make her own, which are the true excellencies of her ſex, and endeavours to appropriate to herſelf the domeſtic virtues, which ſhall one day make her the crown of ſome worthy gentleman's earthly happineſs; and which, of courſe, as you prettily ſaid, my dear, will ſecure and heighten her own.

" That noble frankneſs of diſpoſition, that ſweet and unaffected openneſs and ſimplicity, which ſhine in all her actions and behaviour, commend her to the eſteem and reverence of all mankind; as her humility and affability, and a temper uncenſorious, and ever making the beſt of what is ſaid of the abſent perſon, of either ſex, do to the love of every lady. Her name indeed is not proſtituted on windows, nor carved on the barks of trees in public places : but it ſmells ſweet to every noſtril, dwells on every tongue, and is engraved on every heart. She meets with with no addreſs but from men of honour and probity : The fluttering coxcomb, the inveigling paraſite, the inſidious deceiver, the mercenary fortune-hunter, ſpread no ſnares for a heart guarded by diſcretion and prudence, as hers is. They ſee, that all her amiable virtues are the happy reſult of an uniform judgment, and the effects of her own wiſdom, founded in an education to which ſhe does the higheſt credit. And at laſt, after ſeveral worthy offers, enough to perplex any lady's choice,

choice, she blesses some one happy gentleman, more distinguished than the rest, for learning, good sense, and true politeness, which is but another word for virtue and honour; and shines, to her last hour, in all the duties of domestic life, as an excellent wife, mother, mistress, friend, and christian; and so confirms all the expectations of which her maiden life had given such strong and such edifying presages.

" Then folding my dear Miss in my arms, and kissing her, tears of pleasure standing in her pretty eyes, who would not, said I, shun the examples of the Coquetilla's, the Prudiana's, and the Profusiana's of this world, and chuse to imitate the character of PRUDENTIA!—the happy and the happy-making Prudentia!

" O madam! madam! said the dear creature, smothering me with her rapturous kisses, Prudentia is You!—is You indeed!—It can be nobody else—O teach me good GOD! to follow your example, and I shall be a Second Prudentia —indeed I shall!

" God send you may, my beloved Miss! and may He bless you more, if possible, than Prudentia was blessed!

" And so, my dear Lady G. you have some of my nursery tales; with which, relying on your kind allowance and friendship, I conclude myself,

" *Your affectionate and faithful,*

" P. B."

PEREGRINE PICKLE.

THIS novel was written by the late ingenious Dr. Smollet, and is on a plan in many refpects different from that of Roderick Random. Here a young gentleman is nurfed up in the lap of plenty, and when he arrives at age has an opulent eftate left him by an old fuperannuated naval officer, who had acquired riches in the fervice of his country. With many very good qualities our young adventurer becomes a flave to his paffions, and is led away with the gay diffipation of the age in which he lived, before he knew the right ufe of money. He is reduced to poverty, thrown into a prifon, where he becomes fenfible of his folly, and wifhes for an opportunity of retrieving himfelf outofhisdiftreffed circumftances. His mother, in concert with his younger brother,

deprives

deprives him of his paternal eftate, but being countenanced by an honeft old lieutenant, he procures his inlargement, and recovers his juft inheritance. Upon the whole, there are more ftriking incidents in this excellent novel than in any other that we have feen, and as they are all prefented to the reader they muft afford both inftruction and entertainment.

PEREGRINE PICKLE was the fon of Mr. Gabriel Pickle, who had formerly kept a fhop in London, but the profits of his trade not anfwering to his wifhes, he retired to Cornwall, where he purchafed an eftate, and married a young lady, the daughter of a country gentleman. His fifter, Mifs Pickle, a maid of about forty, had been for feveral years his houfekeeper, but there being no occafion for her in that capacity, after he was married, fhe began to look out for a hufband. She was too old to attract the notice of the gentry, and becaufe her father had been once Lord-Mayor of London, fo fhe could not bear the thought of giving her hand to a tradefman.

It happened that in the fame neighbourhood lived Commodore Trunion, who had been bred up to the fea, and fpent moft of his days in the navy. He lived in a houfe fortified in the fame manner as a caftle, and befides his domeftics, he kept along with him one Lieutenant Hatchway and Tom Pipes, who had formerly been his boatfwain's mate. With thefe two he ufed to fpend the evenings at a neighbouring alehoufe,

where

where he became acquainted with Mr. Pickle, and foon after propofed marrying his fifter. Not that the commodore was in love, but that·becaufe he could go no more to fea, he propofed to take a voyage in the fea of matrimony. Like an honeft tar he was downright in his propofals, and as the lady found it would be needlefs to affume thofe airs peculiar to her fex, fhe foon gave her confent, and a day was fixed for the nuptials.

The commodore had purchafed a couple of fine hunters for himfelf and the lieutenant, on which they mounted at nine in the morning to proceed for the church, but as he had never feen any thing but naval affairs, he refolved to tack about with the wind, as if he had been on the ocean. It happened that the wind fhifted about, and the commodore followed his courfe fo long, that his bride waited for him at church with the utmoft impatience. At laft it was thought neceffary to difpatch a meffenger in queft of him, for he was fo little acquainted with the church, that it was fuppofed he had miftaken the road.

This, however, was not the cafe, for the meffenger found him and his attendants veering about with the wind like a fleet at fea, and told him that the company were waiting for him at church. The commodore anfwered with great deliberation, .that he had weighed anchor about nine in the morning, for the port of matrimony, but the wind had fhifted fo often about, that he believed he would not be able to get to the harbour that day. As the meffenger did not know what he meant, he told him that he had no more to do than turn his horfe's head and follow him, by which they would be at the church in
lefs

less than half an hour. The commodore was so much exasperated at what the messenger said, that he called him an ignorant fellow, who did not understand the trim of a vessel, and therefore desired him to sheer off, or he would pour into him a whole broadside. The messenger, who found what sort of a person he had to deal with, left him, and returned back to the church, where he found the company, and the ceremony was obliged to be defered till next day.

In the mean time the commodore kept shifting about with the wind, till the horse on which he and Lieutenant Hatchway rode, heard the noise of huntsmen, and being well acquainted with the sport, they set out at full gallop, leaving the rest of the company to weather the storm in the best manner they could. Both the commodore and lieutenant believed they were mounted on the backs of devils incarnate, and giving up all for lost, dropped their whips, and held fast by the pummels of the saddles. The horse on which the lieutenant rode, was more nimble than the other, and getting before, he crossed into a field of clover, which circumstance gave Hatchway an opportunity of throwing himself off, without receiving any other hurt than what arose from his fright.

In the mean time the commodore, who had dropped his hat and wig, came up, and seeing Hatchway, called out, " Hilloa! you have got safe into port, I wish to God I was moored." The commodore had some hopes that a five-bar gate that stood opposite to him, would stop the progress of his horse, but no sooner did he approach it, than he jumped over with as much

ease

eafe as a cat would do over a harpficord. He was now in a ftate of infenfibility, he knew not whether he was dead or alive, and at laft coming to a highway, enclofed by two rifing grounds, the horfe jumped over it, to the no fmall terror of a waggoner, who happened to be paffing underneath.

By this time the commodore overtook the horfe on which the lieutenant had rode, and both kept an equal pace together, till they came to the place where the huntfmen were affembled to fee the death of the fox. The ftrange figure of the commodore in his feamen's drefs, joined to the lofs of his hat and wig, attracted the notice of the whole company, and led off their attention from poor Reynard, whofe agility had furnifhed them with fo much diverfion. The two horfes were exceeding good ones, and the 'fquire who conducted the fport, afked the commodore if he would fell them: " Sell them! I mafter; for they are above my weather gage, I have commanded a whole fleet, but was never fo much out in my reckoning as to day." The 'fquire finding that the commodore was a meer novice in land affairs, purchafed the horfes for one fourth of what they coft, and took the commodore home with him to his own houfe for the night. The company made themfelves very merry at his expence, but as he knew nothing beyond featerms, fo he took no notice of them, and next day being properly equipped, he returned to the caftle, where he found his old friend Lieutenant Hatchway. Next morning the wind happened to prove favourable, and left he fhould once more get on the devil's back, he refolved to walk to
the

the church on foot. Accordingly, having difpatched Tom Pipes to inform his bride, the lady
met him at the church, and the nuptial knot was
tied. A grand entertainment was provided at the
caftle, but when the time came for the company
to retire, an unlucky circumftance happened,
which was no other than the want of a bed for
the new married couple. The commodore was
fo much of a feaman, that he obliged every one
in the caftle to lay in hammocks, which were
flung up in the fame manner as in fhips.

The lady remonftrated in the ftrongeft manner
againft laying in fuch an indecent pofture, but by
the perfuafion of her brother and fifter-in-law,
fhe was induced to comply, and being undreffed,
mounted the hammock to wait the arrival of her
fpoufe. Every thing being properly adjufted for
the reception of the commodore, he came into
the room, or rather the cabbin, where having
drank a can of flip, and received three cheers, he
got into the canvas vehicle, to the no fmall terror
of his lady, who imagined every moment that fhe
would tumble out at the other fide. The company being now retired, the new married couple
went to reft, but no fooner did morning arrive
than the lady got up and difpatched one of the
fervants to a neighbouring town, to purchafe a
genteel bedftead, being now determined to affert
her prerogative as a wife, and not be any longer
fubject to the whims and caprice of her hufband.

When the commodore faw the bed, he fwore,
curfed and blafphemed, declaring that it fhould
be immediately configned to the flames, but by
the interpofition of Hatchway and Mr. Pickle,
he was brought into a more reafonable way of
thinking,

thinking, and to oblige his fpoufe, confented to lay in it, though contrary to a refolution he had formed many years before. The lady proceeded to make feveral other alterations in the caftle, by turning off fome of the old fervants, and order- ing that the guns fhould not be fired but in her abfence, left they fhould frighten her fo much as to occafion an abortion. All thefe acts of a new reformation the commodore was obliged to com- ply with, and to confole himfelf under what he confidered as real afflictions, he fpent more of his time than ufual at the alehoufe, curfing the day that ever.he had weighed anchor for the port of matrimony.

The haughty domineering temper of the com- modore's lady, made her odious to every one in the caftle, but as her hufband was made to be- lieve that fhe was pregnant, fo he bore with it for fome time. At laft, all hopes of an heir being vanifhed, the lady took to the bottle and religion for confolation, and the commodore refolved to make young Peregrine his heir. Peregrine had been fometime at a boarding-fchool, where he had played abundance of little knavifh tricks, which were winked at by the ufher, who fre- que..tly recived a gratuity from the commodore. But the ufher going away, Peregrine wrote a letter to the commodore, who was fo much pleafed with it, that he went to his father, and defired he would fuffer him to be brought up under his own direction.

By this time Mr. Pickle, who had another fon as well as a daughter, looked on the propofal as too valuable to be rejected, fo that he inftantly complied with it, efpecially as for reafons unknown,

known, the mother had conceived the utmoſt averſion for her eldeſt ſon. In conſequence of this permiſſion, Hatchway was diſpatched the ſame day in a poſt-chaiſe to the ſchool, and brought young Peregrine home, who was now in his eleventh year, and began to diſplay ſo much genius, that every one was charmed with him. His aunt, the lady of the commodore, was ſo much innured to dram-drinking, that when Peregrine was preſented to her, ſhe ſeemed to take no notice of him, but through the perſuaſion of Hatchway ſhe came down to the parlour, and received him with ſeeming marks of reſpect. Next day the commodore took him to viſit his parents, but how great was his ſurpriſe, when he found that his mother declared that he was not her ſon, for that he had died when only a child. This, however, made no other impreſſion on the commodore, beſides that of making him love the boy more than ever, and therefore he took him along with him to the caſtle, reſolving to beſtow that parental care and tenderneſs upon which his mother had denied him, although ſhe knew it was her duty.

Tom Pipes, who all his life-time had been accuſtomed to the practice of miſchievous tricks, became, as it were by ſympathy, the favourite of young Peregrine, who had one of the moſt fertile geniuſſes that ever fell to the ſhare of one of his age. As the commodore's lady often retired to her cloſet in the evening, under pretence of devotion, but in reality to indulge herſelf with her favourite liquors, ſo our young ſpark, with the aſſiſtance of the artful Tom Pipes, reſolved to torment her with the fear of hell and the devil.

Sometimes

Sometimes they would climb up to the window of her clofet at midnight, and imitate the fcreaming of an owl, or fome other frightful creature, which operated fo ftrongly upon her diftempered imagination, that fhe began to think that the grand adverfary of mankind had come to take her away before her time.

But the bent of their mifchievous inclinations was not confined to the lady, for they actually directed it againft the commodore himfelf. The commodore had the utmoft averfion to attornies ever fince a knavifh one had tricked him in a lawfuit, and therefore our adventurers refolved to try his patience on that head, or rather to torment him, as if they had been devils incarnate. Accordingly, they forged a letter to a country attorney, in the name of the commodore, defiring him to call next day.

The attorney, who doubted not but he would be able to fleece the old commodore of fome hundreds, came to the caftle at the hour of dinner, and Tom Pipes going up ftairs, defired his commander to come down to the parlour, to fpeak to a gentleman who waited for him. This put the commodore into a moft violent paffion, becaufe he was difturbed in the middle of his mefs, but recollecting what Pipes faid of the bufinefs being urgent, he went down, and demanded what the gentleman wanted with him. The attorney told him that he came according to an order he had received from him, and the fooner the bufinefs was difpatched, the better. " True, (faid the commodore, mad with indignation)" and lifting up his ftick, gave him fuch a blow that he fell flat on the

the ground. He then hopped up to his chamber to finifh his dinner, congratulating himfelf that he had knocked out the brains of a roguifh lawyer.

As foon as the attorney had recovered himfelf, fo as to be able to get up, he looked about him, to fee whether he could not procure evidence to fupport an action on the cafe for an affault, but feeing none, he crawled up to the dining-room, where the commodore was finifhing his mefs, and told him that if there was any law in England, he would punifh him to the utmoft rigor of it. He then produced the forged letter, which had been fent in the name of the commodore, but no fooner had the old man read it, than he ordered the attorney to be toffed in a blanket in the caftle-yard. Hatchway and Pipes performed the operation with fo much dexterity, that the fkin of the limb of the law, was as much disfigured as any fheet of parchment that ever iffued from his office. The attorney having received this whole-fome difcipline, was then ducked in a horfe-pond, and left to purfue his journey home in the beft manner he could. Stimulated with motives of revenge, he brought his action for damages againft the commodore, and the affair was tried at the next affizes. Several witneffes were examined, but as ill luck would have it, not one could prove a fingle circumftance, fo that the attorney was nonfuited, to the no fmall pleafure of many perfons prefent, whom he had by his pernicious advice, led into vexatious law-fuits, and actually ruined, under pretence of promoting their intereft.

Their

Their next exploit was much more diverting, and conducted by the very ingenious Tom Pipes. The hide of a large ox was made choice of, and being properly stuffed, the jaw-bone of a shark was fixed to his face, with two large glafs eyes. Within were feveral matches burning, which gave the whole the moft dreadful appearance, and this was fixed near the bedchamber of the commodore. No fooner did the commodore fee the dreadful apparition spewing out blue fire, than he imagined himfelf in hell, for few people in the world are more fuperftitious than feamen. His courage, however, did not forfake him, for lifting up his ftick, he ftruck it fuch a blow, that one of the horns was almoft fractured. He then took to his heels, but could not run long, when he funk down with fear; for he believed the artificial apparition to be the devil. Tom Pipes, who beheld the whole, was not willing to lofe any part of the diverfion, and therefore juft as the commodore was beginning to faint, he ran towards him and tripped up his heels.

The commodore being in fome meafure recovered by his fears rather than the hope of delivery, called out in the moft vociferous manner, upon which the fervants came to his affiftance. They found him in a cold fweat, for fear had impaired both his fenfes and faculties, fo that he was little better than a dead man. Hatchway endeavoured to raife him up, and enquiring into the caufe of his misfortune, was told by the commodore, that he had met Davy Jones, (the name given by the failors to the devil) and that he knew him by his faucer-eyes. It is very remarkable, that of all injuries, thofe that we receive in
youth

youth, make the moſt laſting impreſſion, eſpecially when they are accompanied with circumſtances of an aggravating nature. It ſeems that
while the commodore was only a ſchool-boy, he
had been detected in ſtealing deer, and being carried before a neighbouring juſtice, his worſhip
uſed him in ſo cruel a manner, that he was obliged to content himſelf with a place in the county
gaol. There he remained near a year, and his
relations refuſing to do any thing for him, he was
obliged to embrace the alternative, either to remain in priſon, or go on board of a ſhip. He
choſe the latter, and having undergone all thoſe
hardſhips that are connected with naval affairs,
he conceived the utmoſt averſion to all thoſe related to him, and refuſed to have any connection
with them for the future.

Peregrine, who was acquainted with every particular of this affair, told Hatchway and Pipes
that he would have a notable piece of fun at his
uncle's expence. The propoſal was reliſhed by
the two confederates, and it was agreed upon
between them, that a proper perſon ſhould be
made choice of, to come to the commodore with
a forged letter, in the name of that relation, who
of all others, had uſed him with the greateſt
cruelty. The perſon made choice of for this
purpoſe, was the exciſeman of the pariſh, and
having received proper directions, he went one
morning to the commodore, about two hours
before the uſual time of his getting up. The
commodore ſwore he would not come down till
the uſual time of turning out, but the exciſeman
having told the ſervant that his buſineſs was of
the moſt urgent nature, he reſolved to comply.

Having

Having crept out of his bed, he made a shift to crawl down stairs, grumbling and cursing all the way for being disturbed of his rest. When he came into the parlour, the supposed relation addressed himself to him in all the fulsome flattery that has an effect on weak minds ; but the commodore, who did not relish any thing of that nature, desired him to give over his compliments, and come to the point at once.

Upon that, the stranger presented him a letter, written, as he said, by that uncle who had used him with so much cruelty while he was in prison, for stealing the deer ; and to add the more to the aggravation that it must necessarily occasion, he told him that he had been to him one of the kindest relations that ever lived.

It is impossible to describe the perturbation of mind which the commodore felt, when he read the letter, and at last losing all manner of patience, he tore it into a thousand pieces, and trod upon the fragments on the floor. He cursed all his relations to the lowest pit of hell, and declared that he would not give one farthing, or the value of a rope's end, to keep them above board.

The exciseman, who was no stranger to the character of the commodore, began to consider himself in perilous circumstances, and therefore walked towards the door, in order to procure a retreat, not doubting but he would be able to make the commodore hearken to the voice of reason. He then told the commodore that he was one of the most ungrateful wretches in the world, for using his own relations in so shameful a manner, and concluded, by asking him what

F   he he thought they would fay of fuch an unnatural behaviour.

The commodore could conceal his refentment no longer, and turning to Tom Pipes, ordered him to take his fuppofed relation to the gang way, and there give him a round dozen doubled. Tom, though an accomplice in the whole of the fcheme, yet obeyed his orders with dexterity and punctuality. He called on fome of the fervants to affift him, who readily obeyed, and the poor gauger was conducted over the draw-bridge to the yard, where he was tied to a ftake, in order to undergo proper difcipline. He ftill imagined that Tom Pipes was in jeft, but that arch-rogue who was not too fond of what we call moral obligations, baving tied him fo faft, that he could not well make his efcape, went in fearch of a rope for the intended operation. When he arrived, the excifeman told him that he hoped he was not in earneft, to which Tom anfwered, that he was very forry for the part he was to act, but as his mafter's orders were abfolute, he was obliged to comply with them. He then undreffed the poor excifeman, and gave him fuch a hearty flogging, that he curfed the day he had ever been engaged in fuch an undertaking, threatning at the fame time to reveal the whole fcheme to the commodore. From doing that, however, he was prevented by Lieutenant Hatchway, who told him that if he made the affair public, he would be found guilty of perjury, for he had perfonated the name of a man with whom he was utterly unacquainted. This ferved to filence the excifeman, who as foon as he was loofed from the poft, took to his heels with the utmoft expedition, and ran home to his

wife,

wife, who waited for him with the utmoft impatience.

It cannot be fuppofed that fuch a fpecies of fraud and mifchief, fhould be long carried on without detection, and the commodore having revolved all the circumftances in his mind, charged young Peregrine with it. At firft, the boy denied the whole, but, when he had received a fevere flogging, he made an ample confeffion, which fo much exafperated the commodore, that he refolved to turn Hatchway out of the caftle. But he had been fo long accuftomed to the fociety of the lieutenant, as well as Pipes, that he could not live without them, fo that they were both freely forgiven.

In the mean time young Peregrine made fuch progrefs in learning, that it was propofed to fend him to fome public fchool, and that of Winchefter was made choice of by his tutor, and approved of by the commodore. Indeed, the commodore's lady had feveral reafons for wifhing to get rid of our young adventurer, for, befides his many knavifh pranks, fhe confidered him as a fpy on her conduct. Mr. Jolter, a reverend clergyman, of very high notions, was made choice of and recommended by the parfon of the parifh to be tutor to young Peregrine. Jolter was not a bad fcholar, but he had lived fo long in a college, that his temper was foured, fo that no perfon could have been made choice of more improper for fuperintending the education of a young gentleman. Tom Pipes, who had been long accuftomed to a jacket and trowfers, was put into a fuit of decent livery, in order to attend our adventurer and parfon Jolter as a footman. The

F 2   commodore

commodore propofed, that they fhould fet out to take leave of the· young gentleman's father, but the mother refufed to fee him, fo unnatural was fhe to her child, for reafons that no one could account for. The commodore, however, made up all that was wanting in the affections of the parents, for he adopted young Peregrine as his heir, and fettled him at Winchefter on the moft genteel footing. The commodore's lady made a handfome prefent to Mr. Jolter, as a reward for his piety, and Hatchway infifted on ftaying at the fchool along with Peregrine. He told the commodore, that he had fome thoughts of learning the Latin lingo, although he did not at that time know the difference between a noun and a verb. The commodore expoftulated with the lieutenant on the impropriety of thinking to learn Latin at fuch a period of life, and as he could not bear the thought of living without him, he told him, that if he would return to the caftle, he would give him leave to vifit young Peregrine once every month. Hatchway was not fuch a fool, but he could feel the force of what was faid by the commodore, and therefore having given up all thoughts of learning Latin, he took leave of our young gentleman, though not without fhedding tears. He faid he was fure the young dog had betwitched him, for he could not look at him, without loving him. Indeed, there was fuch an honeft fimplicity in the lieutenant, that he thought well of all the human race, and could not help loving fuch as were young.

Peregrine had not been long at the fchool, when his genius began to diftinguifh itfelf in a moft confpicuous manner. His pupil was fuch an
arrant

arrant pedant, that he feemed a very proper object for him to exercife his ingenuity upon, and
therefore he began by mixing brandy and other
ftrong liquors with his tea, fo that he was often
intoxicated without knowing the caufe. By
fuch practice he brought the character of his
tutor into the utmoft contempt, and to complete
the farce, Peregrine was chofen *Dux* or head of
a felect number of boys, who refolved to fhake
off all obedience to their tutors. The head
mafter having received information of thefe pro-
ceedings fent for Mr. Jolter, and told him that he
muft keep a more ftrict watch over the morals of
his pupils, otherwife he would corrupt one half
of the boys in the fchool.

Mr. Jolter was a good deal difcompofed when
he received the information, but as nothing could
be more juft or reafonable, he went home, and
called Peregrine into his room. He repeated to him
the dangerous confequences of fuch practices,
and the difgrace he would bring upon himfelf
and his relations, unlefs there was fome change
in his conduct.

Peregrine, though a wild youth, was not deftitute of good fenfe, and therefore feeing the
propriety of what was faid by his tutor, he promifed to be more obedient for the future.

Mr. Jolter was fo overjoyed at this inftance of
his pupil's docility, that he refolved to improve
it to the beft advantage, and therefore propofed
to him the ftudy of the mathematicks, as the
only fcience that can enlarge the mind, by leading it off from objects of a trifling nature. The
young gentleman entered upon the ftudy with
the utmoft pleafure, but no fooner had he gone

F 3

through

through the firſt two books of Euclid, than he becan.e ſo much diſguſted with the whole ſcience that he declared he would not purſue it any further. In vain did Mr. Jolter remonſtrate to his pupil on the great impropriety of his conduct; the young gentleman remained inexorable, and nothing cou.d induce him to proceed any furtner. Indeed he ſhook off all manner of reſtraint, he refuſed to be obedient to his tutor any longer, upon which the head maſter deſired Mr. Jolter to write to the commodore, that he might as ſoon a poſſible remove Tom Pipes from attending on Peregrine, for that antiquated ſeaman was now become a general nuiſance to the whole ſchool.

The truth is, Tom Pipes was at the head of every ſcene of miſchief, and nothing ſeemed to give him ſo much pleaſure, as that of tormenting his fellow-creatures. He mingled in all their diverſions, and decided in every controverſy that aroſe between them. He regulated their manual exerciſe by his whiſtle, and he preſcribed rules to each of them according to their different ages. Indeed Tom Pipes was in a manner become ſo neceſſary to the boys, that it could not be ſuppoſed that they would part with him without an inſurrection taking place. Peregrine was ſenſible of this, and therefore on promiſing to be more circumſpect in the reſt of his conduct, Pipes was allowed to continue at the ſchool ſometime longer. This, however, was a reſolution too good to laſt long, as will appear from the following incident.

One day Tom Pipes having conducted ſome of the boys to a garden in the ſuburbs, they were very

rude

rude in pulling the fruit, which so inraged the gardener, that he came to them and demanded satisfaction. The boys refused to satisfy his demands, upon which the great dog was set loose upon them, and in the scuffle Peregrine lost his cap. The engagement now became general, the gardener called his apprentice to his assistance, while Tom Pipes led on the insurgents in battle array. The gardener, who was a stout fellow, took his stand at the turning of one of the avenues, and when Pipes advanced, he gave him such a blow on the head, that his scull rung as if it had been made of bell metal.

Pipes soon recovered from the dreadful blow he had received, and darting his head into the bosom of the gardener tumbled him into a trench, that he had newly digged, nor did it fare better with the dog, who coming up to the assistance of his master, laid hold of the calf of Tom Pipes' leg, and would have eaten it for his dinner, had not the seaman turned about, and in an instant put a period to the existence of the foracious animal.

The gardener was now so much overpowered that he knew not what to do, and his wife having alarmed the neighbourhood, Tom Pipes advised the scholars to desist, lest they should be all apprehended and committed to prison. The scholars complied with his request, but as the gardener was rendered incapable of following his work, and as his children became chargeable to the parish, an enquiry was set on foot to find out the aggressors.

The result of the enquiry was, that our adventurer was found to be at the head of this

unruly

unruly mob of boys, and therefore it was ordered that he should undergo a severe flogging, and a day was appointed for the execution of this solemn decree.

The thoughts of being disgraced in this manner was what he could not bear, and, therefore, he resolved to make an elopement from the school. He communicated his intentions to some of the most active of the scholars, and when the time arrived that he was to receive the threatened discipline, they came with him into the school, and demanded of the master that he should instantly be forgiven. The master, however, behaved with that dignity becoming his station, and Peregrine, notwithstanding his professions of courage, was horsed and whipped, to the terror of all others, who should for the future offend in the like manner. This disgrace had such an effect upon him, that he resolved to detach himself from his disorderly companions, and apply himself in good earnest to his studies. He was now above fourteen years of age, and in stature and shape one of the finest figures that ever was seen. The young ladies began to take notice of him, and there being a ball one evening he went to dance at it, as is the common practice with young gentlemen.

While he was waiting for the company, the master of the ceremonies took notice of him, and singled out for him a partner, a young lady, whose name was Emily Gauntlet, and sister to a young gentleman who happened to be there at the same time. The young lady was extremely handsome, and her exterior appearance was set off by all the improvements that the intellectual

faculties

faculties can receive. When the ball was over
our hero returned to his lodgings, but he could
not sleep during the whole of the night. In
the morning he arose, and having dressed himself in the most agreeable manner, he went to
the lodgings of Miss Gauntlet, and was shewn
into the parlour. Emilia made her appearance
in the most inchanting dress; and the passions of
our hero were now wound up to the highest
pitch. The mother of the young lady was still
in bed, and when she got up she seemed to look
upon Peregrine in no very favourable light, for
she considered him in no other light than a young
spark who wanted to make himself merry at the
expence of such young females as are weak
enough to harken to their solicitations.

The young lady treated him with all the indulgence she possibly could, consistent with the
regard she ought to have had for her own character, and invited him to visit her from time to
time at her mother's house, which was only a
few miles distant. This was just what he wished for, and in the midst of his mutual embraces,
he declared to her, that his passion was the most
pure that ever took place in the human breast.
Being obliged to take leave of his charmer, he
returned to school, but became so pensive and
melancholy, that all his former acquaintance began to shun his company. At last he resolved
to elope, and having tied up a bundle of linen,
with other necessaries, he gave it to Tom Pipes,
and next morning both set out together on
foot, for the village where the mother of Emilia
lived.

F 5

When

When he came to the village, he took lodgings at an inn, and leaving Tom Pipes to take care of his baggage, he let out for the houfe where his charmer refided, ftruggling under all that anxiety of mind that generally takes place in the mind of a lover.

When he came to the gate, he was fo much taken up with the thoughts of the young lady, that when fhe made her appearance he fcarce knew her; for his mind was tortured with all the variety of difcordant paffion. She received him in the moft complaifant manner, and conducted him to the parlour, where her mother was then fitting drinking tea. This was a more favourable reception than he had any reafon to expect; but every thing fucceeding fo far according to his wifh, it was propofed that he and the young lady fhould take a walk together till towards evening. Upon their return, the mother invited Peregrine to fupper, and the young lovers being left alone, many tender things paffed between them. He protefted in the moft folemn manner that he loved her above every one he had ever feen; while fhe on her part chid him gently for running away from fchool. In this fhe was feconded by her mother, whofe circumftances had taught her prudence; for fhe was the widow of a general officer who had loft his life in the fervice of his country, and had left his fon in the humble ftation of a volunteer, waiting for the intereft of fome great man to beftow upon him a commiffion.

While he remained under the influence of this fweet intoxication, his abfence occafioned no fmall difturbance at Winchefter, and Mr. Jolter wrote

wrote to the commodore, giving him an account of his elopement. The poor old commodore received the news of the elopement with the utmost surprise, and cursed Hatchway and Tom Pipes, for having debauched the boy's mind, by leading him off from a sense of his duty. Nor did he spare Jolter, whom he called an old doating fool, because he had not kept a better look out, to prevent Peregrine from foundering. He immediately dispatched expresses to all the sea-ports on the coast, to prevent his going abroad, while Lieutenant Hatchway was dispatched across the country, to make all the enquiries he could concerning the young fugitive. Hatchway spent four days without receiving any intelligence, when being benighted, he took up his lodgings at a village, where he had not regaled himself long, when he heard the voice of his old friend Tom Pipes, entertaining a company of rustics with a song in true sea language. Hatchway flung his pipe into the chimney corner, and grasping a pistol in his hand, went to the room where Pipes was, and swore that he would blow his brains out, unless he produced young Peregrine. Pipes, not in the least intimidated, told the lieutenant that Peregrine was as safe as a roach, and that he would produce him as soon as he had finished his song. Hatchway could not have any objection to this proposal, and Tom having finished his song, and dismissed the company, the two old mess-mates retired to another room. There Pipes recited to the lieutenant every circumstance relating to the elopement, and before they had done speaking, Peregrine came in from his mistress with whom he had spent the evening. Hatchway was over-
joyed

joyed to fee his long-loft young mafter, but much more fo, when he found that he was fenfible of his folly in running away from fchool, and vexing his generous friend the commodore. At laft, it was agreed that they fhould fet out the next morning for Winchefter, and in the mean time, Peregrine went to take leave of his miftrefs. Their parting was truly affecting, but as there was a neceffity for it, the young lady pretended to make no objections, while her mother faid all fhe could in favour of parental authority, and next morning our hero returned to Winchefter, where he was received in the moft kindly manner, by Parfon Jolter, his tutor.

The mafter of the fchool forgave him on account of his youth, but when Hatchway returned to the garrifon, and told the whole of the circumftances to the commodore, the old gentleman was very much grieved, efpecially when he began to confider that there was a young lady in the cafe. He refolved, therefore, to lay the whole of the affair before Mr. Pickle, his father, that proper meafures might be concerted, in order to prevent his ruin. In the mean time, Peregrine fent a love epiftle to his miftrefs, and concluded, by telling her, that he would never place his affections on any other object. This letter was fent by the hands of the faithful Tom Pipes, with ftrict orders that it fhould be delivered into her own hands, without communicating the contents to any perfon whatever befides herfelf.

Tom Pipes being thus employed as ambaffador, took his place on the box of a ftage-coach, and that the letter might not be loft, he put it between the fole of his fhoe and ftocking. This was very confiftent with his own vulgar ideas, but no fooner did he come to the inn, than feeling for the letter, he found that by the motion of the coach, it was all torn in pieces. This was a moft fhocking circumftance for poor Tom Pipes, who curfed both the coachman and the coach. There was, however, no time to be loft, and therefore, after fome reflection, he refolved to fend for the clerk of the parifh, and get him to write a letter of a fimilar nature.

Accordingly, Tom went in queft of the fchool-mafter, who was one of the moft arrant pedants that ever lived, and bringing him to the inn, got him to write a letter in that ftile which thofe of his fraternity call the true fublime. Pipes was fo much overjoyed when he heard it read, that he could not refrain from fqueezing the pedagogue by the hand, telling him at the fame time, that it was light in its timbers, and would for ever remain above water. Flufhed with the hopes of fuccefs, he fet out for the houfe where the young lady refided, not doubting but he would meet with a favourable reception, but when fhe had read the nonfenfical epiftle, fhe concluded that either her lover was mad, or that he had fent the letter with no other view, than to make her an object of ridicule.

Pipes, who doubted not but he would receive a favourable anfwer, was difmiffed with vifible marks of contempt, and next day he arrived at Winchefter. Peregrine, who had waited for his return with the utmoft impatience, no fooner faw him, than he reached out his hand for a letter, but being informed that he had none, he immediately concluded, that Emilia had not an opportunity

portunity to write, and therefore he refolved to wait the return of the poft. But as he did not receive any anfwer during the whole of the enfuing week, his pride was fummoned up to his affiftance, and he began to defpife the woman whom he imagined had treated him with fo much indignity.

His behaviour foon reached the ears of the young lady's mother, and from that circumftance fhe was convinced that he was the fame coxcomb as he had reprefented himfelf in his letter. She therefore ordered her daughter not to think any more of him, and thus a youthful correfpondence was broken off merely by the conduct of Pipes, who took no more notice of it than if he had been affifting in finking a fhip, or preventing one from deftruction.

While things were going on in this manner, the commodore, who never loft fight of the intereft of young Peregrine, confulted the parfon of the parifh concerning the moft proper means to be ufed, and at laft it was agreed upon between them, that he fhould be taken from the fchool, and fent to the univerfity. Accordingly he was fent for home along with his tutor, Mr. Jolter, who had not, during the whole time he was at Winchefter, taught him any thing that could contribute toward promoting his intereft. Mr. Pickle no fooner faw his fon, than he vowed that he was grown up to years of difcretion, and he beftowed a thoufand bleffings on the commodore, for having been at fo much expence in his education, but his mother was of a different opinion, for fhe had conceived fuch an inveterate hatred to her eldeft fon, that fhe looked upon him

as

an object of deteſtation. She ordered that none of the ſervants ſhould for the future grant him admittance to the houſe, which ſo much exaſperated Hatchway, that he ſwore he would be revenged on her one way or other. Indeed, it is not to be wondered at, for the honeſt lieutenant imagined that every one was as innocent as himſelf.

The commodore, who under an outſide of ſavage ruſticity, poſſeſſed real goodneſs of heart, could not hear with indifference the manner in which Mr. Pickle uſed his ſon, and therefore having beſtowed a volly of curſes upon the whole family, he took Peregrine home along with him to the caſtle. It was then reſolved, that our young adventurer ſhould be ſent to the univerſity along with Mr. Jolter, who was ſtill to act the part of his tutor; but he had not been long at Oxford, when he diſcovered ſuch a diſpoſition for ſatire, that every one of the young nobility and gentry courted his friendſhip, not doubting but they would be able to make his ingenuity ſubſervient to their purpoſes. Mr. Jolter, who had the intereſt of Peregrine entirely at heart, in order to divert him from ſuch practices, introduced him to the company of a club of politicians, who were reputed men of knowledge and probity, and who ſpent the evenings in animadverting on the conduct of the miniſtry, and hatching ſchemes for overturning the government both in church and ſtate.

It is not to be ſuppoſed that a youth ſo volatile as Peregrine, would be much delighted with the company of men, who inſtead of ſpeaking conſiſtent with their characters as rational creatures,

were

were like an assembly of quakers, or rather of superannuated or melancholy cats. Indeed, he looked upon them in so mean and contemptible a light, that he soon began to despise them, and one night having made them all drunk, he started a topic of argument that irritated their passions so much, that they got to loggerheads, and bottles and glasses flew about in such abundance, that scarce one in the company could make his escape without receiving a mark that would put him in mind of the nocturnal adventure.

The uproar was so great that the whole neighbourhood was alarmed, and just at that instant, the proctor happening to be returning to his chambers, took them all into custody, except Mr. Jolter, who made his escape at the expence of a couple of black eyes. Next morning he was summoned to attend the proctor, in order to answer for his conduct, which frightened him considerably, but Peregrine, who was an arch-wag, told him that he would, by the help of a certain paint, hide the circles around his eyes, to all which Jolter submitted, but when he made his appearance, the fraud was discovered, and he received a severe reprimand.

For some time Parson Jolter was so much mortified, that he scarce knew how to appear in public, and not doubting but Peregrine had a principal share in the whole scheme, he could not refrain from shewing marks of his resentment. This was what the proud spirit of our adventurer could not bear, and therefore in revenge for the insolence of his tutor, he wrote a copy of verses against him, in such satirical language, that poor Jolter hesitated, whether he should not lay out
his

his laſt ſhilling, in the purchaſe of a rope, in order to deprive the hangman of his *legal* wages.

Peregrine uſed often to make excurſions to different parts of the country, particularly Windſor, where while he was one day walking along with a fellow collegian, he diſcovered Emilia, and made up to her. The young lady had not forgotten the inſult offered her in the odious letter, written by the pariſh clerk, at the inſtigation of Tom Pipes, and therefore ſhe treated him in a cold formal manner. She refuſed to hear any thing that he had to ſay in his defence; but after ſeveral ſolicitations, ſhe agreed to honour him with an interview, during which time the whole myſtery was cleared up, and a mutual reconciliation took place, though not before the amiable young lady had procured a free pardon for poor Pipes and the pedantic clerk. In the mean time, his long abſence from Oxford, gave great uneaſineſs to Mr. Jolter, who with all his faults, ſtill wiſhed his pupil well, and therefore having learned the name of the young gentleman with whom he had made the excurſion to Windſor, he went to his chambers, and was told that Peregrine was ſtill at Windſor along with Miſs Emily Gauntlet, and that it would be no eaſy matter to diſengage them from each other.

In conſequence of that information, Mr. Jolter ſet out for Windſor, where he met with his pupil, and remonſtrated to him on the impropriety of his conduct. This put Peregrine into a moſt violent paſſion, and high words aroſe between him and his tutor. Mr. Jolter could never forgive Peregrine, for the part he had acted, in making him ſo ridiculous at the political club; and,

and, although he was under many obligations to
the commodore, yet he would have given up his
charge, had he not been in expectation of receiving a rich living, which the aged naval officer was expected to have in his power, to present him to after the death of an incumbent, who
was then far advanced in years. The thoughts
of such a valuable acquisition made him keep his
passions under proper restraint, and although often
insulted by Peregrine, yet he resolved to dif-
semble his resentment, till such time as he was
properly provided for.

Peregrine was so much exasperated at the conduct of his tutor, that he wrote a letter to his
aunt, and in answer received one which mortified
his pride to the utmost. She told him, that the
commodore had all along treated him with the
greatest tenderness, and that it was his duty to be
obedient to him in every thing, but th: ..c :.. far
from bringing his passions under the government
of reason, only served to inflame them the more,
and therefore he wrote a letter in the most polite
stile to the commodore, attempting to ridicule
his conduct, by throwing the whole blame upon
Jolter, whom he accused of tyranny and par-
tiality.

The commodore, who knew no other phrases
than such as are made use of at sea, wrote Peregrine an answer, wherein he told him, that if he
would be a good boy, he would yet take him into
favour, but if he continued refractory, he would
discard him for ever.

Hatchway, who had been dispatched with this
letter to Peregrine, said all he could to persuade
the young gentlemen to comply with the commodore's

modore's requeft, and in order to prevail with
him, told him, that if he had feduced the young
lady, he was willing to take her off his hands.
Hatchway had ftrict orders to bring our young
hero home to the caftle, but no fooner had he
mentioned the affair to him, than Peregrine
ftarted up, and declared his refolution that no
perfon fhould compel him to comply with a propofal fo contrary to his inclination. Hatchway
was fo much irritated at what Peregrine faid, that
he tripped up his heels, and laid him flat on the
floor, calling him at the fame time one of the
moft faucy boys that ever walked between ftem
and ftern. Peregrine would have dropped all
manner of altercation with one whom he loved for
the honeft fimplicity of his manners, but nothing
would ferve the lieutenant, unlefs he would fight
him with fword and piftols. The place made
choice of for the deciding this important quarrel,
was Windfor foreft, to which our two combatants walked, but in their way thither, they
were met by Tom Pipes, who had armed himfelf
with a large wooden cudgel. As Pipes had the
utmoft refpect for the lieutenant, with whom he
had ferved many years on board, and as he really
wifhed well to young Peregrine, fo he refolved
to prevent any mifchief that fhould happen, and
in confequence of that refolution, brought both
parties to agree together, and the commodore
wrote a very feeling letter to Peregrine, promifing him that nothing fhould be wanting to
promote his intereft for the future.

When Peregrine had viewed the commodore's
letter, he was fo much chagrined, that he became for fome weeks a perfect flave to melancholy,

choly, but the impetuofity of his paffions getting
the better of every thing, he refolved to affert his
dignity as a rational creature, and not to be any
longer the dupe of a family, who feemed to feek
the promotion of his intereft no farther than was
confiftent with their own inclinations. Stimulated by motives of refentment againft Hatchway,
and ftill a captive to love, he went to vifit his
charmer, not doubting but her converfation
would contribute towards rubbing off that rufti-
city that he had contracted during the melancholy
under which he had laboured. He told her that
his uncle the commodore had propofed that he
fhould make the tour of Europe, and he could
not help expatiating on the pleafure that he would
enjoy in the volatile court of Paris, where nothing lefs than intrigue and gallantry could make
a diftinguifhing figure.

The young lady heard him with emotion, nor
was it in her power to prevent the tears from
dropping down from her lovely eyes, efpecially
when fhe was told that the commodore was offended at their meeting fo often together. To
remove all her fcruples, he told her that he would
be hers to the lateft period of his exiftence, and
at the fame time endeavoured to convince her of
the neceffity he was under of paying an implicit
obedience to his uncle's commands. The young
lady could not help feeling in the moft fenfible
manner the force of what he advanced, and therefore compofing herfelf, fhe told him that fhe was
perfectly fatisfied, and that for the future fhe
would not object to any part of his conduct,
unlefs by fome frefh action of his infidelity, he
fhould give her occafion to do fo. Every thing
being

being thus settled in the most amicable manner, the young lady took her leave, and our hero, who resolved to comply with his uncle's request, dispached the lieutenant and parson Jolter to the castle, to inform the commodore, that as soon as he had settled a few trifling things among his fellow collegians, he would return, and comply with every thing that he had proposed for him, with respect to the regulation of his future conduct particularly, and making the tour of Europe.

In his journey to the castle he took Emilia along with him part of the way, and on the evening of the first day they took up their lodgings at a country inn, which at that time was crouded with great numbers of people, who had been at a neighbouring fair, and were now regaling themselves with beer and tobacco. This was a circumstance that our lovers were obliged to put up with : but in the middle of the night they were alarmed with the cry of fire; and, upon enquiry, it was found, that the country people, having got drunk, had left some candles burning, so that two of the galleries were instantly in a flame. Peregrine and Tom Pipes started up in an instant, and saved the young lady, as well as her companion; and so disinterested was poor Tom, that he refused to accept of a reward which they generously offered him.

Next day they arrived at the house where the young lady's mother lived, but her brother had no sooner seen our hero, than he considered him as one who had a design to injure his sister, and therefore treated him in the most haughty manner. This was more than Peregrine would have

bore

bore with from any other perfon, but the love
he had for Emilia induced him to conceal his
refentment. The young lady, who could not
diffemble her paffion for him any longer, gave
him a ring to keep as a token of her love, which
pleafed him fo much that he embraced her with
all the ardour of the moft tender affection, and
next morning fet out on his journey.

He had not, however, proceeded far on his
journey, when at the end of a lane, he was
met by Godfrey, the brother of the young lady,
and commanded to ftop, till he had given him
the fatisfaction of a gentleman. For fome time
Peregrine infulted him on account of his poverty, and told him in plain terms, if he did not
go inftantly about his bufinefs, he would order
his footman, Tom Pipes, to give him a moft
hearty drubbing. This laft expreffion fo much
exafperated Godfrey, that he drew his fword, fo
that our hero was obliged to do the fame, and
a furious combat enfued. Each of the contending parties were wounded, but Peregrine having
broken his fword, the other refufed to take any
advantage of him, but, leaving him, told him,
that for the future he muft never infult any gentleman on account of his poverty.

Peregrine, who with his foibles had a large
fhare of humanity, no fooner heard the laft
words uttered by the young gentleman than he
was ftruck with remorfe, for having treated him
fo difrefpectfully, and therefore going up to him
defired that he would alight from his horfe, till
he fhould have an opportunity of explaining his
fentiments. The young gentleman, who was
no more than a cadet in the army, though the
fon

son of a general officer, fuppofed he wanted to
finifh the combat, and therefore alighting, walked with him into a room, where he expected he
would prefent him with a brace of piftols. But
how 'great was his furprize when Peregrine gave
him to underftand, that he was willing to do any
thing to promote his intereft, and that his paffion for his fifter was the moft pure that could
be imagined. He added that he was going to fet
out for France, and Godfrey having promifed to
meet him at the commodore's, they both parted
on the moft friendly terms.

The commodore was now turned of feventy,
and fo much crippled by the gout, that he was
fcarce able to ftir abroad. Mr. Pickle, his brother-in-law, gave him but very little of his company, fo that the old gentleman, was in a manner, reftored to a new ftate of life, in confequence of having young Peregrine once more to
attend him. Gamaliel, the younger brother of
Peregrine, was now about fifteen years of age,
but of fuch a perverfe difpofition, that although
his mother confidered him as her favourite, yet
every one in the houfe, as well as in the neighbourhood, treated him with the moft fovereign
contempt.

One day while young Gam. was riding out
along with his tutor, the curate of the parifh,
Peregrine happened to come in fight, and Gam.
who had been taught to offer him all the indig-
nities he could, rode up againft him, in order
to unhorfe him. Peregrine, who gueffed his intention, acted in fo fpirited a manner, that young
Gam. was flung from his horfe, and before he
had time to recover himfelf, Peregrine dif-
mounted,

mounted, and gave the curate such a hearty drubbing, that he was not able, for several weeks after, to make his appearance in the church, so that he was obliged to say, " Lord have mercy upon us," at home.

Complaints were made to the commodore, but the good old seaman, instead of paying any regard to them, declared that he wished young Gam. had broke his neck, so as Peregrine was out of the scrape.

As Peregrine could not put up calmly with the affront that had been offered him by the curate, so he resolved to take a severe revenge on that reverend gentleman. Accordingly he and Hatchway set out for the alehouse where the curate spent his evenings, and having engaged a parlour for themselves, the lieutenant was placed to keep a good look out, while Peregrine, who was an excellent mimic, went into the yard, and personated a dialogue between the curate and the wife of the publican. It was not long before the landlord heard what passed, and concluding that his spouse was gone into the barn with the priest, he run thither in search of the adulterers, while Peregrine got in at the window, and set down in the most demure manner with Hatchway. As the poor publican was too much agitated to seek for his wife in the barn, he left the door open, and returned to the house, where he saw her go in at another door. His suspicions were now fully confirmed, but much more so when he heard Hatchway in his arch leering manner, tell him that he believed the curate of the parish had some regard for his wife.

A few days after this, in order to carry on the farce somewhat farther, at the expence of the curate, a boy was difpatched to inform that reverend gentleman that the publican's wife was extremely ill, and that fhe could not bear the thoughts of dying without fpeaking with him. The curate obeyed the fummons; and, in the mean time, Peregrine, with Hatchway, went to the place as ufual, where they had not been long, when our young hero told the publican, that the parfon was juft gone in at a private door to the kitchen. This was more than the publican could bear; and, therefore, not doubting but he would meet with the curate at the end of one of the lanes in his return, went into the barn, and armed himfelf with a flail. From thence he fet out to the place where he expected to meet him, and feeing him come up he extended the flail, which, if it had done the execution, there would have been a new place for another poor prieft. Exafperated that he had not felled the prieft to the ground, the publican once more extended the flail, but a fecond time miffing his aim, he ftruck himfelf on the head fuch a terrible blow, that for fome time he ftaggered in the fame manner as he had often feen fome of his cuftomers do. In the mean time the curate, who imagined that he had been befet by fome robber, grafped his cudgel, and took to his heels, but the publican getting up, purfued him, and gave him fuch a drubbing, that had not fome labourers come up to his affiftance, he would have inevitably perifhed.

Hatchway and Peregrine fat waiting in the parlour till the landlord arrived, and feeing the

marks

marks of his rencounter upon him, they began to
make themselves very merry at his expence. He
could not conceal from them the manner in which
he had treated the curate, whom he called a
parish bull, let loose upon the wives of all the
honeft men in the neighbourhood.

He had fcarce done fpeaking, when his wife
came in, and told him, that fome waggish boy
had fent Mr. Sackbut, the parfon of the parish to
pray with her. The publican, whofe jealoufy
was now wound up to the higheft pitch, could
conceal his indignation no longer, and therefore
turning to his wife, told her that he had difabled
the parfon from praying with her for fome time.
This was what the publican's wife could not
bear, and therefore cafting a look of ineffable
contempt on her hufband, told him that he had
no bufinefs to fit in company with gentlemen,
while the company in the kitchen wanted his attendance. It was in vain for the poor hen-
pecked hufband to make any reply, for knowing
the fuperiority that his wife had over him, he
left the room, and went to obey her orders.
Next day it was reported throughout the parish,
that Mr. Sackbut had been attacked by footpads
and almoft murdered, and an advertifement was
affixed to the church door, offering a reward to
thofe who would make a difcovery, but no perfon
came to claim it, fo that the poor parfon was
obliged to put up with his drubbing.

It was not long before the curate began to
fufpect that the whole was a fcheme projected by
Peregrine, for he knew that the whole county
could not produce fuch two cunning rogues as
Hatchway and Mr. Thomas Pipes, under whofe
direction

direction our young hero acted. He therefore refolved to be revenged on Peregrine, and imparted
his fcheme to young Gam, his pupil, but as
good luck would have it the fifter of Peregrine,
an amiable young lady, overheard the whole of
their converfation, and communicated it to a
young gentleman, who was in love with her, and
who gave by her direction an account of it to
Peregrine.

To counteract this diabolical fcheme, it was
propofed that a perfon fhould be fent to watch in
an adjacent field, in order to give them an account at what time the confpirators came up.
One whole evening was fpent in vain, for none
of them came up, but on the fecond the meffenger came to the caftle, and informed the lieutenant that three men were fkulking behind a
hedge near the road that led to the public
houfe.

This news was no fooner told, than the company fallied forth, in order to wreck their ven-
geance on the curate and his pupil, but when
they came to the place, they found young Mr.
Gauntlet, the brother of Emily, exercifing his
cudgel on a fellow whom he had got down. Peregrine, with the reft of the company, ran to his
affiftance, and having taken the fellow prifoner,
conducted him to the caftle along with the young
gentleman, who had left his horfe at the inn.
The prifoner being brought before the commodore, confeffed that he had been employed by
the curate of the parifh, to affaffinate Peregrine,
upon which he was fuffered to go about his
bufinefs, to the great mortification of Pipes, who

G 2   wanted

wanted to give him a round dozen at the gang-
way.

The commodore treated young Gauntlet with
every mark of refpect, and one day, in the courfe
of their converfation together, difcovered that he
had been formerly acquainted with his father,
who at that time was only a lieutenant of marines,
though an officer of experienced conduct.

Young Gauntlet had fuch fcrupulous notions
of honour, that before the commodore could prevail on him to accept of as much money as would
purchafe a commiflion, he was obliged to tell
him that he was fo much indebted to his father,
but not knowing what was become of him, had
never till then an opportunity of repaying it.
Thefe things being fettled, and French fervants
hired to attend our young hero in his intended
tour, Gauntlet left the caftle, and the commodore ordered that Tom Pipes fhould remain at
home, becaufe he was ignorant of the French
lingo. Before Peregrine fet out, he received a
letter from his fifter, informing him that fhe
would meet him at a cottage near her father's
houfe, in order to converfe with him on fome
things of importance.

He obeyed the fummons, and when he came
to the place, found his fifter, and was furprifed
to find her poffeffed of fo many accomplifhments
beyond what he expected. He propofed taking
her away from her unnatural parents, but before
he had done fpeaking, his mother, who had
placed fpies on her daughter, rufhed into the
apartment, and would have torn the poor young
lady to pieces, had not Peregrine interpofed in
her defence. The mother was fo tranfported
with

with rage that she seemed like a bedlamite, and when
Peregrine began to expostulate with her in favour
of his sister, she declared that for the future she
should never be admitted into her father's house.
Peregrine was much troubled in what manner he
should dispose of his sister, but finding no other
method of providing for her than putting her
under the protection of his generous benefactor,
he took her home to the castle, where she met
with a welcome reception from the commodore.
Old Pickle was obliged to comply with the dictates of his wife, which so enraged the commodore, that he sent him a challenge, but the
other had no intention of accepting it. Hatchway, however, was extremely unwilling to lose
a little fun, and therefore returning to the castle,
told the commodore that old Mr. Pickle would
meet him.

As the commodore never knew what it was to
be afraid to fight, he resolved to go, and in the
mean time it was proposed that young Peregrine
should personate his father, and mimic his
voice. A real farce ensued, and the poor commodore was defeated without knowing that the
conqueror was his godson.

The time for his departure drawing nigh, Mr.
Jolter was made choice of to attend him as a
tutor, and having taken leave of all his friends at
the castle, he set out in a post-chaise for Dover.
Young Gauntlet went with him, to see him safe
on board, and before they parted, a plan was
settled in what manner they should correspond
with each other. When they came to Dover,
Parson Jolter ordered an elegant supper to be got
ready, and some of the best Burgundy wine, but

scarce.

scarce had they sat down, when they were alarmed with a dreadful uproar in the next room. It happened that the dispute was between a furious Welchman and a poor Italian quack, who not finding proper encouragement in other countries, had come over to England. The Welchman, whose Cambrian blood was all on flame, had got the poor foreigner down, and would certainly have killed him, had not Peregrine and the rest of the company come to his assistance. The Welchman said, the Italian was a conjuror, and young Gauntlet swore that he was a Jesuit, because those gentlemen never travel without charms and inchantments. Peregrine, however, was not so very superstitious, but told the foreigner, that he was at liberty to proceed on his journey, and that no person would molest him.

Mr. Jolter, who had now joined the company, and heard the whole affair, declared that he differed in sentiment from his pupil concerning witchcraft, and supported his opinion by many quotations from scriptures, as well as from the writings of some divines in the last century. Young Gauntlet, who had been brought up in the army, corroborated all that was said by Jolter, and told the company that he had seen many apparitions, and was well convinced in his own mind of the reality of witchcraft. To all this the Welchman assented by declaring that the empire of Pelzebub was far more extensive than that of Rome, for it had extended to Glamorganshire, which the Romans could never conquer.

Peregrine did not chuse to enter the list with three such formidable combatants, but contented himself, by telling them, that he was convinced

in

in his own mind, that witchcraft was nothing more than a scare-crow, or bug-bear, invented to frighten the vulgar, after which they all went to supper together in the moſt amicable manner. In the courſe of their converſation, it appeared that the Welchman was the ſame Mr. Morgan, who makes ſuch a diſtinguiſhing figure in the adven-tures of Roderick Random, and who had been ſome years ſettled at Canterbury. It happened, that he had been ſent for to wait on a ſick perſon at Dover, and the Italian being there at the ſame time, a moſt violent diſpute aroſe concerning the nature of the medicines that ſhould be adminiſter-ed to the patient.

The emperic preſcribed ſpecific medicines, which the patient accepted of, ſo that poor Morgan was diſmiſſed without his fee. This exaſperated him ſo much, that he ſwore revenge againſt the Italian, and not being properly qualified, or rather not having a ſufficient ſhare of patience to reaſon coolly, he called the Italian a necromancer, becauſe his medicines had the deſired effect. That every thing might be made agreeable to Morgan, who was really an honeſt fellow, Peregrine made him a preſent of as much money as he could have expected from the patient, and for that night the company ſeparated, in order to retire to their ſe-parate apartments. In the morning, when they got up, they went to viſit the caſtle, with every other curioſity that was to be ſeen at Dover, after which they breakfaſted together, waiting till the packet ſhould be ready to ſail. Morgan declared that he would not leave our hero till he ſaw him ſafe on board, and he was as good as his word, for he kept ſtanding on the ſhore till the packet

hoiſted

hoifted fail, after which he and young Gauntlet marched back to the inn, and having refrefhed themfelves, fet out in a poft-chaife together for Canterbury.

Our hero had not got far out to fea, when the wind fhifted about, and blew directly in their faces, and the tide running high, they were in great danger of being loft. Mr. Jolter, who had been bufy in attempting to folve one of the moft difficult problems in Euclid, happened in the midft of his reveries, to hear the boy call to put out the dead lights, which frightened him fo much, that he ftarted up, and called out, " Lord have mercy " upon us." Peregrine gave up all for loft, and juft when he was expecting that the fhip would go to the bottom, the individual Tom Pipes made his appearance on the deck. It feems that this original genius had left the caftle the day after Peregrine departed, and getting to Dover fome hours before he embarked, took his place in the packet, and concealed himfelf in the hold.

Alarmed by the danger he was in, Pipes got up from his lurking place, and gave fuch directions to the feamen, that the mafter confidered him as an angel fent from heaven to deliver them. By his fkill in naval affairs, they were enabled to weather the ftorm, and foon after the fpiers of Calais prefented themfelves to their view. Jolter, who was a real enemy to his own country, no fooner faw France, that land of defpotifm, than he began to launch out in praife of the French government. Peregrine, who had the moft contemptible notion of his tutor's abilities, could not refrain from giving him the lie, and in proof of his opinion, no fooner had they landed, than they were

were furrounded by a parcel of cuftom-houfe officers, who began to tofs and tumble their baggage about, without any regard to the fo much
boafted politenefs of their country. As Jolter
had been often in France, and confequently was.
well acquainted with the manners of the people,
he gave the officers a bribe, and told them that
his pupil was a young Englifh nobleman, upon
which they defifted from fearching any farther.
They told him, however, that the baggage muft
be fealed up at the cuftom-houfe, and that there
were fome men ready to carry the trunks thither,.
This fo enraged Peregrine, that he knocked fome
of them down, calling them by the moft oppro-
brious names, but in an inftant a whole file of
mufquetteers furrounded the houfe.

Peregrine was not fuch a madman as to difpute
the authority of men under arms, and therefore
turning to the corporal who commanded the party,
defired him to accompany his baggage to the
cuftom-houfe, and fee that no harm happened to
it. The corporal was fo mortified at what our
hero faid, that he darted him a look full of contempt, telling him at the fame time, that he was
forry he was fo little acquainted with the French
laws. As foon as they had befpoke a poft-chaife
for Paris, our hero found that there was an Englifh gentleman and his lady in the fame inn, and
therefore he fent Tom Pipes to the kitchen, in
order to fcrape an acquaintance with their footman. In the mean time he and Parfon Jolter
went to view the fortifications, and upon their
return, Pipes told Peregrine, that the gentleman
was an old debauchee, who had in his youth defpifed marriage, but now in his advanced years
had

had been led into a match with an oyſter-wench, whoſe impudence was equal to the ſtation in which ſhe had been brought up. He added, that her huſband, upon mature deliberation, being aſhamed of his conduct, had, in order to avoid the reproaches of his friends, and the ſcoffs of his companions, brought her over to France, where it was not likely that ſhe would betray her ignorance, ſeeing ſhe did not underſtand one word of the language. Her temper was violent as well as vulgar, and it was with much difficulty that her huſband had prevented her from engaging in an intrigue with an officer, during one ſingle day that they ſtopped at Canterbury.

Peregrine's paſſions were now wound up to the higheſt pitch, and ſeeing the lady at the window he made a moſt reſpectful bow to her, which ſhe returned in a very low curtſey. She was neatly dreſſed, and had he not been informed of the nature of her former ſtation, he would have taken her for one of thoſe pert ladies, who in general have that ſort of impudence about them which their ſtation in life conceals under another name. He did not imagine there would be any great difficulty for him to ingratiate himſelf into her affections, and with that view he ſent a card to her huſband, whoſe name was Hornbuck, telling him that as he was to ſet out for Paris next day, ſo he would be glad of his company. Mr. Hornbuck, who had ſeen all manner of ſcenes of debauchery, no ſooner received the meſſage, than he ſent a very civil anſwer, telling our hero that he was ſorry he could not have the pleaſure of his company, becauſe his wife had been for ſome days indiſpoſed.

Peregrine

Peregrine was no ſtranger to his motives for ſending ſuch an anſwer, and being extremely uneaſy that he could not gratify his inordinate paſſion, he ſet out next morning with Parſon Jolter in the poſt-chaiſe, being attended by his French ſervants, and Tom Pipes on horſeback. They breakfaſted at Bologne, and it being propoſed that they ſhould reach Abeville that night, the driver went on at ſuch a rate, that the axle-tree broke before they had got a few miles out of the town. This accident obliged them to return to Bologne, where being under the neceſſity of waiting till next day, they ſaw ſome unfortunate Scotch gentlemen who had been engaged in the rebellion, looking earneſtly at that happy iſland, from whence they were for ever baniſhed. Peregrine, who had a moſt compaſſionate heart, could not help ſympathiſing with them, although he differed from them in political principles.

He invited them to ſpend the evening with him, but no ſooner had they got heated with wine, than they forgot their unhappy circumſtances, and launched out in invectives againſt the illuſtrious houſe of Hanover. Our hero, however, had too much generoſity to triumph over their want of prudence, and although one of them, who was the principal aggreſſor, had given him a challenge, yet next morning he was ſo ſenſible of his folly, that he came to his chamber, and aſked pardon in the moſt ſubmiſſive manner, telling him that his many misfortunes had almoſt deprived him of the uſe of his natural reaſon. His requeſt was granted, and having breakfaſted with, Peregrine, they took the moſt affectionate leave of each other.

Next

Next day the chaise having been got ready, our adventurer, with his retinue, proceeded on their journey, and Parson Jolter continued to bestow the highest encomiums on the French government. Peregrine interrupted him by pointing to the barren desolate state of the country, and the miserable appearance of the inhabitants in their ragged cloaths and wooden shoes. Jolter finding it in vain to dispute with one who could refute him, from the evidence of his senses, said no more till they came to an inn, where they partook of a small refreshment, and in the evening arrived at a small village called Bernay, where they called for fresh horses, but were informed by the landlord, that none could be had, for the gates of Abbeville were shut up, and there would be no possibility of their procuring admittance till next morning.

Mr. Jolter, who had often travelled that road before, did not chuse to contradict the landlord, and while supper was getting ready, our hero strolled about the yard, where to his great surprise, he saw another chaise come in with Mr. Hornbuck and his spouse. The landlord, though conscious that he had not victuals sufficient to serve both his guests, yet admitted the gentleman and his lady, and Peregrine, not doubting but he would find an opportunity of conversing with the lady, sent Mr. Hornbeck an invitation to sup with him.

Mr. Hornbuck, who was really hungry, accepted of the invitation, and Peregrine having led the lady into the room, placed her at the head of the table. During the evening, while they were at supper, the lady could not help darting some

significant

fignificant glances at our hero, which he took care to return, but that only ferved to encreafe the jealoufy of Hornbuck, who was no ftranger to intrigues.

For fome time he endeavoured to conceal his refentment, but not being able to contain him-felf any longer, he reached out his foot to tread on hers, but as ill luck would have it, he trod on the toe of Parfon Jolter, who happened at that time to have a fevere corn. The application was made with fo much good will, that the parfon ftarted up, and roared about the room like a madman, to the no fmall diverfion of Peregrine and the lady, who laughed in fuch an immode-rate manner, that they had almoft thrown them-felves into convulfions. Hornbuck was fo much confounded at the miftake he had committed, that he begged pardon of Jolter, who with tears in his eyes, forgave him, and then they fat down again to fupper. The reft of the evening was fpent in the moft agreeable manner, and when the time came that they fhould retire to bed, Pere-grine handed the lady into her chamber. Mr. Hornbuck had gone down to the yard, and during that time, our hero declared his paffion to the lady, but fhe advifed him to retire, leſt her hufband fhould come in. He was not fo blind as to negleft taking a hint upon which the fafety of the lady depended, and therefore retiring to his chamber, fpent the whole night in revolving in his mind what fchemes would be moft proper, in order to make Mr. Hornbuck a cuckold. The lady fpoke to him in the moft favourable manner, previous to his departure, and as it had been agreed upon that they fhould travel together next

day,

day, he doubted not but he would find an opportunity of completing his defign.

Next day they breakfafted at Abbeville, where
they learned that the landlord in Berney had played
them a French trick, for the gates were not fhut
till fome hours after they arrived at the village.
It was late in the evening before they reached
Chantilly, which is not much to be wondered at,
when it is confidered that the journey was one
hundred miles. Mr. Hornbuck was fo much fatigued, that he knew not what to do for a little
reft, and no fooner had he fupped, than he fell
faft afleep in his chair. Jolter, whofe conftitution was not fo delicate, had fwallowed fuch
large draughts of wine, that he began to yawn,
fo that Peregrine and the lady had fome time to
improve to their mutual wifhes. Indeed Peregrine had taken care to have opium adminiftered
to Jolter in his wine, which operated fo ftrongly
upon him, that he dreamed the moft horrible
dreams, and often ftarted up in violent agonies.
At laft being put to bed as well as Mr. Hornbuck,
they both fell faft afleep, for the gentleman was
fo much over-powered, that he even forgot his
fpoufe. Peregrine, who longed with impatience
to enjoy the lady, went foftly to her room, where
he found her in a loofe gown and petticoat, and
was juft about completing his wifhes, when Jolter
got out of bed in the next room, and exclaimed
fire! fire!

Women are very fertile at contriving fchemes,
efpecially where they are under the neceffity of
vindicating their honour from any afperfions that
may happen to be thrown upon it, and therefore Mrs. Hornbuck, not doubting but her
huſband

hufband would awake, ran into the room where Jolter was, and cried out, " Lord have mercy " upon us, where is it ?" Jolter, who was walking in his fhirt, with his eyes fhut, made no anfwer, but Peregrine vexed even to a ftate of madnefs, gave him fuch a flap on the fhoulder, that in an inftant he was brought back to the ufe of his reafon. Mean while, Hornbuck having awaked from his fleep, and miffed his fpoufe, doubted not but fhe was along with our hero, and jealoufy inftantly took place in his mind. In going in queft of his wife, he found that fhe had dropped her under petticoat, and there being no doubt remaining of her infidelity, he walked up to her, and fhewed it to her. Her natural prefence of mind hinted an excufe, for fhe declared that the petticoat was not her's, fhe not having fuch a one in her poffeffion. Peregrine, who was very fertile at invention, told him that the petticoat belonged to the inn-keeper's daughter, with whom he had an intrigue, and wondered how he could be fo foolifh, as to prevent him from enjoying a little pleafure.

Hornbuck was too well acquainted with the tricks practifed by young gentlemen, not to fee into our hero's intentions, but without difcovering the leaft mark of refentment, haftened to his bed-chamber with his fpoufe, and next morning fet out three hours before Peregrine got up.

Our hero was obliged to put up with his difappointment, and as foon as he had taken lodgings at Paris, he fent an account of his journey to the commodore. His next bufinefs was to have clothes made in the fafhion, and then he joined himfelf to a company of young gentlemen, who
fpent

spent the evenings in every species of debauchery. Most of these were his own countrymen, and as they had much money to spend, so it is not to be wondered at that they were guilty of many irregularities. In particular, they went one evening to a tavern, the landlady of which was extremely handsome, and our hero soon ingratiated himself into her good graces. The lady was one of those who are willing to bestow favours, so as they could be conducted with propriety, without giving offence to the husband ; but as ill luck would have it, her husband was extremely jealous of her, and coming home one evening, found her in such an attitude with our adventurer, that he could not help testifying his resentment. Peregrine, who happened to be then on the eve of enjoyment, was so much vexed, that he knocked the husband down, upon which the watch was called, and all the young gentlemen taken into custody. It happened that the officer of the night was a man of prudence, and therefore finding that little mischief had been done, he discharged them with a gentle reprimand.

This affair made such a noise, that it could not be long concealed from Parson Jolter, and as he respected the French government above all others in the world, he considered this part of his pupil's conduct as a high indignity offered to its laws. Indeed, the tutor was such a biggoted Jacobite, that his acquaintance reached no farther than among some of the English and Irish priests, who being extremely poor, spend much of their time in teaching foreigners the French language, and instilling into the minds of youth the utmost aversion to the English government. Such a
person

perfon was not in the leaft qualified to be the tutor of a young gentleman of our heroes fpirit, who looked upon him as a moft arrânt pedant. He defpifed every word that under the name of inftruction dropped from his mouth, fo that poor Jolter, in order to make the commodore believe that he had, at leaft, in fome meafure difcharged his duty, contented himfelf with writing down, from time to time, an account of the money that Peregrine fpent.

Peregrine having procured a chariot, and all other forts of equipage, according to the fafhion of Paris, he made his appearance at all the places of public diverfion, and vifited the gardens and palaces. But one day as he was returning home, two carmen happened to meet in the ftreets, and their carts being entangled, they both fell a boxing according to the mode of France. Pipes, who was then behind his mafter's coach, feeing one of the carmen on the ground, and the other belabouring him in the moft unmerciful manner, jumped from his ftation, and having fet the defeated combatant on his legs, told him to fight boldly, and he would fee fair play. Accordingly the combat was again revived, and there being another coach as well as our hero's, interrupted by the engagement, one of the footmen, who ftood behind, ftruck one of the combatants with his cane.

Pipes, who had true notions of honour, according to the fyftem of Englifh boxing, laid hold of the cane, and began to lay it about the aggreffor with great dexterity. The other footmen, who were behind the coach, ran to the affiftance of their brother. This new reinforcement

ment did not in the leaſt intimidate Tom Pipes, for graſping the cane, he drove two of the footmen off, and belaboured the other in ſuch a manner, that he was glad to beg for mercy. The whole ſtreet was now in an uproar, for the perſon whoſe ſervants had been aſſaulted in this manner, was one of the princes of the blood, but being a nobleman of age and experience, and Peregrine having made ſome ſubmiſſion to him on account of his quality, his highneſs took him into his chariot, and treated him with every mark of reſpect. The prince, who ſoon perceived that our hero had more ſpirit and education than generally falls to one of his age, took him home to his own houſe, and treated him as if he had been his own ſon. He introduced him to his lady, and ſome other very reſpectable perſons, but he ſoon found that the French ladies paid no regard to any but ſuch as ſpent the whole of their time in gaming. Not that he had any intention to deſiſt from gaming, but he could not ſee with what propriety, ladies, who pretended to the higheſt rank, could ſo far demean themſelves, as to ſpend their time in acting a part that ſet them on the ſame footing as thoſe wretches whom we call common ſharpers.

These conſiderations induced him to enter himſelf into a celebrated academy, where he became acquainted with ſeveral ſenſible people ; but volatile diſpoſitions and habits are not ſoon eradicated. This will appear evident from the following anecdote. Peregrine, who like moſt other young gentleman, was conſtantly in ſearch of new ſcenes of pleaſure, became acquainted with one of the polite girls of the town, and accordingly

cordingly took her into keeping. For fome time he imagined that fhe was one of thofe, who in confequence of receiving a fufficient fubfiftance, would be at leaft faithful to him, but he was moft wretchedly miftaken, for one morning Pipes came into his room, and told him that he faw a young fpark in laced cloaths go out of her chamber.

Peregrine, who had at fometimes a large command of his temper, took no notice of what was faid by Tom Pipes, but going towards evening to the houfe of his dulcinea, told her that he was obliged for that night to go on fome bufinefs of importance to a diftant part of the country. The lady, who was no ftranger to all the arts of her profeffion, pretended to be very much affected, but Peregrine taking leave of her with the ftrongeft profeffions of love, returned to his lodgings, in order to prepare himfelf for the executing a fcheme that he had formed. About twelve at night, having given Pipes the cue, they both fet out for the place, and knocked at the door, which was opened to them by the footman. Peregrine bolted in, and leaving Pipes to take care of the door, ran up ftairs, and knocked moft violently at the door of his dulcinea's apartment. Affairs were now in a very critical fituation, but there being a window to the ftreet, the vifitor dropped out of it, and fo made his efcape. Pipes, who happened to fee him defcend, made up to him, and belaboured him with his cudgel, from one end of the ftreet to the other, till being wearied with thrafhing him, he gave him up to the patrole, who took him into cuftody for the night in a moft wretched condition. Next morning the French gentleman was difcharged, but the difhonour of
having

having been beaten in so vulgar a manner, by an English footman, induced him to send a challenge to Peregrine, and both met together, where our hero came off conqueror, to the great mortification of the Frenchman, who was one of the officers of the guards.

Parson Jolter was so much offended with the conduct of his pupil, that he threatened to leave him and return to England, but Peregrine having made some concessions, he was diverted from his design, and once more resolved to spend some time longer in his beloved France. But still nothing could restrain the impetuosity of our hero's passions, for intrigue seemed to give life to all his actions.

One day as he was walking abroad to see some of the public places, he met Mrs. Hornbuck, and in the most imprudent manner agreed to elope with her. Accordingly they set out together to a village near Paris, where they gave themselves up to voluptuous pleasure, till the poor husband having found out the place of their residence, procured an order to take them both into custody. The affair began to make a considerable noise in Paris, and it might have been attended with fatal consequences, had not the English ambassador, a nobleman of great prudence, interposed so far as to represent our hero as a young man who had launched out into public life before he was acquainted with the world. In consequence of that representation our hero was set at liberty, but at the same time received a severe reprimand, with a positive injunction never to behave in the same manner for the future.

Soon

Soon after he was set at liberty, he went one day to visit the public places, and in one of the galleries he met with two of his countrymen, one of whom was a physician, but one of the most arrant pedants that ever lived; on the other hand the painter, who was the companion of the doctor, was an ignorant fellow, who had such an opinion of his own abilities, that all the ancient painters were considered by him as objects of contempt. With these two real originals in their way, our hero contracted an acquaintance, not so much from motives that could attach him to them on the principles of virtue, as that they were objects whom he could laugh at. He attended to every thing said by them, and could scarce refrain from laughing, when he heard that the painter condemned all the painters, whose works had done honour to the Italian schools; and the doctor, instead of minding the duties of his profession, spent the whole of his time in studying the most superficial parts of the Greek language.

Peregrine took the first opportunity to introduce his two new friends into the company of Parson Jolter, who received them in his usual formal manner, but as ill luck would have it, the doctor, who had borrowed his notions of government from the Greek classicks, spoke with the utmost contempt of the French government, as being entirely despotic. On the other hand, Parson Jolter insisted that no form of government could be so good as that which enabled the prince to support his prerogative, because in consequence thereof, the people were kept in humble subjection, and none of them could find fault with
the

the meafures of adminiftration. At laft the difpute arofe to fuch an height, that both parties
would have gone to blows, had not Peregrine interpofed, and with the utmoft difficulty made the
contending parties good friends. In the mean
time, the doctor, who was in every fenfe of the
word, abforbed in the ftudy of the claffic authors,
propofed to have an entertainment at Paris, according to the forms ufed by the old Romans, and
our hero, with Parfon Jolter, were both invited
as guefts. Some other foreigners were invited at
the fame time, among whom was a German
count, and an Italian baron. Among other in-
gredients was a dormoufe pye and a fow's ftomach,
ftuffed with a hundred different forts of herbs.
The painter exclaimed that the Romans were the
moft beaftly fellows he had ever heard of, and
the Italian taking the pye on his knees, the
whole contents burfted into his breeches, and
made him roar out in the moft vociferous manner.
The whole company was now one fcene of riot
and confufion; the doctor faid all he could to
apologize for the conduct of poor Pallat, the
painter, but all to no purpofe; for every one was
difgufted.

It was in vain to call the company to order, and
Peregrine, who was ftill fond of intrigue, per-
fuaded the painter to accompany him to the
Opera. There having fpent the evening, they
made affignations with fome girls, and were juft
on the point of returning home, when their coach
was interrupted by one belonging to a prince of
the blood. Peregrine would not give way, and
Tom Pipes having acted in the moft extravagant
manner, the whole body of them were taken into
cuftody,

cuſtody, and Peregrine, with the poor painter, were committed to the Baſtile.

The faithful Tom Pipes, as ſoon as he return- ed home, went and informed the Engliſh ambaſ- ſador, and in conſequence of his interpoſition, our hero and the painter were both ſet at liberty. Their releaſe, however, was procured upon con- dition that our hero ſhould leave Paris in a uuur time ; and, accordingly, as ſoon as he had taken leave of his friends, he ſet out for Flanders.

The painter now began to have the moſt con- temptible opinion of the doctor, and during the whole of their journey the time was ſpent in mutual quarrellings, the one calling the other a fool, and his companion retorting by the epithet *pedant*. During the firſt day nothing was to be heard but diſputes concerning the difference be- tween a monarchial and limited government, Parſon Jolter always taking part with the French, and the doctor at the ſame time condemning them.

About ſeven in the evening they arrived at an inn, where a ſupper was provided for them, and as the principal part conſiſted of rabbits, Pere- grine had a ſtrong inclination to enjoy a little fun. He perſuaded Tom Pipes to come into the room, and tell the gueſts, that there was the ſkin of an old ram cat hanging in the kitchen, and he was ſure the body was then ſerved up at the table. The painter, who had juſt then cut up a leg of the ſuppoſed cat, began to recollect that he had read the ſtory in Gil Blas of Scipio's, and therefore he would not eat any more. Parſon Jolter, whoſe ſtomach was not ſo very ſqeamiſh, told him that the people on the coaſt of France eat both cats and

and dogs, and that there could be no difference in the use of the animal, except what arose from vulgar apprehension or common inclination. This gave so much encouragement to the poor painter, that he proceeded to eat a little more, till a claw, that had been properly placed in the dish by Pipes, happening to fall out, he dropped his knife, and fell into a swoon. The doctor did all he could to relieve his friend, the painter, to a state of sensibility, and at last, having in some measure effected it, they all went to bed, and next day continued their journey to Flanders.

During their journey, the doctor expatiated on the excellency of the roads of the antients, while Parson Jolter represented those in France as far superior to any that had ever been seen.

In the evening they arrived in the neighbourhood of Arras, but the gates being then shut, they were obliged to lodge in the suburbs. It is true, they might have spent the evening with a great deal of pleasure, but, as ill luck would have it, two French officers happened to come to the inn, and engaged in gaming with our hero. They were so well acquainted with the principles of gaming, that Peregrine soon found he had to do with a couple of sharpers, and in the morning, when the landlord presented his bill, which he did with fear and trembling, they told him that he was a most wicked rascal, who thus thought to impose on the king's officers.

As soon as they were gone, the inn-keeper came into the room, and told our hero, that it was common for the military officers to do so, for such was the nature of the government in France. Peregrine, who had the most inlarged notions of

government,

government, could not help looking upon him
in any other light than as an enemy to the
natural rights of mankind; but making the hoft
fome amends for the injury he had received, he
proceeded on his journey along with his company. From Arras they proceeded to Lifle,
where our hero foon contracted an acquaintance
with feveral Scotch officers in the Dutch fervice,
who had come there, during the fummer feafon,
to learn the art of war. One of the Scotch
officers happened to be as great a pedant in the
Greek language as the doctor himfelf, but then
he had this advantage, that he had read over the
commentaries of the chevalier Follard.

Acquainted with fortification, as laid down by
Vauban, he was convinced in his own mind that
there was at leaft fome difference between ancient
and modern fortifications. The doctor and the officer took a walk round the ramparts, and a difcourfe
enfued upon the difference between ancient and modern fortifications. The Scotchman endeavoured to
fhew, that all towns fortified according to the
modern method, muft be conftructed in fuch a
way, as to be able to refift the force of balls,
whereas the doctor faid, that there was nothing
could equal the methods ufed by the Greeks. This
enraged the Scotchman fo much, that he chal-
lenged the doctor, but as the fon of Efculapius
had no intention to fight, he applied to our hero,
who accommodated matters in the moft amicable
manner.

One day as Peregrine was walking along the
ramparts, he happened to fall into converfation
with one of the knights of Malta, who bore a
H   commiffion

commiffion in the French fervice. The difcourfe turned upon the Englifh drama, which
our hero vindicated to the fatisfaction of the
knight, who was himfelf a man of letters : but
before they had done fpeaking, parfon Jolter arrived in a great hurry, and told them, that Tom
Pipes, having affronted a foldier, a great mob
were gathered together, and that he was in danger of being killed. Peregrine hearing the danger his faithful Pipes was in, ran up to his affiftance, and took along with him the knight of
Malta, who ordered the folder to be taken into
cuftody, and brought before him. It feems,
that Pipes, in his walk through the town, had
got into company with fome Irifh foldiers in the
French fervice, who treated him with great civility, but the fubject of difcourfe happening to
turn upon politics, Pipes curfed the pope, the
pretender, and the French king, as well as all
thofe who were connected with either.

This was too high an indignity for the foldiers
to put up with, upon which a battle enfued between them and Pipes, in which the latter would
have had the advantage, only he had no other
weapon to defend himfelf but his fifts.

Peregrine was fo much exafperated at the conduct of Pipes, that he immediately difmiffed him
from his fervice; and next day the whole company fet out for Ghent.

The whole company, befides our hero, the
painter, the doctor, and Mr. Jolter, confifted of
a lady of pleafure, a Jew broker, a capuchin
friar, and a young lady committed to the care of
the latter.

Jolter

Jolter difputed with the Jew about the mean‑
ing of fome words in the fcriptures ; the doctor
ridiculed the capuchin ; while the painter made
love to the kept miftrefs ; and Peregrine attached
himfelf to the young lady, When the company
had fupped in the evening, they all retired to
their own apartments ; but Peregrine having
made an affignation with the young lady, got
up about midnight, and went privately to her
chamber.

It happened that the woman of pleafure lay
in a bed in the fame room, and the painter hav‑
ing got to the bedfide, juft at the fame time
that Peregrine got to the other, the capu‑
chin, who had fome fufpicions, crawled
upon his all fours, in order to make a dif‑
covery. He had fcarce got up to the middle
of the room when the painter felt his fhaved
head, and the prieft, who was an arch wag,
turning his jaws round, bit the finger of the
painter in fo fevere a manner that he fcreamed
out fire ! murder ! thieves ! Peregrine was fo
much inraged, that he knocked the painter down,
and then returned to his own apartment, in or‑
der to prevent a difcovery.

Next night when they came to Aloft Pe‑
regrine made another attempt on the young
lady, but Pallat, the painter, who had not yet
relinquifhed his fcheme, once more got into the
room at the fame time. This fo much exafpe‑
rated Peregrine, that he knocked him about till
there was fcarce any life left in him, and then
decamping, in the dark, the poor painter was
put to bed. The doctor, who had been ca'led
out of bed to attend the patient, declared that

H 2　　　　　　　　　　　　　he

he had been bit by a mad dog, and taking up
the chamber-pot, emptied the whole contents of
it upon him. In the midſt of his fury the painter got up, and would have done ſignal execution on the doctor, had not he taken to his
heels out of the room, and overturned Jolter in
the paſſage, who tumbled like a dead log of
wood into the kitchen. In the morning every
thing being adjuſted, our travellers ſet out for
Bruſſels, where Peregrine had not been long
when he met accidentally with Mrs. Hornbuck,
from whom he had been ſeparated at Paris.
The two lovers met together every evening at
a private houſe in the ſuburbs, but Mr. Hornbuck having diſcovered their retreat, hired two
ſoldiers to lay hold of Peregrine upon his return
home, and actually make him a eunuch.

As good fortune would have it, Tom Pipes,
who had ſtill kept near his maſter, though not
perceived by him, happened to hear the con-
ſpirators talking of their intended ſcheme, at a
public houſe, and went and gave Peregrine information of the whole: our young hero had
too much ſpirit to forget the behaviour of Pipes
at Liſle, and therefore refuſed at firſt to
ſpeak with him, but the other convinced him of
the neceſſity he was under of being on his guard,
upon which he was once more taken into favour.

A plan was now laid to defeat the ſcheme
projected by Hornbuck; and in the evening
when the poor cuckold came to the place, he
was dragged to the river, and ducked over head
and ears; but his cries having brought the patrole to his aſſiſtance, our hero was taken into
cuſtody. Parſon Jolter was quite confounded at
the

the conduct of his pupil, but as he was still under his care, he went to the governor of the city and procured his release. They then set out for Antwerp, where they had not been long when Peregrine fomented a quarrel between the painter and the doctor, and nothing less than a duel was to decide the merits of the controversy.

Pipes was made choice of as second to the painter, and Peregrine to the Doctor; but when they went on the ramparts, being both arrant cowards, they trembled like criminals who were going to be hanged. In vain did the seconds endeavour to force them to action, they shrunk back, and the painter at last taking to his heels, Tom Pipes gave him a knock on the breach, which tumbled him down. The fall of the painter gave fresh spirits to the doctor, who, making up to him, terrified him with a number of Greek verses, which he repeated from Homer, and forced him to acknowledge that he had been defeated.

From Antwerp they proceeded to visit the most noted places in Holland, where they met with nothing worthy of their notice, upon which, Peregrine, with his companions, set out for Harlem, and took shipping for Harwich in England, being desirous of once more visiting his native country.

As soon as he arrived in England, he went to visit some eminent persons, whose relations he had met with abroad, and then set out for the castle, where he was received by the good old commodore, in the most gracious manner. All the poor cottagers who lived in the neigh-

H 3   bourhood.

bourhood, came to wiſh him joy on his return, and within a few weeks after he had the plea- ſure of ſeeing his beloved ſiſter married to the young gentleman who had made his addreſſes to her before he went abroad. In the mean time his parents treated him in the ſame inhuman manner as before, but all this was made up by the goodneſs of the commodore.

Having attended the commodore with the moſt filial tenderneſs during a fit of illneſs, occaſion- ed by the gout, the old gentleman propoſed making over to him his whole eſtate, and to de- pend on him for a ſubſiſtance during the re- mainder of his life ; but this was what our hero would by no means comply with. The commo- dore being in ſome meaſure recovered, he gave Peregrine leave to return to London, and in his way thither he met with Emilia, and offered ſuch rudeneſs to her, that ſhe reſolved not to have any thing more to do with him. This cha- grined him ſo much, that he left her mother's houſe in diſguſt ; and ſoon after his arrival in London, met with her brother Godfrey, who, in conſequence of his good behaviour, had been advanced to a lieutenancy. After ſome days ſpent in the pleaſures of the town, they both ſet out for Bath, where, by their cunning and ingenuity, they diſperſed a whole gang of ſharp- ers. At the ſame time they practiſed ſo many roguiſh tricks on the phyſicians, that thoſe ſons of the great Eſculapeous were put to the bluſh amidſt the whole circle of their acquaintance.

At Bath they became acquainted with a cer- tain lady, whoſe ſole buſineſs was to entertain every promiſcuous company in her houſe, with

no

no other view fave that of procuring a name. Among others who vifited her was one Mr. Crabtree, an old Welch gentleman, who, in confequence of fome tricks that had been put upon him in his youth, became an enemy to all mankind, and was in the ftricteft fenfe of the word a mifanthrope. That he might have it in his power to retail as much fcandal as poffible he feigned himfelf deaf, fo that the moft fecret things were mentioned in his company, without the leaft fufpicion that he heard any of them.

With this perfon our hero contracted an ac-quaintance, and he foon conceived that he was no more deaf than himfelf. Peregrine was aftonifhed to hear him repeat a vaft number of anecdotes relating to the nobility, and the frailty of nature among the females, ferved only to fti-mulate his defires, in order, if poffible, to be able to add one to the number of thofe, who in confequence of their levity had been fe-duced,

The commodore had been for fometime in a bad ftate of health, and Peregrine thought that he could not confiftent with his duty neglect to wait upon him. Accordingly he arrived at the caftle, where he was received with open arms of affection, and next day his generous benefac-tor departed this life. He had given the moft particular directions concerning his funeral ; and our hero notwithftanding his volatile difpofition in other things, took care to have it celebrated according to his defire.

The fervants, whofe hairs had become grey fince they came to live with the commodore, lamented the lofs of an indulgent mafter, and

the

the next day after his funeral the gentlemen in the neighbourhood came to congratulate our hero on his being left in poffeffion of fo ample a fortune.

Their principal defign was to try, if poffible, to bring about a reconciliation between him and his mother, but all to no purpofe, for fhe remained as obftinate as ever, and declared that Peregrine was not her fon.

In the mean time, Peregrine having fettled all his domeftic affairs left the caftle in order to return to London, but in his way thither he called at the houfe where Emilia lived, and in a moft audacious manner made an attempt on her virtue. The young lady treated him with that contempt his conduct intitled him to, but as her heart was not deaf to tender impreffions fhe confented to give him her company at a mafquerade. She imagined that he would not purfue his fcheme any further; but fhe was miftaken, for no fooner was fhe mixed with the crowd, or rather the *herd*, than he made a fecond attempt on her virtue, but was repulfed in the fame manner as before, and to complete her misfortune, her uncle, who was her guardian, and had her under his protection, forbad him from coming any more to his houfe, unlefs he thought proper to be ducked in a horfe pond.

Baffled in all his attempts, he was filled with the utmoft chagrine, for fuch is the violent impetuofity of youth, that they are in general deaf to the voice of reafon. They go on from one degree of extravagance to another, till it is too late to change, and they feek for pleafure where

'It

ft can never be found. Peregrine, in order to vindicate his character, wrote a long fubmiffive letter to Mrs. Gauntlet, the mother of Emilia, but the anfwer he received, ferved only to convince him that fhe looked upon him as an object of the utmoft deteftation. This ftimulated him to fuch a height, that he refolved never more to vifit the place, upon which, after returning to fpend a few weeks at the caftle, he refolved once more to drown his cares in London. Upon his arrival in London, he met with his old friend Cadwallader, the mifanthrope, who informed him concerning many curious paffages relating to the intrigues of the ladies of quality. One of them was a duchefs, who had on all occafions proftituted herfelf to thofe who were kind enough to difcharge her debts contracted at a gaming table, fo that upon the whole fhe was in a manner a difhonour to her fex. Another was one of thofe ladies who pay no regard to moral obligation, and therefore having loft her firft hufband, whom fhe married from motives of love, fhe was by the orders of her father, who at that time was one of the commiffioners in the cuftom houfe, obliged to give her hand to an Irifhman, who taking him altogether, was one of the moft infignificant wretches that ever lived. They had not been long married, when the lady difcovered fuch an averfion to her hufband, that fhe began to intrigue with feveral of the young nobility, and actually went over with one of them to France, where they fpent a whole fummer together. At laft, fhe returned to England, and finding no other way left, in order to fupport her in extravagance, fhe once more threw herfelf into the arms of her

hufband,

hufband, and fpent the remainder of her time in
privacy.

Peregrine, had fo much art, that fcarce
any thing could deceive him, refolved to make
himfelf merry at the expence of his fellow creatures. Accordingly he got Cadwallader to affume
the character of a fortune-teller, and in confequence thereof, he foon got acquainted with
the many fecrets that would otherwife have been
buried in perpetual oblivion. To a young gentleman like our hero, this could not fail of yield-
ing a confiderable degree of entertainment, and
in confequence thereof, he was at all times able
to triumph over the moft dignified female characters. Nothing was more common for him than
to enter into an intrigue with a lady of quality,
and as he knew well her prior character, he
thought there could be no hurt in expofing her
for the favour fhe had granted him. Peregrine,
who never knew where to ftop, when he wanted
to indulge his favourite paffion for ridicule, refolved to give fuch a mark of his ingenuity, as
would tranfmit his name to all future ages.

Among the circle of his friends, he became acquainted with two notorious free-thinkers, or as
we call them, deifts, and thefe men having made
a mock of all forts of apparitions, he contrived
to raife a fictitious one, that actually frightened
them into the utmoft ftate of fuperftition. The
devil was reprefented as arifing from hell, to take
thefe infidels along with him to the infernal
regions, and notwithftanding all the pretenfions
that our deifts had made, yet when they faw the
old gentleman with the cloven foot appear, they
trembled as an afpen leaf, and for once declared,

that

that their deiftical notions were not able to carry them through in a day of adverfity. They could not help reflecting that the heathens believed there was a future ftate of rewards and punifhments, and that brutal fortitude to which they had fo long attached themfelves, vanifhed into nothing.

It was not long before our hero became celebrated for being one of the greateft wits of the town. He took notice of the conduct of the different nobility and gentry, who happened to be in his company, and he drew their characters according to the obfervations he had made. One in particular, who had been long reprefented as a patriot, or in other words a lover of his country, he reprefented, according to juftice, as a moft vile infamous debauchee, who had pretended to fet up a fcheme of reformation for the whole kingdom, while he knew at the fame time that he was wallowing in luft with feveral common proftitutes. However volatile he might be in his own difpofition, he could not help treating, with the utmoft abhorrence, thofe wretches who fet up for reformers of the nation, while at the fame time their own houfes exhibits nothing but fcenes of debauchery. In the pub ic news papers, and many other periodical works, he endeavoured to reprefent thofe wretches in their lively colours, and furely nothing could be more commendable. Shall the debauchee fet up to reform the nation and promote charity, when at the fame time he knows that he is going on in a courfe of impunity. Shall the fpendthrift attempt to teach œconomy to the people, while he knows at the fame time that he is living above his circumftances. In a word, Peregrine was convinced in

his

his own mind, that private virtue and patriotifm, muft, or at leaft, ought to go hand in hand together, and therefore it will appear to fome of our more fenfible readers, that thofe who are not able to take care of their own affairs, will never be able to attend to thofe of a public nature. Indeed it is a notion that has been too much cultivated in the prefent age, that people may be wicked at home, and at the fame time virtuous abroad, but this is inconfiftent with the firft principles of natural reafon, for he that is faithful over little, will be faithful over much.

Lieutenant Hatchway had now been married fome time to the widow of the commodore, but that lady had fo far given herfelf up to drinking, that fhe was feized with a dropfy, and there being no hopes that fhe would recover, her hufband fent Peregrine a letter in the ftile of a feaman, defiring his immediate attendance at the garrifon.

Peregrine no fooner received the honeft lieutenant's epiftle, than he fet out for the garrifon, where he found his aunt in the agonies of death, and ftaid to perform the laft offices to her, after which he returned, in order to vifit his companions in London. In his way to London, he called on his friend Gauntlet, and had the good fortune to fee him happily married to the young lady whom he had courted feveral years. Indeed Peregrine would have willingly married Emilia at the fame time, but fuch was his attachment to gallantry, that he ftill entertained hopes, or rather wifhes, of having it in his power to feduce that young lady, and to triumph over her fhame.

Baffled, however, in all his attempts on her virtue, he fet out for London, but had not been
long

long there, when he returned to the garrison on a visit to honest Lieutenant Hatchway, who treated him with the utmost respect.. Having settled several of his domestic affairs, he took leave of the lieutenant, and in his journey picked up a young gypsey, whom he resolved to take into keeping.

Tom Pipes was ordered to see her washed clean and dressed in a proper manner, and although her countenance had something ferocious in it, yet she was in many respects as agreeable as some of the court ladies. He introduced her to all the noted gaming tables, where she made a very distinguishing figure, for it was but a short time before she made herself acquainted with all the tricks practised in those polite circles. But notwithstanding her natural rusticity, yet she had the seeds of honesty in her mind, for one evening at a gaming-table, having discovered that one of the ladies was a dexterous hand at cheating, she called her a damned bitch, and walking towards the door, bid her kiss her arse. The ladies present upbraided our hero with having palmed upon them a common trull, and he having been cloyed with possession, gave her some money, and left her to make her fortune in the world in the best manner she could, so that she soon after became one of the women of the town.

Soon after he had discarded the young gypsey, he was visited by his old acquaintance Pallat, the painter, who had accompanied him in his journey from Paris to Flanders. The painter had got some poor daubings of several capital works of the Flemish schools, and had proposed to sell them by subscription, so that he was under the necessity
of

of making himself acquinted with as many of the nobility and gentry as poffible. Peregrine looked upon him with the utmoft contempt, but as he knew him to be poor, he did not fay any thing to difcourage him.

In the courfe of their converfation, the fubject turned upon gaming, and our hero, who was altogether of a volatile difpofition, embraced an opportunity that Pallat offered him of being introduced to the acquaintance of Lord Sweepftakes, who had for many years made the moft diftinguifhing figure at Newmarket. As Peregrine had a confiderable fum of money at his difpofal, it was not long before he was fleeced of the greateft part, for gamblers, let their ftations be what they will, are no better than cheats.

Vexed to find himfelf bubbled in that fcandalous manner, he refolved to get into the miniftry, and for that purpofe ingratiated himfelf into the favour of a nobleman, who propofed fetting him up as a candidate for one of the rotten boroughs. This led him into a frefh feries of expences, but the other candidate having by oppofite intereft become more fuccefsful than Peregrine, he was obliged to fit down with his lofs, and curfe both government and minifters.

As Peregrine had good natural parts, he refolved to become a dependant on the miniftry, and in their vindication he wrote feveral very fatirical papers. This employment, however, was of too mean a nature to fupport a young gentleman of our hero's fpirit, efpecially as the dignified nobleman gave him nothing but promifes for all his trouble. It was natural for him under fuch circumftances to defcend gradually to meannefs,

meannefs, and notwithftanding the elegant manner in which our hero had been brought up, yet
he became every day more and more an object of
contempt among all thofe with whom he had been
formerly acquainted.

Tortured with thefe melancholy reflections, he
one day took a walk to the park, where he had
not been long, when he was accofted by his old
friend Gauntlet, who foon after his marriage, had
been advanced to the command of a company.
Gauntlet was accompanied by his wife and fifter,
and no fooner had our hero feen the latter, than
all thofe former emotions took place in his mind,
that her perfon had firft infpired. He faid every
thing he could think of in vindication of his conduct, but the young lady was extremely fhy, and
told him that nothing but a conftant perfeverance
in the practice of every moral duty, would entitle
him to her favour. They converfed together
fome time, and when they took their leave, he
fwore everlafting conftancy to the object of his
love, after which they parted for the prefent with
very different fentiments, for our hero was tortured with the thoughts of having incurred the
difpleafure of his Emilia.

He next affociated himfelf with a club of
authors, moft of whom were very defpicable
wretches, but they were at the fame time fo
proud, that they would not for fome time make
him acquainted with all their fecrets. As his
wants were daily encreafing, he had recourfe
once more to the minifter, who had fo long filled
his mind with promifes, that he never intended to
perform ; but although feveral very lucrative
places were then vacant, yet he was given to underftand

derſtand that they had all been diſpoſed of. This declaration of the miniſter mortified him ſo much, that he could not conceal his reſentment any longer, and therofore turning about, he left the preſence chamber in the utmoſt diſguſt. From the miniſter's houſe, he went to viſit the authors, whom he found engaged in a moſt violent diſpute concerning the merits of ſome of their performances.

Peregrine had but little to ſay, for as yet he was no more than a novice, but as ill luck would have it, in the midſt of the diſpute, a bailiff came with a writ againſt one of them. The defendant who was no ſtranger to the power of catch-poles, no ſooner heard of his danger, than he jumped out of the window, and pitching upon the top of a ſedan, overturned it with a young maccaroni, who had been dreſſed out in the higheſt taſte, in order to make his appearance at the opera. In the mean time he became acquainted with ſome of thoſe inſignificant wretches called antiquarians, who ſpend moſt of their time in looking over old coins and manuſcripts, that cannot be read but by the help of a magnifying glaſs, or an index to explain the contractions. He had the good fortune, however, in conſequence of his political writings, to procure a ſmall penſion from the miniſter, which for ſome time was regularly paid, but as he ſtill wiſhed for a ſettlement, he one day put the miniſter in mind of his promiſe, and having not received a ſatisfactory anſwer, he went home, and wrote him a letter, wherein he taxed him with duplicity, and the conſequence was, that he was inſtantly diſcharged. The affair of his being diſcarded made ſome noiſe among thoſe at the head of affairs; but the minifter, who was hackneyed in all the ways of iniquity, told them that our hero was difordered in his mind, and for fome time the ftory was believed. In revenge for being treated in fo difgraceful a manner, he commenced a writer againft the miniftry, and treated the whole of their conduct with fuch ridicule, that they became objects of deteftation to all ranks of people in the nation.

But this did not anfwer his expectation, for the minifter who had never entered into any agreement with him, caufed him to be arrefted, and from a fpunging-houfe he was removed to the Fleet-prifon. There he found his confinement much better than is common in other prifons, and he met with feveral perfons who did all they could to make his confinement as agreeable as poffible. Among others, he met with a perfon who had fpent his whole fortune, in order to procure juftice to an injured young gentleman, but by a quibble in law, which will ever remain a difgrace to juftice, he had been nonfuited, and in confequence thereof, not being able to pay his cofts, he was arrefted and committed to prifon.

The news of Peregrine being committed to prifon foon reached the ears of Lieutenant Hatchway, who with all his foibles was really a good man. The honeft lieutenant, in company with Tom Pipes, fet out for London, and not knowing Peregrine was to be confined for life, propofed taking lodgings along with him in the Fleet.

Peregrine faid all he could to diffuade them from fuch a refolution, but all that he could prevail

prevail upon them to do was to take lodgings in the same neighbourhood. As it was their constant practice to visit our hero two or three times in the day, and to spend the evenings with him, so one night while Crabtree, the misanthrope, was there, they happened to quarrel, and the poor Welchman was tossed in a blanket. This was considered as such an outrage, that the warden ordered that Hatchway and Pipes should never be again admitted to the prison, and in the mean time Peregrine gave himself up to all manner of sloth and nastiness.

While he continued in this deplorable situation, his old friend Gauntlet, who had come to town in order to procure advancement in the army, came to the Fleet to visit him, and condoled with him on the unhappy state of his then circumstances.

As good luck would have it, a person, to whom Peregrine had lent some money to equip him for an East-India voyage, happened at that time to arrive in the Downs, and as he had met with considerable success, he came to the prison and paid the debt for which our hero had been arrested.

Being thus at liberty, he went to visit his old friend the lieutenant, who, notwithstanding some disputes that they had before, received him with open arms of friendship. He was informed by Hatchway that his father had been dead some time, and that he had left his whole fortune to his son Gam. That was a most mortifying stroke to our hero, who, notwithstanding all the unnatural usage of his parents, yet imagined that his father would have done him justice at last. This

This induced him to hold a confultation with his friends, who were all of opinion that there was fomething unfair, and that it would be ne-ceffary to make a proper enquiry into the nature of the will. This led to a difcovery that the whole was a collufion carried on by the intrigues of his mother who had got a falfe will fubftitut-ed in the room of the true one, to the injury of her eldeft fon. This led to a further enquiry, and, upon the moft mature deliberation the whole cheat was difcovered. The noife occa-fioned by this affair reached all over the country, but our hero, confiftent with his common no-tions of benevolence, made a fettlement on his mother and brother, after which he took poffef-fion of his eftate, and proved himfelf to be the real hair at law to his father, notwithftanding all that had been done to injure him.

Having fettled every thing of importance, he went to fee his friend Gauntlet, and it was agreed upon between them to fpend fome time in the country. This was in a manner abfolutely neceffary, for our hero who had been confined feveral months in a prifon, but the principal reafon was to bring about a match between the two lovers.

Gauntlet had a real friendfhip for Peregrine, and told him, that he would do every thing to bring about an ecclairciffement between him and his fifter. Accordingly our hero was indulged with an interview with his beloved Emilia, but fhe was fo much on the referve that it did not give him any fatisfaction. Mortified at his dif-appointment he retired into another room, but had not been there long when he heard a dialogue

logue between the brother and sister, that gave him the most inexpressible pleasure. Emilia said, she had no objections to Peregrine, except such as arose from the nature of his conduct, which on many occasions had been very irregular. To this her brother answered, that whatever might have been his foibles, yet they were merely owing to the unguarded sallies of youthful imprudence, but as he had now returned both to a regular discharge of his duty as a man of honour and virtue, she could not with the least colour of reason have any objection to him.

Peregrine, who overheard this discourse, was in a manner quite transported, and waited for an opportunity of embracing his charmer, and running into her room flung himself at her feet in humble prostration.

As she could not bear to see him in that attitude, she gave him encouragement to rise, and then clasping her in his arms, he told her that he was for ever devoted to her, and that he would live and die with her. She told him, that he had been so wicked, that he ought to have undergone a severe punishment, but as things then were, she was willing at once to pardon him, and put up with a man for a husband whom she believed would be an arrant tyrant. In answer to this, as he was scarce able to speak, he told her that he had eighty thousand pounds in money, which should be at her service, and as a proof of his sincerity, he offered to lay the whole in her lap. So saying, he clasped her again in his arms, and sealed the conract into which he had entered with bestow-

ing

ing a thoufand kiffes upon her who was more dear to him than his life.

Every thing being fettled for the nuptials, our hero fet out for the commons, in order to procure a licence, by which his happinefs was to be fealed. It is true Emilia made fome objection to his being fo precipitate in an affair of fuch importance, but her brother, the captain, having interpofed, fhe was brought to harken to the voice of reafon, and gave her confent to the performance of the ceremony. Lieutenant Hatchway, who had never loft fight of our hero, refolved to be prefent at the ceremony of the marriage, and as he always liked a little fun, he propofed to make Peregrine drunk, previous to his going to bed. In that, however, he was difappointed, for our hero was on his guard, and took care not to drink any more liquor than was neceffary.

The ceremony being over, Tom Pipes danced like a madman, as if he had been on the forecaftle of a man of war, while Hatchway regaled himfelf over his bowl of rum and water, in the fame manner as if he had been on the quarterdeck of the commodore's fhip. At laft the new married couple retired, and next day was fpent in the utmoft degree of feftivity. From London they fet out for the country, where our hero ordered the caftle to be put in proper repair, and having fettled every thing with his tenants, he went to vifit his fifter, whom he found the mother of two beautiful young children.

He was, as well as his fpoufe, received by her with every mark of refpect, and rejoiced in having it in his power to contribute towards promoting

moting her happinefs. He lived agreeably and happily with his dear Emilia, and fhe foon made him a happy father.

Their friends and acquaintance looked upon themfelves as happy in being connected with two perfons of fo much worth, and their fame for the exercife of every benevolent action, reached to the exterior parts of the country, where their names were known.

Peregrine detached himfelf from every vicious practice, and day after day convinced his wife that he was far from being an object unworthy of her choice, or improper for her to place her affections upon.

To conclude this work it is neceffary to take notice of what happened to the other celebrated perfonages who have been fo often mentioned in it. We have already configned the commodore to the filent grave, and have feen that his widow, after having been married fome years to Lieutenant Hatchway, paid the debt of nature, and was depofited befide her firft husband, or to ufe the fea phrafe, fhe was fafely moored.

Lieutenant Hatchway furvived the marriage of our hero about two years, moft part of which was fpent in drinking his can of flip, and fmoaking his pipe. He often wifhed for a war that he might have one opportunity more of giving orders on the quarter-deck; but as nothing of that nature happened, he was obliged to come to an anchor, and be laid up in an everlafting dock.

Tom Pipes furvived him about three years, and was treated by Peregrine with every mark of refpect, and what added moft to his pleafure

was,

was, that the lovely Emilia fuffered him to have a hammock to fwing in, as if he had been ftill on board, or in the garrifon. At laft a violent ftorm obliged him to flip his anchor, and as there was none ready to take him in tow, he went to the bottom and was never after heard of.

'The doctor whofe feaft had made fuch a diftinguifhing figure at Paris and Antwerp, returned to London, where he publifhed propofals for a tranflation of Pindar from the original Greek; but not meeting with the fuccefs he expected, he commenced writer for a bookfeller, and did every thing in his power to ridicule the Chriftian fyftem. At laft he became fo notorious for his licentious writings, that an indictment was preferred againft him, and being found guilty on the cleareft evidence, he was committed to Newgate, till fuch time as he fhould pay a fine according to the judgment of the court. There he continued near two years in the utmoft ftate of penury, till at laft being forced by neceffity, he wrote in defence of adminiftration, and in confequence thereof procured his releafe, and at the fame time received a penfion of three hundred pounds a year, by the interceffion of thofe in power.

The minifter of ftate, by whofe cruelty our hero had been fo long cruelly oppreffed, was, in confequence of a change at court, turned out of all employments, and fpent the remainder of his time in fomenting fchemes to crofs the meafures of government. At laft he died, not only unpitied, but even hated by all thofe who had formerly known him, nor was there one left to fhed a tear over his grave. He had domineered

over

over his fellow fubjects while he was intrufted with power, but no fooner were his remains laid in the grave, than fome of the meaneft of them trod on them. '

Pallat, the painter, who was one of the moft arrant blockheads that ever lived, publifhed propofals for fome of his daubings, but they were executed in fo wretched a manner, that he became an object of deteftation to all thofe who knew him. His family was reduced to want, and his creditors becoming clamorous, he was arrefted, and glad to take up the fame lodgings in the Fleet, from which our hero had been fo fortunately delivered. There he remained till he was fet at liberty by an act of infolvency, and the reft of his days were fpent in penury, which would have been ftill greater, had not our hero contributed towards his affiftance.

With refpect to our hero, he foon obtained a feat in parliament, and made a moft diftinguifhing figure as a Britifh fenator. His family increafed in the courfe of time, and fuch was his benevolence, that he never loft fight of fuch opportunities as put it into his power to be ferviceable to his fellow creatures. From the whole of thefe circumftances we may learn, that it is never too late to refrain from vicious courfes, and that wherever reformation takes place, beneficial confequences will follow. Such is the nature of things in this world, that we never know when to form a judgment till we are directed by the confequences, and this fhould teach us to watch over every part of our conduct, and fo make it appear to the world that we are not unworthy members of fociety.

ADVENTURES

OF

AMELIA.

THIS novel was one of the last produc-
tions of the late ingenious Mr. Field-
ing, and is written on a plan very different
from the rest of his compofitions. In it the
reader is entertained with a vaft variety of occur-
rences, and upon each of them the author has
made the moft judicious reflections. A worthy
family is here reprefented as fuffering the utmoft
hardfhips, in confequence of the unnatural conduct of a fifter, and the villainy of an attorney.
Such fcenes of diftrefs are laid open to which too
many of our fellow creatures are no ftrangers,
and characters are introduced entirely confiftent
with nature.

The character of Mrs. Bennet, ferves to fhew
that a parent may act in an imprudent manner

by giving his daughter too much education, and that there is a line to be drawn between what is peculiar to each fex. In Mr. Booth we find a brave young man, endowed with the purest notions of honour and benevolence, ftruggling under a load of afflictions, with none to comfort him befides thofe whofe fufferings he was the innocent caufe of. In Amelia we find piety and benevolence fo blended together, that each became affiftant to the other, in all their operations. She fubmits to thofe evils to which it feems Providence had thought proper to vifit her, but at the fame time fhines with a redoubled luftre, under all her fufferings. Profperity does not induce her to look down with contempt on her fellow creatures, and fhe even feeks to extend her benevolence to thofe perfons whofe crimes had occafioned all her fufferings.

In the firft edition of this work fome things were inferted, which, although innocent in themfelves, yet were inconfiftent with the common character of the author. In the correct edition of the authors works, publifhed by Mr. Murphy, all thefe exceptionable places have been expunged, and in this abrigment that edition has been followed. The reader will here find that no fact of any importance has been omitted, nor has any of the reflections been curtailed, except where they appeared to be fuperfluous. Upon the whole great pains has been taken to make this abridgment much more ufeful to ordinary readers than ever it could be in perufing the whole, and young perfons will be here gradually led to embrace virtue, as the moft defirable thing in life.

Amelia

AMELIA was the daughter of a country gentleman, but deprived of her father in her more
tender years, fo that fhe had not the happy opportunity of being brought up under his direction. Her mother, however, fupplied the defi-
ciency, and fhe was brought up in fuch a manner
that fhe foon became an object of admiration to
all who knew her. One day as fhe was going to
vifit a friend, the chaife in which fhe rode, had
the misfortune to be overturned, and fhe received
fuch a violent wound in her nofe that disfigured
her lovely countenance ever after.

A misfortune of that nature would have made
her an object of ridicule to the vulgar and un-
thinking wretches, who do not deferve the name
of men, and yet fuch as were endowed with fen-
fibility, could not refrain from pitying her. The
inward graces of her mind fhone in fuch a confpicuous manner, that all exterior imperfections
were forgotten, and the perfon was beloved, in
confequence of the intellectual faculties.

As foon as fhe was able to fee company, Mr.
Booth, a young gentleman, was invited to drink
tea at her mother's, and no fooner had he feen
the depredation that had been made on her lovely
countenance, than fhe appeared to him with her
intellectual graces the moft lovely object in the
univerfe.

Mr. Booth foon found himfelf in love, but he
had not courage to declare his fentiments, becaufe he was in diftreffed circumftances. But
love is all powerful, and no motives can induce

the

the real lover to defift. This was the cafe with Mr Booth, for although he had refolved never to fee his charmer any more on the footing of a lover, yet happening to come again accidentally into her company, he was more enamoured of her than ever. He made a declaration of his love, and his dear Amelia was touched with humane feelings, when fhe confidered his diftreff-ed circumftances on the one hand, and her own deformity on the other. Being now on the footing of lovers, all reftraint was thrown off, ex-cept fuch as is confiftent with modefty and de-cency, and Mr. Booth would have looked upon himfelf as extremely happy, had he not turned his thoughts back to his circumftances. Like an honeft man he laid every thing open to her, upon which, fetching a deep figh, fhe faid, that fhe wifhed they had never met, for fo far as it appeared to her they could not be happy, unlefs married, nor happy then while the means of fub-fiftence were wanting.

One day while the lovers were giving a vent to their mutual forrows, the mother of Amelia burft out of a clofet where fhe had concealed herfelf, and running up to her daughter told her that fhe had abufed her indulgence by fuffering a perfon to vifit her on the footing of a lover who had nothing in view befides that of pro-moting her ruin.

This was an unexpected ftroke to both the lovers, who knew nothing of her being there, and it is not certain what might have been the confequence, had not one Dr. Harrifon, a Reve-rend Divine, who was at that time in the houfe, interpofed, and put an end to the difpute. The
doctor

doctor was one of thofe men who are an honour to their profeffion, and telling Mr. Booth that he had fomething of the utmoft importance to communicate to him, took him away, leaving Amelia and her mother to fettle the controverfy between them in the beft manner they could.

When Dr. Harrifon had got Mr. Booth into his ftudy, he reprefented to him, that nothing in the world was more improper than his entertaining thoughts of marrying a young lady who had been tenderly brought up, while he knew it was not in his power to fupport her according to her rank. In anfwer to this, Mr. Booth told the doctor that fo far from having any mercenary views, he only defired to call Amelia his own, and with refpect to what might be left her by her mother, it fhould be entirely at her own difpofal, for he had refolved to purchafe a commiffion in the army.

His anfwer was fo fatisfactory to the doctor, that he went to the mother of Amelia, and procured liberty for his being admitted on the footing of a lover. This was much more than he had ever expected, but he had not enjoyed the privilege long, when he was fent for to attend his fifter, who then lay on her death-bed, and in confequence of a violent fever, foon after paid the debt of nature.

Mr. Booth was fo much concerned for the lofs of his fifter, that for fome days he forgot to write to his beloved Amelia, but on the very day of the funeral, a meffenger arrived from Dr. Harrifon, defiring him to return as foon as poffible. Having called the meffenger into the room, he extorted from him, that a great gentleman had come with propofals of marriage to Amelia, and that

I 3   he

he was defired to return inftantly to Dr. Harrifon's houfe. Upon that, he left the dead corpfe
of his fifter, and fet out for the houfe of Dr. Harrifon, by whom he was received with open marks
of friendfhip. The doctor told him that a few
days before, a rich old gentleman had come with
a grand equipage, and had made very advan-
tageous propofals of marriage to Amelia, and
although fhe had rejected them with the utmoft
difdain, yet her mother had given but too much
countenance to them. The doctor faid all he
could to diffuade the old lady from a fcheme that
muft in the end make her daughter unhappy, but
all to no purpofe, for fhe ftill remained obftinate
in hopes that her daughter would be enabled to enjoy all thofe indulgences that are the natural confequences of an opulent fortune.

In the mean time a wine merchant came into
the doctor's houfe, and informed him that he was
going to fend a hamper of wine to the houfe of
Amelia's mother, upon which it was propofed
that Mr. Booth fhould be clofed up in the hamper
and fent thither. Mr. Booth gave his confent,
and accordingly he was conveyed to the houfe,
and fet down in one of the out-houfes, where he
remained till two of the fervants came to take out
the contents. It is natural to fuppofe that the
fervants would be furprifed, when they faw a
man in the hamper, and indeed both of them
took to their heels, not doubting but the devil
had come to fetch them away before their time.
Poor Booth was obliged to remain in his unhappy
fituation, till fuch time as Amelia arrived, who
with her mother and fifter had been out on a vifit
to a friend.

The

The mother of Amelia had received some intimation of what Mr. Booth had done in getting into the hamper, and therefore she no sooner arrived, than she went to the place where he had concealed himself, and upbraided him in the severest terms. She then led him to the gate, and having conducted him out, told him never more to be seen at her house. It was not a proper time for him to dispute the orders of a woman so imperious as the old lady, and therefore taking his leave he walked several hours in an extreme cold evening, before he came to a place where he could get lodgings.

However, before he arrived at a house, a woman came up just as he was getting over a stile, and threw herself into his arms. He embraced her in the most tender manner, and having lifted her over the stile, they proceeded together till they came to a hedge, where they concealed themselves till those who had been sent in pursuit of them were past. The pursuers being gone, the two lovers proceeded on their journey till it began to rain in the most violent manner, upon which being directed by a light that attracted their notice, they went into a cottage without any sort of ceremony. It happened that the good woman, who lived in the cottage, had been nurse to Amelia, and the mutual surprise that took place between them, may be conceived, but it cannot be expressed. The well-meaning good woman did all she could to accommodate them in the best manner, and having dried their cloaths, it was agreed upon between the lovers, that the nurse's son should be sent with a letter to the worthy Dr. Harrison.

It

It happened that when the young gentleman's letter was received by the doctor, he was engaged in company, so that they did not receive any immediate answer, and while they were deliberating on more proper means to be used, the mother of Amelia came into the cottage with the picture of a fury painted on her countenance.

Amelia no sooner saw her mother, than she fell into convulsion fits, and in the mean time Dr. Harrison arrived with a licence, and next day they proceeded to the church and were married.

During the first two or three months after their marriage, nothing remarkable happened, for both were fond of each other on the principles of the most unsullied virtue, and the mother of Amelia seemed to be reconciled to the match.

Mr. Booth, who had hitherto been no more than an ensign, was advanced to a lieutenancy in consequence of two additional companies having been added to the regiment. Soon after this small promotion took place, the mother of Amelia insisted that her daughter's fortune should be settled on herself, and that as Mr. Booth had obtained his commission gratis, it was necessary that no deductions should be made on account thereof. This proposal Mr. Booth complied with without the least hesitation, but from this time forward there was a visible alteration in the countenance of Miss Betsy, the sister of Amelia. She took every opportunity to traduce the character of Mr. Booth, and although some persons made use of the warmest arguments, in order to bring her to a sense of reason, yet something so selfish had taken place in her mind, that she
became

became an object of detestation to all those that knew her. However, from motives which afterwards appeared to be of a political nature, the young lady became more cordial to her sister, and her brother-in-law, and all that resentment which formerly had made her appear more odious, seemed now to have vanished ; but alas ! it was only to break out anew with a more redoubled fury than ever had appeared, for it was first discovered by her own relations, who had no suspicion of her cunning.

Dr. Harrison, who in all the affairs of this family, took care to act like every honest man, an indulgent part, no sooner heard what the contending parties had to alledge against each other, than he proposed becoming a mediator, in order to reconcile them and make them once more friends. He proposed that as nothing was so dear to a soldier as honour, so he was not on any account whatever to forfeit his title to it. In this the worthy doctor was seconded by Amelia, who fell on her knees, and implored her husband that he would not do any thing inconsistent with his honour. This affair being settled, Dr. Harrison spent the remainder of the evening with the old lady, and said every thing he could think of, in order to reconcile her to her daughter and her husband. When the evening was almost spent, Mr. Booth returned to his chamber, where he found his Amelia on her knees, praying to that Divine Being, whose providence superintends all the affairs of the children of men.

He did not think proper to disturb her, but as soon as her devotions were over, he took her in his arms, and told her that the nature of his em-

ployment

ployment required his attendance in another part of the world, upon which a moft tender fcene enfued. Amelia was willing that her hufband fhould do his duty, but fhe could not bear the thoughts of being fo long feparated from him. The nature of his bufinefs, however, admitted of no delay, and therefore next moining he was obliged to take leave of his beloved Amelia, and fet out on his journey.

He had rode only about two miles, when he difcovered that he had forgot fomething that Amelia had given him to keep in memory of their love for each other; and therefore he fent his man back to bring them, for it would have been imprudent for him to have gone himfelf, becaufe he would have been reduced to the fame difficulty as before, when he firft took leave of her.

This young man, who attended Mr. Booth, in the quality of a fervant, was the fon of that woman who had given fuck to Amelia, and therefore there is no doubt but he would be treated by Mr. Booth with the utmoft refpect. When he returned, his face was covered over with tears, and Mr. Booth having afked him the reafon, he told him it was only fomething of a private nature, upon which he was not preffed any farther. Next day they joined the regiment, which then lay at Plymouth, and having embarked on board the tranfports, they fet fail for Gibraltar, but were foon after overtaken with a moft violent ftorm. The diftrefs to which they were reduced, was more than can be expreffed, and feveral of the fhips, with all the people on board perifhed. This was a moft awful fcene to Mr. Booth, who had never been at fea before, but.

but he endeavoured to reconcile himfelf to it with a philofophic firmnefs. The thoughts of his Amelia were ftill uppermoft in his mind, 'and the confideration, or rather hope that fhe was alive, reconciled him to the dangers of the rageing ocear, and induced him to fet a proper value upon all the affairs of human life, fo as not to prefer any thing above its real intrinfic value.

Soon after their arrival at Gibraltar, Mr. Booth was fent on a party againft the common enemy, and received a wound in his leg, but his fervant, who ftill adhered to him, carried him off in his arms, and fo fayed his life. . When he was brought back to the garrifon, his pain was fo great, that it threw him into a violent fever, but Atkinfon, his fervant, and one Mr. Jones, who commanded a company in the fame regiment, both fympathized with him in fo tender a manner, that he was foon brought to the ufe of his reafon, and in a fhort time afterwards he was able to walk abroad.

As foon as he was once more able to join the regiment, he was fent on another meffage, namely, to attack one of the enemy's forts, but received fuch a violent contufion, that he was once more obliged to be carried back to the garrifon.

During the time he was confined with this wound, his lovely Amelia rufhed into his chamber, without having given him any notice of her intention to vifit him. After the mutual congratulations were over, Amelia told her hufband that fhe had been informed by a letter from an unknown hand, that his life was in danger, and that therefore fhe had croffed the feas, in order to vifit him.

As

As foon as Mr. Booth recovered from his in-difpofition, Amelia fell ill, and it was thought that her life was in danger, for the nature of her diforder was not underftood by the phyficians who attended her. To increafe the affliction of this amiable couple, Amelia, when in a ftate of the utmoft weaknefs, received a letter from her fifter, wherein fhe was informed, that her mother had utterly difcarded her, but that fo far from aliena-ting her affections from her hufband, only ferved to endear him the more to her. The refpect which the governor of Gibraltar had for Mr. Booth, induced him to fuffer him to go to Mont-pellier, where his wife, as well as herfelf, would have an opportunity of drinking the waters, and confequently being again reftored to their former ftate of health. Accordingly they embarked on board a fhip at Gibraltar, and failed for Mar-feilles, from whence they proceeded over land to Montpelier.

They had not, however, been long there, when the good fenfe of Amelia gained her many admirers, and Mr. Booth, notwithftanding his ufual philanthropy of temper, began to be jealous. Among other perfons who had come there for the benefit of their health, was one Mr. Bath, who had been fome time major of a marching regiment, but was then on half pay, and along with him was his fifter, a young lady, who had fhone as one of the moft diftinguifhed coquettes in En-gland, but in confequence of her reputation, having began to decline, fhe had gone over to France, not doubting but that at Montpellier fhe would meet with a certain perfon who had not ufed her in the moft generous manner. At that place of diffipation fhe continued fome time, but

not

not meeting with what she expected, she began to intrigue with some of the French gentry, who of all others, are the most volatile persons in the universe, and never happy unless they find themselves attached to one of the fair sex.

These intrigues brought on a duel between the major, who stood up for the honour of his sister, and the French gentleman who wanted to seduce her. The combat itself, however, was no more than an affair of honour, and although the major received some wounds, yet he soon recovered from them, and then the whole company set out together for Paris. Upon their arrival in that celebrated city, they were treated with great respect by some of the English nobility, who happened to be at that time spending the season in Paris. It is natural to suppose that Mr. Booth's circumstances were of too circumscribed a nature to admit him to launch out into fashionable follies, and therefore he and his spouse contented themselves with private lodgings. They had not, however, been long there, when Mr. Booth received a letter from Dr. Harrison, wherein he informed them that the mother of Amelia was dead, and that she had bequeathed the whole of her estate to her other sister. He added at the same time that he had sent them one hundred pounds, which they would receive in consequence of their calling at a certain place, and that he would as far as was in his power, endeavour to promote their interest in the world, and make some amends for the injury that had been done them, consistent with the laws of this country.

Soon

Soon after this, our travellers left Paris, and set out for England, but as nothing happened to them in their journey, so it is not worthy of being taken notice of. When they arrived in London, Amelia was too much attached to the interests of the child, whom she had left in Wiltshire, to spare one moment till she had seen it, and therefore she set out for the place as soon as she had received proper refreshment.

The humanity of Dr. Harrison was such, that she knew not of any person to whom she could with propriety address herself more than to him, and as he had been her friend, as well as the friend of her husband, on every occasion, she went to his house and knocked at the gate.

The doctor received them with the same good nature that distinguished all his actions, and the evening being spent in the most agreeable manner, she and her husband retired to an apartment, which the doctor kept for the use of his friends. During the whole of the night Amelia could not sleep one wink, so full was her mind of the distress to which she was reduced, and next morning having breakfasted with the good doctor, they all set out together to visit the young infant, whom she had left behind, and whom they had not seen for some time.

A parent only can know what Mr. Booth and his dear Amelia felt, when they saw their beloved infant; every little prattling word served to endear it to them ; and from thence, though with reluctance, they set out to visit the place where Amelia had been brought up with the
utmost

utmoft tendernefs, and which was then inhabit-
ed by her fifter. They were received with a
fort of diftant formality; for the young lady,
in whofe favour the will had been made, behaved with fo much referve, that vifiting her
was rather a pain than a pleafure. She told
Amelia that it had pleafed heaven to remove her
mother by death, and that as fhe had left the
whole of her fortune to her, fo there was not
the leaft doubt but fhe muft have had her reafons
for doing fo. It is true fhe pretended to fympathize with her fifter, but inftead of alleviating
her diftreffes, fhe fuffered her to remain in the
fame diftreffed condition as before.

It could not be fuppofed that Amelia could
hear all this without emotion, for fhe burft into
tears and took her leave foon after. Next morning her fifter wrote her a letter, wherein fhe
told her, that as fhe had married without her
mother's confent, fo fhe had no reafon to expect
that any thing fhould be left to her. In the
mean time Dr. Harrifon, who had the intereft
of Amelia at heart, and wanted to fee it pro-
moted as far as it lay in his power, propofed
that Booth fhould occupy a farm that belonged to
him. The farm lay contiguous to the parfon-
age houfe, and as the doctor was obliged to go
abroad to fuperintend the education of a young
nobleman, fo Booth complied with the propofal, and for fome time lived extremely happy.

He might have continued fo to the laft, had
he been able to bring his mind down to his circumftances, but unhappily for himfelf he fell
into difputes with a 'fquire, who was the principal

cipal perfon in the parifh, and the curate, whom Dr. Harrifon had left to officiate in his room.

Mr. Booth, in order to make himfelf appear the more refpeflable, vamped up an old coach, but the fupporting it in a proper manner, was attended with fuch expence, that in the compafs of four years he become indebted for the fum of three hundred pounds. His goods were feized on, and having nothing left, he fet out for London, where he arrived in a few days afterwards. His misfortune, however, was, that the firft night after his arrival, he was taken up for having been concerned in a riot in the ftreet, and although he was entirely innocent, yet a certain juftice of the peace committed him to prifon.

While Mr. Booth was in prifon he became acquainted with one Mifs Matthews, a young lady of but a loofe character, who had been committed on fufpicion of having murdered one of her lovers. She was not deftitute of generofity, and feeing the diftrefs to which Mr. Booth was reduced, gave him money to fupply his immediate wants, and a mutual friendfhip took place between them. A criminal converfation enfued, which continued above a week, when they both procured their difcharge, but juft as they were going to take their leave, Mr. Booth heard a female voice exclaim, Where is he! and immediately recollected that it was his Amelia. She had fcaice fpoken when fhe fainted away, but the wife of the goaler, who was a notable woman, in her way, came to her affiftance, and endeavoured to bring her back to the ufe of her fenfes,

Amelia

Amelia had no fooner come to her felf, than turning her eyes to her husband, fhe faw Mifs Matthews ftanding befide him. She was no ftranger to the character of that young lady, and wondering what could be the reafon why fhe was fo intimate with her husband, afked her feveral queftions, but did not in the leaft exprefs any ill-nature. In the mean time one of the turn-keys came in and told Mr. Booth that his coach was waiting, upon which he and Amelia went into it, and Mifs Matthews, to her no fmall mortification, was fuffered to go home by her-felf.

Mr. Booth and his lady retired to private lodgings, where they found the children wait-ing for them, and at the fame time imploring every bleffing upon them. The remembrance of paft follies put Mr. Booth to the blufh, efpe-cially when he recollected the difference between an amiable wife, and one, who in the utmoft fenfe of the word, was no better than a com-mon proftitute. He gradually funk into a deep melancholy, and as his wife did not in the leaft fufpect the caufe, fhe imputed it to the diftrefs he was under for the happinefs of his children, who were likely to be left miferable objects, and to be defpifed by all thofe that knew them.

Amelia told him that nothing in her power fhould be wanting to make his life as agreeable as poffible, upon which he began to recover a little of his former vivacity, and one morning at breakfaft he afked her in what manner, or by what means fhe had learned where he was con-fined. She told him that it had been reported

all

all over the country that he had been committed for murder, and as all she had was at stake she took her passage in the Salisbury stage along with the children, and arrived safe in London. Upon further enquiry he found that Miss Matthews was the person who had propagated the story, for Amelia pulled a letter out of her pocket signed by that lady. The contents of the letter were, that Mr. Booth had committed a capital offence, and that whatever might be the consequence, he had one in prison along with him who would stand by him to the last. Booth had no sooner read the letter than he tore it in pieces, with all the marks of indignation, and then threw the contents into the fire. He was sorry to think that he was under any pecuniary obligation to Miss Matthews, and much more so when he began to discover that she had made them public; but still he resolved to dissemble his resentment, and as soon as ever he should have it in his power, make her an ample amends, especially as she had been of service to him in the most trying of all difficulties, namely the horrors of a prison.

While Mr. Booth was reflecting on the subject matter of this scandalous letter, he received one from the doctor, reflecting on his conduct, for having set up a carriage while he was indebted to him for two years rent. The doctor informed him that his conduct had been entirely inconsistent with reason, and although he did not chuse to make use of any violent methods to inforce the payment of what was owing, yet he could not help looking upon him as an object of contempt

contempt for involving his family in fuch difficulties.

He could not conceal the contents of the letter from Amelia, and although it gave her much trouble to perufe it, yet fhe said every thing fhe could to comfort him. In the mean time Mr. Booth went to take a walk in the Park, and while he was gone his little boy afked his mother what was the matter with his pappa; Amelia looking at the child with the greateft maternal tendernefs, told him that his pappa was only a little thoughtful, but that he would be merry after dinner, upon which the child was fatisfied, and fhe returned to give vent to her grief in tears.

When the hour of dinner arrived, Mr. Booth brought along with him his old friend Mr. James, who had been formerly married to Mifs Bath, and Amelia received him with open arms of friendfhip. She made fome apology for the dinner not being dreffed up in the fame elegant manner as when they were in affluent circumftances, but good nature and good humour foon put an end to thefe formalities.

When dinner was over, Amelia went to attend her children, and in the mean time, Mr. James, who had rifen in the army to the rank of a lieutenant-colonel, told Mr. Booth, that nothing in the world was more likely to promote his intereft as that of going into the army. He promifed to give him all the affiftance in his power, and at the fame time propofed backing his petition to fome of the great men, who were at the head of public affairs.

It

It is not to be wondered, that Mr. Booth, who had a family to fupport, would embrace any fcheme that was confiftent with honefty could fupport their wifhes, and therefore he refolved to comply with what Colonel James had propofed. The next day as he was fitting at breakfaft he received a letter from Mifs Matthews, wnich he put into his pocket unopened. When breakfaft was over he went to take a walk in the Park, where he met with the colonel, and told him of the diftrefs to which he was reduced, and then they walked to a coffee-houfe at the end of Spring Gardens. There they converfed together in the moft friendly manner, but from a variety of concurring circumftances, it appeared that. the colonel was no ftranger to the contents of the letter. Mr. Booth, who was no ftranger to real courage, and at the fame time did not chufe to wifh his life in the hands of every ruffian, wanted to come to an ecclairciffement with the colonel, and to know whether or not he had acted in conjunction witn Mifs Matthews, in order to difturb the peace of his family.

Indeed he was not left long in the dark, for that fame hour he received a letter from Mifs Matthews that ferved to unravel the whole myftery, and he found that James was his rival in the affections of that lady. As nothing in the world could give more fatisfaction to Mr. Booth than that of making his wife happy, fo he hefitated whether he fhould not make an open confeffion to her of the imprudencies he had been guilty of, or conceal them till fuch time as fhe found them out by the information of another perfon, who, perhaps might fix fuch a ftigma upon

upon them as would for ever render them inferviceable towards promoting any beneficial purpofe.

The next evening Mr. Booth and his lady went to take a walk in the park, with the children along with them, and coming near the parade, Mr. Booth began to defcribe to his wife the different buildings adjoining. In the mean time the little boy, their eldeft fon, happened to flip away among the croud, and Mr. Booth, cafting his eyes to a little diftance, faw a footfoldier fhaking the little boy in a menacing pofture. Mr. Booth, without the leaft hefitation, jumped over the rails, and tripped up his heels. A ferjeant, who happened to be then on duty, ran up to the foldier, and beftowed upon him a hearty curfe, telling him at the fame time that he ought to be hanged.

The ferjeant then went up to Booth, and made an apology for the behaviour of the foldier, but how great was his furprize, when he faw one that had been long dear to him, namely, his fofter fifter Amelia.

The faithful Atkinfon, for that was the name of the ferjeant, was received by Mr. Booth with open arms of refpeft, and added that whatever might be his prefent ftation, he was under every obligation to him. Amelia was fo much pleafed to fee poor Atkinfon, that fhe wifhed him joy of his commiffion; for becaufe he had laced clothes, fhe thought that he had been in a much higher ftation than he really was.

The ferjeant, who had all the good nature that any man could poffefs, walked home with Amelia, while Mr. Booth conducted the children. When they arrived at the houfe, the
good

good woman, who faw that Amelia was difordered, begged her to walk into the parlour, where fhe gave her a glafs of wine and water, upon which fhe began to recover her fpirits, and the ufual bloom returned into her amiable countenance.

She then gently chid Mr. Booth for being fo rafh, and pulling her little boy to her faid, Billy you muft never do fo any more, for you fee that your poor father's life was in danger. La, mamma, faid the child, what harm did I do? Can there be any harm in walking in the green fields? If I have done a fault, I am fure I have been punifhed enough for it, for the man almoft pinched a piece out of my arm. He then fhewed his arm, which was greatly difcoloured from the injury it had received, upon which ferjeant Atkinfon returned to attend his duty on the guard.

This accident, however trifling it may appear to fome perfons, ferved to make the landlady of the houfe better acquainted with her lodger than fhe had hitherto been. Mrs. Ellifon, for that was the name of the landlady, was one of thofe women, who, without any large fhare of beauty, had learned to make herfelf agreeable to every perfon with whom fhe converfed, and fuch was her good humour, that Amelia could not help taking notice of her, and actually folicited for the continuance of her friendfhip, as long as fhe lodged in the houfe.

In this manner they continued on very good terms during the fpace of two weeks, at the end of which Colonel James fent Mr. Booth a letter that gave him no fmall fhare of uneafinefs.

Amelia

Amelia wanted to fympathize with her hufband, but he not chufing to communicate to her the contents of the letter, fhe defifted from afking him any queftions. In the afternoon, Mrs. Ellifon, who was all good nature, could not help taking notice that her lodgers were under fome fort of a cloud, and therefore having received a prefent of feveral tickets for an oratorio at the Hay-market, fhe told Amelia that fhe would make her a prefent of one, and at the fame time accompany her to the place.

Amelia thanked Mrs. Ellifon for her kindnefs, but in the politeft manner declined the favour, becaufe, as fhe juftly obferved, it was inconfiftent with one in her circumftances, to go to places of public entertainment, while fhe had fcarce fo much as would fupport her and her children, with the common neceffaries of life. Mr. Booth faid all he could to perfuade his wife to accompany Mrs. Ellifon to the opera, but fhe dropped fome hints with the moft becoming propriety. Mrs. Ellifon did not, confiftent with good manners, chufe to infift any futher, but fet out for the opera houfe by herfelf.

She was fcarce gone when an officer of the regiment to which Mr. Booth formerly belonged having enquired of Serjeant Atkinfon where Mr. Booth lodged, came that day to vifit them. He told Mr. Booth that he and fome of his brother officers were to dine next Wednefday at a tavern, and Amelia, who was all compliance, made no objection againft her hufband going thither, efpecially as fhe thought it would in fome meafure difpel the melancholly that they feemed to hang over his mind.

It

It may be afked by the reader, what could induce Mr. Booth to go the tavern, and at the fame time refufe to accompany his wife to the opera-houfe. The reafon was, (and perhaps a very good one) that the tavern where they were to meet was within the verge of the court, and every one of the officers had at that time writs iffued out againft them. Thefe confiderations, indeed, brought him to comply with the requeft of his brother officers, and the evening was fpent in the moft agreeable manner, efpecially when it was confidered that no catchpole could come to moleft them. Indeed, in fome cafes, many of thefe gentlemen become objects of compaffion, for this reafon, that they have had liberal educations, and been taught to expect more than Providence has put in their way to enjoy. Unacquainted with that prudence which fhould regulate all the affairs of human life, they are apt to live above their circumftances, and feed themfelves with vain hopes, till their creditors become clamorous, and then they are obliged to feek an afylum in any place where they can obtain protection. In all cafes of that nature we fhould look upon thofe gentlemen as perfons who are entitled to our refpect, for although they have been guilty of imprudencies, yet they are not to be hunted down as beafts of prey, and driven out of the fociety of all rational creatures, as is too much practifed in fimilar cafes.

Through many perfuafions, Mrs. Ellifon prevailed on Amelia to accompany her the week enfuing to the opera, where they remained above two hours before the performers made their ap-

pearance

pearance. A gentleman who fat next them did every thing to make the time as agreeable as poffible, and when they came out he conducted them home. When he took his leave he promifed to call next day to drink tea, and in the mean time a long difcourfe took place between Amelia and her landlady.

Mrs. Ellifon was a woman of extreme gaiety, for no fooner had Amelia mentioned to her, that fhe thought fhe had acted imprudently in admitting the gentleman to vifit them, than the other burft out into a loud laugh, and told her, that there was no wonder that all the men in the world fhould be in love with her, could they only find an opportunity of feeing her. Thefe words uttered in fo light and fo volatile a manner, gave Amelia but a mean opinion of her landlady, efpecially as fhe feemed to make fo light with the moft facred of all duties between the fexes, namely, that of marriage.

About twelve o'clock at night Mr. Booth came home, rather flufhed with wine, but fo good natured, that Amelia received him with open arms of love; and for that night they went to bed in the moft peaceable manner.

In the morning as foon as Mr. Booth got up, honeft ferjeant Atkinfon came and told him, that he had been at an alehoufe the preceding night, where he heard one Murphy, an attorney, fay, that he had a writ againft one Captain Booth, which he would next morning get backed by the clerks of the Board of Green Cloth.

Mr. Booth thanked honeft Atkinfon in the moft obliging manner, telling him that he had too much reafon to fear that he was the perfon

mentioned;

mentioned ; becaufe his circumftances had been long in a very diftreffed condition. Atkinfon told him, that as he was a houfe-keeper he would give bail to the writ as far as his intereft would go ; upon which Mr. Booth, who was much troubled in his mind, told the ferjeant that he would take the utmoft care of himfelf he poffibly could ; but at the fame time did not neglect to thank an honeft fellow who had thus generoufly undertaken to ftand by him in his diftrefs, without being folicited to do it.

Mr. Booth was of opinion that the writ muft have been taken out by Colonel James, becaufe all the other debts he owed had been contracted in the country ; but he could not account for Murphy having been made choice of as the attorney to carry on the fuit. However, he made no doubt but he was the perfon, and therefore he refolved to confine himfelf to his lodgings, till he faw the event of the affair.

It feems, that, the evening before, while he was at the tavern, a gentleman took fuch notice of him, that he promifed to ufe all his intereft in recommending him to the fecretary at war ; and there being at that time a vacancy in a regiment abroad, he thought that it could not be unacceptable to Booth.

The afternoon was fpent with Mrs. Ellifon, who waited for the gentleman who promifed to drink tea with them, but he did not come ; and therefore Amelia, who only dreaded his appearance, was in high fpirits ; for from the whole of his behaviour he feemed to be one of thofe who pay no regard to moral duty, while a lovely woman is the object of a brutal gratification.

A young

A young lady with whom Mrs. Ellison was well acquainted, came to spend the afternoon with them, and as she was extremely grave in the whole of her deportment, Amelia conceived so strong a desire to be acquainted with her character, that she could not help asking Mrs. Ellison some questions, and from her she learned that her name was Bennet, that she was the widow of a young clergyman who had died of a consumption, and left her exposed to all the hardships that necessarily arise from a state of penury. The curiosity of Amelia was stimulated to the utmost, in order to contract an acquaintance with an unfortunate lady in distress, and, therefore she begged of Mrs. Ellison to introduce her to her. The good woman promised to comply with her request, telling her at the same time, that Mrs. Bennet was a lady of no ceremony, so that she might be introduced to her at any time.

The two next days Booth spent at home with his dear Amelia, which was no small comfort to her, who was never happy out of his company. On the Saturday following, a noble lord came to drink tea at Mrs. Ellison's, who was actually a distant relation of that lady's, for although she had been reduced in her circumstances, yet she had some persons related to her of the highest rank among the nobility and gentry.

During their conversation, Mrs. Ellison took occasion to mention to his lordship, what a happy circumstance it would be, if he could by his interest provide for Mr. Booth in the army; for although this nobleman was not in the ministry, yet his influence was great with every one at

the

the head of public affairs. His lordfhip, who,
like many others of the fame rank, cannot look
upon an amiable woman without wifhing to
have fuch connections with her as are inconfiftent with modefty, declared, that nothing fhould
be wanting on his part to perform fo benevolent
an action, and Mr. Booth made him the moft
grateful acknowledgments.

When that happy day arrived on which the
moft wretched debtor may walk abroad without
being afraid of catchpoles, Mr. Booth went
out to take the frefh air, and after walking
about an hour in the Park, he went to the lodgings of Colonel James, in order to know why
he had taken out a writ againft him. He was,
however, denied admittance, under pretence that
the colonel was not then ftirring, and after he
had walked another hour, was told by the fervant that he was gone out.

Difappointed in this manner he went into a
coffee-houfe near St. James's, where he had not
fat long when he heard one officer call out to
another, that there was the perfon come whom
he wanted. This perfon was no other than
Major Bath, with whom Mr. Booth had been
long acquainted. He afked Mr. Booth feveral
queftions concerning the ftate of his affairs,
when Booth told him in a whifper, that he had
a great many things to communicate to him,
particularly relating to Colonel James, whofe
friendfhip he was afraid he had loft.

Accordingly they took a walk into the Park,
where Mr. Booth informed the major in what
manner the colonel had ufed him, and how he
had firft taken out a writ againft him, and then

had

had got it backed by the clerks of the board of Green Cloth. He added that he had called on the colonel for an explanation, but was denied admittance to him ; upon which the major propofed that he fhould once more go and deliver a challenge to the colonel.

Mr. Booth was too much convinced of his own deplorable circumftances to venture upon a projeƈt fo dangerous in its own nature, and likely to be attended with fatal confequences. The major, however, was all on fire, and infifted that there fhould be a duel confiftent with the charaƈter of gentlemen, or he would look upon them as the greateft poltroons ever after : upon which they both departed for the prefent, diffatisfied with each other.

Such was the end of this converfation, fo little to the fatisfaƈtion of Mr. Booth, that he began to wifh he had never mentioned one word of what had happened, and to add to his misfortune, he found upon his return home, that one of the children had been taken extremely ill. As Amelia had been extremely uneafy, fhe had fent for a phyfician, who arrived foon after with the apothecary at his heels. A curious dialogue enfued between the two phyfical gentlemen, but fo little to the fatisfaƈtion of Booth that he ordered them both to be difcharged, and fent for another, who, in a few days, by a proper adminiftration of medicines, reftored the child to a proper ftate of health.

Poor Mr. Booth was obliged to remain at home all the week, till Sunday arrived, and then finding the child perfeƈtly recovered he went abroad with him in his hand. His defign

K 3

was

was to vifit the noble peer who had treated him with fo much refpeēt, at the houfe of Mrs. Ellifon; and when he came there he met with a much different reception than he had from his old friend Colonel James.

No fooner had he knocked at the door than the porter opened it to him in the moft refpeētable manner, telling him at the fame time that his lordfhip was at leifure to wait upon him.

His lordfhip was a nobleman of fuch politenefs, that he told Mr. Booth that he would fpeak to the minifter in his favour, not doubting but he would receive a favourable anfwer, and therefore defired him to call again as often as he pleafed, until fuch time as the bufinefs fhould be completed. Booth foon after took his leave with the moft profufe acknowledgments for fo much goodnefs, and haftened home to acquaint his amiable Amelia with the profpeēt he had of making fome provifion for his young family.

It feems his lordfhip had propofed that Mr. Booth fhould go to fome of the fettlements abroad; but no fooner had Amelia heard of that, than fhe hinted that he fhould take her along with him, as fhe was determined that fhe would ftand or fall by him, wherever he went. This affair being fettled, Booth and Amelia, with the children, fat down to eat a bit of a leg of mutton, which was all that their finances would allow, and in the afternoon they drank tea with Mrs. Ellifon, where they had the pleafure of meetting once more with Mrs. Bennet.

While they were fitting at tea, ferjeant Atkinfon happened to pafs by the window, and Mrs. Ellifon, as well as Amelia, having afked

fome

fome queſtions concerning him ; it was propoſed to call him in, which was accordingly done, but as the poor fellow, though one of the moſt handſome that ever appeared at a public aſſembly, yet was utterly unacqainted with dancing, ſo when he came into the room he made but an aukward appearance.

There is ſomething in real goodneſs that makes amends for the want of formalities, which in their own nature, are often little more than trifling, and ſuch was it with the honeſt ſerjeant. He had a moſt benevolent heart, and although he had ſeen many of his fellow creatures cut down in the field of battle, yet on all occaſions, and in every place, he diſcovered ſuch generoſity of ſentiment, as ſeldom falls to the ſhare of one who has born a halbert. To entertain the company, he repeated many ſtrange ſtories relating to what had happened to him, while he was in the army, and Mrs. Elliſon, who ſeemed quite captivated with him, inſiſted that he ſhould ſtay ſupper.

Indeed ſhe was ſo pleaſed with his handſome appearance, that although he made uſe of ſome expreſſions rather improper while he had got heated with wine, yet ſhe found no fault with them, although they ſeemed to offend the delicacy of the chaſte Amelia.

The remainder of the evening was ſpent in the moſt innocent manner, and at the time of going to bed arrived, the ſerjeant took leave, and Mrs. Bennet was conducted home by the ſervant of Mrs. Elliſon.

Next day when they were all ſitting together in the parlour, except Atkinſon, Mrs. Elliſon called him

him her clever ſerjeant, and added that he was worthy of the beſt woman in the kingdom, for ſhe did not ſee how any one could refuſe him. Mr. Booth ſaid that he had already ſaved one hundred pounds, and if he had a little more he would be able to procure a commiſſion, which would put him on the footing of the genteeleſt man in England, for although his courage was truly heroic, yet he had the ſpirit of a lamb when not engaged in war.

While they were talking in this manner in praiſe of the handſome ſerjeant, a footman came to the door, and alarmed the whole houſe with his dreadful rap. It is not to be wondered at that poor Booth ſhould be afraid, eſpecially as he knew that there was a writ out againſt him, but the little girl ran down ſtairs, and told her mamma, that there was a gentleman on the ſtairs that appeared to be no other than the noble lord who had already made them ſo many pro-miſes.

Amelia received his lordſhip with that good nature that ſeemed on all occaſions to mark her character, and Mr. Booth, her poor afflicted huſband was ready to attend him, in the moſt obſequious manner. His lordſhip ſpoke in the true ſtile of a courtier; to which Mr. Booth (and it is to be hoped every other man) is an utter ſtranger, and concluded by making a thouſand promiſes, which he had no intention ever to perform. Poverty, however, lays hold of the moſt diſtant ray of hope, and poor Amelia, who had never harboured a criminal thought in her mind, began to imagine that his lordſhip

was

was not fo bad a man as his behaviour had induced her to think he was.

The company having how refumed a lively
turn, his lordfhip began to entertain them with
ftories, which although well enough in the detail,
could not be read, were they committed to
writting. He was fo highly pleafed with Amelia, that he could not help taking particular notice of her, but fhe was deaf to all that he faid,
that was in the leaft inconfiftent with the funda-
mental rules of virtue.

On the other hand, Mrs. Bennet declared
that fhe was not in the leaft entertained with
what his lordfhip had mentioned, for although
his words had been expreffed confiftent with
the higheft degree of politenefs, yet fhe thought
the honeft fimplicity of the ferjeant was far fuperior to it. She faid there was fomething fo
amiable in the whole of his behaviour, that fhe
wondered how any perfon could converfe with
with him without being in raptures, and in that
fentiment fhe was feconded by Mrs. Ellifon,
who faid fhe would give all the world, were it
in her power to be entitled to fo high a privilege
as to call him her husband.

Indeed the whole ftate of the cafe was this,
both Mrs. Ellifon and Mrs. Bennet were in love
with the ferjeant, which is not much to be wondered at, when it is confidered that he was fuch
a handfome fellow, and at the fame time endow-
dowed with fo many amiable qualities. Envy,
confiftent with the nature of female characters,
took place in both their minds, and as neither
of them were able to hold out the converfation

K 5   any

any longer, without giving a fally to irregular paffion, they agreed to part for the night.

It is a maxim among moralifts, and it can certainly be realized in real life, that no woman will ever allow another to be fuperior to herfelf in beauty, wit, or fenfe. Nay, let any woman tell another that fhe is ugly, or that her character has been ruined in confequence of an imprudent ftep, then fhe will never forgive the perfon who has faid fo. Such was the cafe with Mrs. Ellifon and Mrs. Bennet, who had both good qualities, but who were at the fame time women who had not paid fo much regard to their characters as they ought to have done, confiftent with the rules prefcribed for the prefervation of modefty among the female fex.

Amelia was no fooner alone with her husband than fhe congratulated him on the fuccefs that he had had with his lordfhip, and then asked him his opinion concerning Mrs. Bennet. Mr. Booth told her, that as fhe had loft her husband fhe muft in confequence thereof be an object of pity; but before they had done fpeaking, Mrs. Ellifon came in and told Mr. Booth that fhe was afraid he was in fome trouble, for fhe had feen two ugly ill-looking fellows lurking about the door; but to comfort him, fhe added, that fhe could find him a lawyer, who would do fomething in his favour with the Board of Green Cloth.

Mr. Booth thanked her in the kindeft manner, and as foon as fhe was gone, ferjeant Atkinfon came in, and told him, that he had fcraped an acquaintance with Murphy, the attorney, and found

found him to be one of the greateſt villains in the world.

The honeſt ſerjeant told him further, that he had ſome money, which was entirely at his ſervice, which ſo much overcome the poor lieutenant that he could not help ſhedding tears. It was agreed upon between them, that the good-natured ſerjeant ſhould for two or three days wait in the parlour, to act as a porter at the door, in caſe the bailiff ſhould come.

During theſe days that the ſerjeant waited in the parlour, he was conſtantly viſited by Mrs. Bennet, who took every opportunity of waiting upon him, for he was ſo handſome, that it was almoſt impoſſible not to fall in love with him.

Nothing material happened during theſe three days, only that Amelia received a card from Mrs. James, the lady of the colonel, deſiring to ſee her at her lodgings. Amelia was a good deal ſurprized to hear from one of whom ſhe had formed but a very indifferent opinion, but ſtill ſhe was reſolved to wait on her.

When they met, Amelia could not help aſking her, what was the reaſon that ſhe had treated her with ſo much coldneſs ; to which the other anſwered, that ſhe knew of no ſort of coldneſs ; and theſe matters were for the preſent happily adjuſted. The ladies parted, ſeemingly, on good terms of friendſhip ; and, at the end of three days, Mrs. Elliſon's lawyer had the good fortune to make ſuch intereſt with the Board of Green Cloth, that Mr. Booth obtained liberty to walk abroad in the verge of the court.

Next

Next morning Booth took a walk to the Park, where he met with Major Bath, and accofted him in the moft humble manner; but the old major looked upon him with fo much contempt, that he would not fpeak to him. Booth not being able to account for this part of the major's conduct, waited till he was alone, and then ftepping up to him, asked him what offence he had given him. The major anfwered that he was a fcoundrel, and infifted that he fhould give him the fatisfaction of a gentleman. Accordingly they both walked up through the Green Park to Conftitution Hill, and from thence to Hyde Park, where, when they had reached the ring, the major pulled off his hat and wig with his coat, and laid them all on the grafs. Booth did not ufe much ceremony, but drawing his fword put himfelf in a pofture of defence, upon which the combat became ferious. Two or three paffes put an end to the difpute, for Mr. Booth having wounded the major, it was propofed that he fhould be immediately fent to the houfe of a furgeon, who undertook to reftore him to the fame ftate as before, upon which Mr. Booth, taking leave of him in the moft tender manner, returned home to his family.

This affair had fo much abforbed Mr. Booth's thoughts, that he forgot the time of dinner, while Amelia, 'who knew that he was one of the moft punctual men alive, after waiting for him above an hour fat down to dinner with her children, not doubting but he had ftaid to dinner with one of his friends. When he arrived the cloth was juft removed, upon which, forgetting the

the hour of the day, he asked her if dinner was not ready; ever obliging, .and willing at all times to make her husband as happy as poffible, fhe ftarted from her feat, and ordered the victuals that had been left to be again brought upon the table. Amelia was of fo good-natured a difpofition, that fhe never enquired any farther what had detained her husband, except in a friendly manner, where natural affection induced her to fympathize with him.

Booth made fome little apology for having ftaid fo long, but as he was ignorant of what is commonly called deceit, he could not help betraying himfelf, and therefore began to difcover fome little confufion. Amelia did not want to prefs him any further, but at laft overcome by her goodnefs, he told her, that he had had an affair of honour with Major Bath, but no dangerous confequences were likely to flow from it.

In the evening Mr. Booth propofed to wait on the major, who lived in the verge of the court as well as himfelf; and fo pofitive was he in his refolution, that although Amelia remonftrated againft it, yet he ftill infifted on going. He found the major in his night-gown, without the leaft appearance of having received a capital injury, and adjourned with him to the next room, for he was then engaged at a game at chefs.

The major told Booth, that his friend Colonel James had depreciated his character in fuch a manner that he could not help demanding fatisfaction, but as he had now received it he was fully convinced that there muft have been fome miftake in the cafe. He added, that he would

take

take the firft opportunity of fpeaking to the colonel, and in the mean time, confiftent with his
notions of military honour, he declared that
Booth was the braveft fellow he had ever met
with.

This affurance of the major's gave Booth the
utmoft fatisfaction, for he was confcious he had
never given the colonel any offence, he having
been his particular friend for feveral years. Every
thing being amicably fettled, Booth returned
home, where he found his dear Amelia and Mrs.
Ellifon engaged at cards with the noble lord
whom we have already mentioned. His lordfhip
it feems had had a fecond interview with the great
man ; his ufual good nature brought him there
that night to communicate the news that he
had not yet had an abfolute promife. As he did
not find Mr. Booth at home, he fat down with
the ladies, and the rather fo, as he had not at
that time any particular affair that demanded his
prefence in another place. He faid every thing
he could to pleafe Amelia, but whatever might
be his thoughts, or his intentions, certain it is
that fhe acted with all the decorum becoming the
character of the moft virtuous woman in the
world.

His lordfhip made fo many offers to ferve Mr.
Booth, that the whole company were in raptures
when they confidered his benevolence. Mrs.
Ellifon told them, that although his lordfhip was
not married, yet he was extremely fond of
children, and fhe doubted not but he would
marry, were it not that his fifter was a widow,
and therefore he would do every thing in his
power to ferve her. She added, that there was

nothing

nothing would more contribute towards promoting Mr. Booth's intereſt, than that of making
his lordſhip acquainted with the children, for ſhe
was ſure he would be extremely fond of them.
It was then propoſed that Mr. Booth's children
ſhould wait upon thoſe of his lordſhip's ſiſter,
and Amelia, whoſe tenderneſs as a mother, could
not hinder her to do every thing to promote the intereſt of her progeny, willingly gave her conſent.
Booth expreſſed his diſapprobation, becauſe he
ſaid his children would be conſidered as on the
footing of beggars, but Mrs. Elliſon endeavoured
to make him entirely eaſy on that head, becauſe
ſhe ſaid his lordſhip was one of the beſt men in
the world, and would always treat him with the
moſt particular friendſhip. Next morning ſerjeant Atkinſon came to wait on Mr. Booth, and
deſired him to take a walk into the park. A
requeſt of that nature was what Booth could not
refuſe to comply with, and therefore they both
walked into the mall, where they had not been
long, when the ſerjeant aſked him whether he
would keep a ſecret that he had to communicate.
Mr. Booth, who could not tell the meaning of
all this preface, asked him to be explicit, and
not keep him any longer in ſuſpenſe.
Upon that, Atkinſon told him that he was
really in love with Mrs. Bennet, in conſequence
of the character he had heard of her from Mrs.
Elliſon. Mr. Booth told him he might do as he
pleaſed, and that nothing ſhould be wanting in
his power to promote his intereſt. He ſaid he was
willing to ſee him happy, upon which they both
parted, in order to return home. When they
arrived at the houſe, Mrs. Elliſon, who was in
. love

love with the ferjeant as well as Mrs. Benner, could not help coming up to Mr. Booth's room as foon as there was a proper opportunity. Amelia rallied her on an account of the handfome ferjeant, to all which fhe anfwered, that fhe did not know what they meant by fo much mirth, but as for the ferjeant, to be fure he was an extremely handfome fellow, who would at all times endeavour to make a woman happy. Amelia then told her all that fhe knew concerning him in his youth, and the little petty follies only ferved to revive love, and make him more adorarable to her than he had ever been before, but for the prefent the converfation broke off, becaufe Amelia wanted to go to reft.

Next morning Booth went to wait on Major Bath, and found Colonel James along with him. As he doubted not James was the perfon who had injured him, he told him that he demanded the fatisfaction of a gentleman. Colonel James, without any hefitation, defired the lieutenant to walk out. Accordingly he did fo, and upon enquiry, it was found that the perfon who had caufed all the mifchief, was Mifs Matthews, who wanted to be revenged on Booth, becaufe he had left her in fo abrupt a manner when they came out of prifon. It feems that lady had been for fome time kept by the colonel, and therefore, like moft other women, when they think themfelves flighted, fhe fpread a falfe report of both parties. The news of their going out together, foon alarmed their friends, but no bad confequences followed, for after walking an hour in the park, they returned home to their lodgings.

Upon

Upon their arrival they found no perfon at home but the maid, for Amelia had gone out along with Mrs. Ellifon and the children to pay a vifit to the noble lord whom we have already mentioned, becaufe he had expreffed a great defire to fee her. Booth had fcarce ufhered the colonel in, when a fervant arrived, and told them that Mrs. James had fallen into violent convulfions, in confequence of having heard that a duel had been fought between her hufband and Captain Booth, at which the colonel fmiled, and then fent the fervant back to contradict the account. The fervant was fcarce gone, when Amelia came in, adorned with all that is amiable in female charms, and produced a great many trinkets, which fhe had received from his lordfhip, amongft which was a gold watch. Mr. Booth did not look on the prefents as given without fome finifter view, and therefore he gravely afked his wife in what manner fhe was to make a proper recompence for them. Mrs. Ellifon anfwered, that they were prefents from one of the moft generous noblemen in the kingdom, and therefore there was no occafion to think of a return, becaufe it was below his dignity to accept of it. In this fhe was feconded by Amelia, and then the parties fat down together to a frugal meal, without any of that oftentation which in a great meafuie diftinguifhes the tables of the great.

Amelia, during the whole time they were at dinner, difplayed fo many charms without defign in the moft artlefs manner, that the colonel became entirely captivated with her. Love for her perfon, and compaffion for her diftreffed circumftances,

ftances, operated upon his mind in fo powerful a manner, that he could not help ftealing a glance as often as poffibly he could. At laft decency obliged him to retire, and Mr. Booth with his fpoufe went to bed.

Next day in the afternoon they took a walk into the park, where Amelia told her hufband that Mrs. Ellifon had mentioned fome things to her concerning the noble lord, her coufin, that were not confiftent with the rules of virtue. It feems Mrs. Ellifon, who was a volatile woman, had been converfing with her on the character of Mrs. Bennet, and that led them to fpeak of his lordfhip, who in an affair of diftrefs had been very bountiful to that lady. Amelia had told her that there was no perfon in the world whom fhe efteemed more than her hufband, nor did fhe believe there was one endowed with fo many accomplifhments, upon which Mrs. Ellifon laughed, and told her fhe was deaf to her own intereft. To this Amelia replied, that fhe might think as fhe pleafed, but as for her own part fhe was determined to live and die in fuch a manner, as no perfon fhould have any occafion to reflect on her conduct.

When they returned home, Amelia was not a little furprifed to find feveral things tumbled about the room, and calling the fervant, who was only a young girl, fhe asked her the reafon. The girl told her that a perfon knocked at the door, which fhe having opened, let him in, upon which he ran up ftairs and committed the robbery. She faid, that fhe ftill thought he was in the houfe, but Booth having made the moft diligent fearch, could not find him. Upon farther enquiry,

quiry, it was found that nothing had been taken away, and as the things had been only tossed about, Mr. Booth and Amelia began to suspect that the girl had had some person along with her. They questioned her upon it, but she denied the whole, and Amelia, who was all good nature, said she was extremely thankful they had not lost any thing, but at the same time cautioned the girl against letting any person into the house for the future whom she did not know.

Mr. Booth, in consequence of his unhappy circumstances, had reason to imagine that the person was a bailiff, but before he had time for much, or indeed any reflection, a violent knocking was heard at the door, and Mrs. James, the lady of the colonel, made her appearance ; her principal motive for coming at that time, was to convince Amelia that she had not lost any respect for her, but was the same friend as before, and indeed she had profited so much in consequence of some instruction that she received from Amelia, that she had shaken off all that stiffness and formality so peculiar to the former part of her conduct.

While Mrs. James was sitting in the parlour, the little boy, son of Mr. Booth, was playing with the gold watch, and Amelia having informed her that it was a present from his lordship, Mrs. James answered in such a manner as to fill Booth with the utmost jealousy, for he began to imagine that the peer had a design on the virtue of his wife. He turned pale all of a sudden, which Mrs. James, who had made use of the words on purpose, observing, ordered her carriage and rode off,

She

She had scarce got from the door, when Mrs. Ellison came up in a great fit of laughter, and told him that the thief, who had made so much disturbance in the house, was no other than his lordship, who being enraged because he had not found them at home, had tumbled the things about, and then went to spend the evening at Almacks along with some other persons of the most dignified stations. She added, that he had left a ticket for Amelia to go to the masked ball at Ranelagh, but Mr. Booth interposing, declared his wife should not go to any such place. A smart dialogue ensued, but Amelia was too good a wife to oppose her husband's inclinations, and therefore told him, that if the masquerade was a heaven on earth, she would not go to it without her husband's consent, whom she looked upon as the only valuable person in the world.

Mrs. Ellison having taken her leave, and indeed with some marks of disdain, a dialogue ensued between Mr. Booth and Amelia concerning the nature of the masquerade. She told him that she did not imagine there was any harm in it, but in answer to that, he informed her, that the accepting a ticket to go to such a place from a lord, would be an indelible stain upon her character. As Amelia was utterly innocent, she burst into tears, and asked Mr. Booth whether she had done any thing to make him suspect her virtue, upon which he clasped her in his arms, and told her she had not, but added, that she must not for the future receive any presents from his lordship.

For that night they went to bed in the most agreeable manner, and in the morning Booth having gone out to take his walk, Amelia went
down

down to the parlour to spend a few minutes with Mrs. Ellison. She found that lady alone, and notwithstanding the difference that had taken place between them the preceding day, yet nothing but good humour ensued. Mrs. Ellison, however, told Amelia that she had not treated his lordship as she ought to have done, and in consequence thereof, there was reason to fear that her husband would be deprived of all those hopes he had formed, in consequence of his application to the ministry in his favour.

When Mr. Booth returned, his wife communicated to him what Mrs. Ellison had said, and as he had seen much of the villainy of the world, he began to be fearful for the consequences. In the afternoon Mrs. Bennet came to visit them, and Mr. Booth, who had formed no high notion of her before, now began to entertain a quite different opinion. Indeed she discovered what few women know, namely, a perfect knowledge of the Greek and Latin classicks, and could quote them on every occasion with the same facility as a girl can a single passage out of one of our common plays. Nay, she even went further, for she repeated in the course of her conversation, some of the most striking principles in the Roman law, and she seemed to be as well acquainted with the Justinian institutions as we are with a common news-paper. There is no wonder that such a person should attract the notice of Mr. Booth, who although brought up the greatest part of his time in the army, was no stranger to common life, and could not help wondering how a woman could acquire the knowledge of the dead languages, while many men, who loll about the

streets

ftreets in their chariots, are totally ignorant of
the firft principles of them.

Mrs. Ellifon having made her fecond appearance, Amelia told her that fhe would go to the
mafquerade, upon condition that fhe could procure a ticket for Mrs. Bennet, but fhe was given
to underftand, that it could not be done, for his
lordfhip had a great many friends to oblige, and
as for Mrs. Bennet, fhe was one of a very doubtful
ful charaƈter. In the mean time ferjeant Atkinfon
came and informed Mr. Booth, that he had been
in company with Murphy, the attorney, and that
he had told him that the board of green cloth
would, in a few days, iffue their warrant, for
him, Booth, being apprehended on an aƈtion of
debt in the verge of the court. Mr. Booth, as
foon as the ferjeant was gone, communicated
the news, unwelcome as they were, to his dear
Amelia, for indeed he could not conceal any
thing from her.

Next morning, as Mr. Booth was going out
to take his ufual walk, he received a note from
an unknown hand, importing that he was in
fome danger, which he concluded was the effeƈt
of the information he had received from ferjeant
Atkinfon, but upon a more clofe and ftriƈter
examination, he found he was miftaken, and
fhewing it to his wife upon her return home, fhe
knew the hand-writing to be that of Mrs. Bennet's.
She immediately fet out for her lodgings, where
fhe found her at home, though in fome confufion;
at leaft it appeared fo, in confequence of her
making Amelia wait fo long before fhe came to
give her an anfwer.

When

' When the note was produced Mrs. Bennet could not deny it, but owned it . to be her own hand writing, though fhe faid fhe hoped it had not been fhewn to Mrs. Ellifon. Amelia told her it had not, and feeing her in the utmoft confufion was loth to prefs her any further, than by telling her that the happinefs of her family depended upon an explanation. Mrs. Bennet told her, that nothing was in her view beyond that of promoting her intereft, and preferving her from ruin, and therefore propofed relating to her the following narrative.

Mrs. Bennet had been very thoughtful fome . time, which induced Amelia to ask her the caufe of her melancholy. Upon which Mrs. Bennet burft into tears, and fpoke to her in the following manner :

" My father was a country clergyman in Effex, who brought me up with great tendernefs till I was fixteen years of age, at which period I may with propriety begin my hiftory. On the birth day of my mother, my father gave an entertainment to his friends ; but, alas ! my mother having gone to affift the old fervant maid, went for a tea-kettle of water, but ftooping too low, fhe fell into the well, and was drowned. My father, though as tender a parent as ever lived, yet he bore his misfortune with refignation, and finding me of a ftudious difpofition, fpent a few hours every day in teaching me the Latin and Greek Languages.

" When I was in my nineteeth year my father removed to Hampfhire, taking me along with him, for he where had a good rich living conferred on him. We had not been long there, when

when my poor ancient father fell violently in love with a young lady, which gave me the greateſt uneaſineſs, but the mrriage took place, notwithſtanding my remonſtrances to the con-´ trary. It was not long before I found my life very much altered, for my new ſtepmother was little better than a devil. She was continually forging ſtories to my prejudice, and at laſt my father, one day, giving me a letter, deſired me to pack up my clothes, and inſtantly remove from his houſe. The place to which I went was the houſe of an aunt, a woman of great vanity, without any mental qualifications. Her houſe was about forty miles diſtant from ours ; and I can aſſure you, I went there without ſo much as eating victuals, for grief can fill the ſtomach as much as meat. When I had beeń there about ſix months, I was informed that my ſtep-mother was delivered of a fine boy, and ſoon after my aunt began to treat me with very little reſpect, and, in ſome caſes, even con- tempt.

" The curate of the pariſh was a young gen- tleman of twenty-four, who had been left an orphan, and his uncle had provided for his edu- cation, but had left him nothing in his will, ſo that when he entered into orders, he was glad to accept of a ſmall curacy. ´ It was not long be- fore the young gentleman became extremely fond of me, but´the worſt was, that my aunt was in love with him. While we were one day in an arbour, my aunt ſurprized us, and flew upon me like a tygreſs ;´ſo that my life being now a burden to me, I gave my hand to Mr. Bennet, who treated me with the greateſt tenderneſs,

dernefs, fo that I confidered myfelf as the happieft of women.

"We had not been long married when Mr. Bennet propofed coming to London, where he obtained a curacy, and to promote his intereft took lodgings near the houfe of a noble peer, who had been h's fellow-collegian. We had not been above three months in town when I was delivered of a fon; and, notwithftanding my diftrefs on account of poverty, yet I could not help rejoicing as much as if I had been delivered of an heir to an eftate.

"As foon as I was perfectly recovered, we removed to the fecond floor of the houfe, where you now lodge, and Mrs. Ellifon treated us with great tendernefs.

"At that time the noble lord, who has been fo affiduous to ferve you, lodged in the fame houfe. He pretended to be much in love with my little boy, and was often taking him on his knee, nor did he for fome time proceed to take any greater liberties. But little did I fufpect the enjoyment of my own perfon was the object he had in view. All this time he was foliciting (as he faid) for the futrender of a living for Mr. Bennet, and actually propofed writing down to the country in order to procure it. This however was not his intention, for under pretence of having fomething of importance to tranfact in London, he prevailed on Mr. Bennet to go in his room.

"As foon as Mr. Bennet was gone, Mrs. Ellifon came into the room under pretence of comforting me, and told me that his lordfhip had propofed accompanying me to Ranelagh,

L   and

and for that purpofe had fent me a ticket. At firft I made fome objection, but Mrs. Ellifon, by her arguments, prevailed fo far upon me, that I confented to go.

" It was a mafquerade, and the different, whimfical dreffes pleafed me fo much, that I beheld them with admiration. When I had been there about two hours, his lordfhip came up and began to be very familiar, with me, which did not give me fo, much offence as before, for to tell the truth I had conceived an efteem for him. About two in the morning we returned home, where we found a fine collation prepared for us, and the wine being exceeding good as I thought, I drank rather too freely, without confidering that it was mixed with fomething of a ftupifying nature. —— I need not proceed any further, for that night my ruin was completed, and I became the moft wretched of women.

" Next morning his lordfhip left the houfe, and went into the country, and, in the mean time Mr. Bennet returned home. He embraced me in the moft tender manner, and although my face was all confufion, yet fuch had been the fatigues of his journey, that he took no notice of it. He told me that there was no fuch thing as a living to difpofe of, and that he had been only treated with contempt by every perfon to whom he mentioned it. Next day he went and performed his duty in the church, but I refufed to accompany him, which was the firft time I had ever done fo fince our marriage : but, alas ! the thoughts of my difhonour diftracted me fo much, that I was afhamed to be feen any where,
                                                                  or

or by any perſon, much more ſo by a man who had treated me with ſo much tenderneſs.

"For ſome days I ſaw my husband looked dejected, and often darted ſtrange looks at me, and next Saturday evening he turned from me in bed, and refuſed to ſpeak with me. All night he ſeemed in the utmoſt agonies, and getting up in the morning, went out with tears in his eyes. He did not return till evening, when ſitting down by me in a ſtate of diſtraction, he took up a book and threw it at my head. Confounded, and not doubting but he had in ſome manner or other diſcovered my ſhame, I burſt into tears, and begged to know why he uſed me in that manner. He darted at me a look of horror, and with tears in his eyes told me that I had polluted him, by communicating to him a fatal diſtemper.

"When I found the fatal ſecret with which I was utterly unacquainted before, I fell at his feet and begged that he would that moment kill me, for I had been betrayed by a villain. I then related to him every particular, upon which he told me he believed me, and as he was convinced of Mrs. Elliſon being an accomplice, he reſolved not to ſleep one night longer in the houſe.

"The artful woman, who was conſcious of her guilt, told them, that ſhe ſo much abhorred the crime that had been committed in her houſe, that ſhe could not blame us for going away; and as for the ſmall debt that was owing, ſhe would never demand it.

"We had not been above ten weeks in our new lodgings, when my poor husband died of a broken heart, and I was left in the moſt de-

plorable

plorable circumstances; but Mrs. Ellison, not-withstanding the base part she had acted, yet treated me with the utmost tenderness, and necessity drove me back to her house. There I remained some time, when his lordship settled an annuity upon me, but I solemnly declare he never offered me any indecencies after. Indeed, I was informed, that he was so inconstant, that after he had seduced a woman, he took no more thought of her, and as for his making a settlement on me, I believe it was in consequence of the fate of my husband."

Such was Mrs. Bennet's account of herself, and Amelia embraced her with the greatest tenderness, when she found in what danger she herself was in from his lordship, who had been hatching schemes to betray her in the same base manner. Amelia, who had the greatest regard for Serjeant Atkinson, asked Mrs. Bennet if he did not lodge in the same house with her, and being answered in the affirmative, she soon learned that they had been married some time. Amelia approved of her choice, and the serjeant coming in at that time, they all sat down together in the most friendly manner.

The honest serjeant could not refrain from dropping a tear, which Amelia taking notice of, told him that she hoped nothing had happened to her husband. He begged she would not discompose her spirits, but Captain Booth had been arrested at the suit of Dr. Harrison, and was then in a spunging house, but he had sent a lawyer to him, and he doubted not but he would be set at liberty in a few hours. It seems that as Mr. Booth was taking his morning's walk, a bailiff came

came up and arrested him, and took him to a spunging-house in Gray's-Inn lane.

When they arrived at the doleful mansion where many had been ruined, he was first obliged to pay for the coach-hire, and then he was told he must comply with the rules of the house, which was no other than to pay for ten times more than he either eat or drank, all which he was obliged to comply with, otherwise he would have been sent to Newgate.

Booth, who was a real practical philofpher, asked the bailiff, who were his fellow prisoners, upon which he told him that the first was an author, who wrote for the bookfellers, and was extremely clever in his way, but being very idle, he had been arrested for a debt of about eleven pounds. This (he added) was done in order to make him mind his business, and to be sure, said the bailiff, I love the fellow, because he is a friend to liberty. Liberty, (cried Booth) why sure, Sir, as you live by depriving men of their liberty, you cannot wish for any such thing as real liberty taking place. The bailiff answered, that if men were not arrested for the payment of their debts, then officers could not live, upon which Booth, finding him to be an ignorant fellow, did not ask him any more questions concerning so important a subject. He proceeded to tell Mr. Booth, that they had a poor tradefman there, who had lost some money, by neglecting to infure his goods, and he had a wife and five children fo ragged, that they seemed more proper to be sent to the house of correction than to the workhouse. They often came after their father, but as they were such miserable objects, he had ordered his

L 3   followers.

followers to deny them admittance, left they should bring a dishonour on his house.

In the mean time Serjeant Atkinson having left the ladies, Amelia, with Mrs. Ellison and Mrs. Atkinson, went to see Booth's children, who were drowned in tears, and the artful Mrs. Ellison desiring Amelia to compose herself, told her that her husband was arrested for debts to the amount of five hundred pounds, but if she would go with her to the masquerade, she would make every thing easy; she would either give bail herself, or get another person to pay the money.

Amelia had heard such a character of that lady from Mrs. Atkinson, that she told her she would not hesitate one moment in giving her an answer, which was that should her poor husband die in misery, she would preserve her innocence to the last. · Mrs. Atkinson, who heard all that passed, told Amelia to beware of a masquerade ticket, with which to her ruin she had been once honoured herself, upon which Mrs. Ellison looking upon them with the utmost indignation, went out of the house, declaring that she would never after come back to the place.

Soon after Mrs. Ellison was gone, Colonel James arrived, and having heard of Mr. Booth's misfortunes, insisted on Amelia's accepting of a bank-bill of fifty pounds to supply the immediate wants of her husband, telling her at the same time that he would visit them next morning.

Amelia, who thought every person of as condescending a disposition as herself, was not a little shocked when she heard the colonel propose putting off his visit so long, but upon her expostulation with him, he declared that he would

go

go immediately. Amelia told the colonel that Serjeant Atkinson, whom he had formerly known at Gibraltar, was then in the house, and that he would accompany him thither. Atkinson being called, paid his respects to the colonel, and was received with particular marks of respect, after which they set out together, Amelia having first begged of them that they would not stop by the way, but give her an account of her husband as soon as possible. The colonel was all compliance, and honest Atkinson did not hesitate one moment to assist the afflicted.

As soon as Mrs. Atkinson, who was now married to the serjeant, arrived at Amelia's lodgings, she told her what a generous man the colonel was, and endeavoured to perfuade her that there was no doubt he would extricate Mr. Booth out of all his difficulties. This served in some measure to comfort Amelia, whose spirits had been in a great measure sunk in consequence of her misfortunes, and therefore they both sat down together in the most harmonious manner.

In the mean time the colonel and Serjeant Atkinson arrived at the spunging-house, where they found Booth engaged in conversation with the author already mentioned, and after the colonel had given the son of Parnassus a guinea as a subscription, he began to ask Mr. Booth how much the debts amounted to for which he had been arrested. To this question Booth answered that he could not well say how much they amounted to, only that he believed the whole did not exceed four hundred pounds. Upon that the

colonel

colonel told him that all he had to do was to get bail, and for his own part he was ready to be one. Booth was filled with gratitude, but no sooner did the bailiff hear that bail was to be given, than he came into the room, and asked in a surly manner who was to be the other person, because he was obliged to have two. The colonel told him, that as for his own character, it was well known, and he doubted not but Serjeant Atkinson would join with him.

The bailiff, who on the whole acted consistent with the character of all those in the same employment, told the colonel that he knew neither him nor the serjeant, and that he must have time to search the office, left some fresh detainers should be lodged. The serjeant, who could not bear such insolence any longer, told the catchpole that the gentleman was a member of parliament, upon which being terribly frightened, he begged pardon for what he had said, declaring at the same time that he had no intention to give his honour any offence. Upon that the colonel having expressed the utmost desire to serve Mr. Booth, took his leave for the night, promising at the same time to call on Amelia, and in the mean time left the serjeant along with him.

When the colonel arrived at Amelia's lodgings he found her in company with Mrs. Atkinson's, and said every thing he could to comfort her, telling her that her husband would be set at liberty next day. Amelia seemed to be as easy as the nature of her circumstances would permit, but still she declared that the night in which her husband was in a state of confinement, would be the most grievous to her that ever she had known since

she

she was born. The colonel, who was much
pleafed with her company, did not take his leave
till one o'clock in the morning, and when he was
gone, Mrs. Atkinſon told Amelia that ſhe was
ſure he had a defign on her virtue. This was
what Amelia could not form the leaſt notion of,
for ſhe was ſure that if he had the leaſt regard for
her husband, he would never ſeek to injure her.
The other, however, after asking her a few
queſtions, cautioned her to be upon her guard,
for from the whole of the colonel's behaviour,
ſhe was convinced that he was in love with her,
and would leave nothing undone to promote her
ruin. At that inſtant, the ſerjeant arrived, and
Amelia having received from him the moſt ſatiſ-
factory account of her husband, took leave of her
two viſitors, and with a mind filled with ſerenity,
addreſſed herſelf to the Supreme Being, and then
retired to bed.

The colonel ſpent the whole night on his bed,
tortured with envy and luſt. Envy, that Booth
ſhould enjoy ſuch a fine woman as Amelia, and
luſt, to ſeduce her to his lewd embraces. In the
morning Serjeant Atkinſon came to inform him,
that he had procured a reputable houſe-keeper to
be bail along with him, to whom he had, by his
wife's conſent, given a bill of indemnification.
The ſerjeant, however, did not find the colonel
ſo ready to go as he expected, for he told him that
he did not think proper to give encouragement to
ſubaltern officers, who without a ſhilling in their
pockets, would marry ladies of quality, while at
the ſame time they knew not in what manner
they were to ſupport them. He then took leave
of the ſerjeant in the moſt haſty manner, telling

him

him that he would be ready to ferve him, but he muft excufe him, if he could not, 'confiftent with his honour, become bail for a young fellow who had acted in fuch an imprudent manner.

The honeft ferjeant was obliged to retire, and having communicated the difmal news to Amelia, fhe propofed that moment going to vifit her husband, and Mr. Atkinfon propofed going along with her. Juft as they had dreffed themfelves, Mrs. James came up to the door, and being ufhered in, made the ftrongeft profeffions of friend-fhip to Amelia, promifing to do all that lay in her power to extricate her out of her difficulties, and then fhe took her leave. Mrs. Atkinfon, who had fome fufpicions of the colonel's lady, told Amelia that fhe did not like her, for fhe feemed to be a bawd for her husband.

In the mean time Mr. Booth fpent his time in the fpunging-houfe in a very difagreeable manner, for the bailiff, who was a difgrace to human nature, told him, that unlefs he would drink, he would immediately commit him to Newgate. Booth, who could not bear fuch infolence, knock-ed him down, upon which he called two of his followers, but at that inftant the honeft ferjeant arriving, laid one of them fprawling on the floor, while Booth knocked down the other. The bailiff then called out a refcue; to which the ferjeant anfwered, no refcue was intended, and then an attorney, with Colonel James and another perfon, and Dr. Harrifon came into the room.

The bailiff no fooner faw the attorney, than he began to draw in his horns, for he had had many jobs from him before, but as for the reft of the gentlemen he knew nothing of them. Dr.

Harrifon

Harrifon told Mr. Booth, that he did not expect
to meet him in fuch a place, to which the other
anfwered, that fpunging-houfs were the moft
proper places for people to meet their friends,
becaufe they were fure of finding them there.
Poor Booth could fay no more than that he did
not expect to have been fent there by fo worthy
a gentleman as himfelf, to which Dr. Harrifon
anfwered, that the attorney, Mr. Murphy, who
had taken out the writ againft him was there,
and that he would do every thing confiftent
with the duty of his profeffion. Proper bail
having been given, Mr. Booth was accofted by
the bailiff, who wanted fome civility-money, as
they call it in fpunging-houfes, but Mr. Booth
declared that he had been fo ill ufed that he
would not pay one farthing. Murphy, the attorney, faid all he could to induce him to comply, but to no purpofe, and Dr. Harrifon being
called in as an arbitrator between the two contending parties, declared that Mr. Booth did
right, for what reafon in the world could there
be for men who acted in fuch an inhuman manner to expect a gratification from thofe unhappy
perfons over whom they had domineered, and
whofe miferies they had ridiculed in fuch a way
as was fhocking to be mentioned whc a civil
government exifted, or where there was a perfon
living who deferved the name of a Chriftian.

It is neceffary to inform the reader, that when
Dr. Harrifon arrived in England, he went to
his parfonage-houfe, and found that Mr. Booth
had deferted it, upon which, enquiring the caufe,
he was informed by the curate's wife that he had
fet up a carriage, and that he had fpent his mo-
ney-

ney in the moſt extravagant manner. This naturally brought him to London, where he ſoon
found out Booth's lodgings, and going into the
room one evening while the poor lieutenant was
taking a walk in the park, he ſaw a gold watch
that had been given to one of the children by
the noble lord already mentioned. This confirmed him in his ſuſpicions of the extravagance
of thoſe whom he intended to ſupport, and
meeting with Mr. Murphy the attorney, that
gentleman perſuaded him to take out a writ
againſt Mr. Booth, contrary to his natural diſpoſition, which was all humanity and compaſſion.

He was not, however, eaſy in his mind, he
wiſhed well to Booth, and he had ſome doubts
whether he would act in ſuch an imprudent
manner, unleſs there was ſome reaſon to be aſ-
ſigned for it. Ruminating on theſe thoughts he
accidentally met with ſerjeant Atkinſon; on
the morning after Booth was arreſted, and taking him into a coffee-houſe was informed of the
whole affair, upon which the doctor deſired by
any means whatever to be conducted to Amelia,
whom he ſtill looked upon as virtuous.

The doctor had no ſooner ſeen the afflicted
mother with her lovely children, than his breaſt
melted into tenderneſs, and he dropped tears of
real compaſſion. He then went with Murphy
to the ſpunging houſe, from whence he releaſed
Booth in the manner we have already mentioned.

When Mr. Booth, with his friends, arrived at
home, they were received in the moſt affectionate

ate manner by Amelia, who had no hopes of feeing her beloved husband fo foon.

Dr. Harrifon was fo much captivated with the children, that he could not help playing with them, and taking the little boy on his knees, asked him if he would forgive him for taking his pappa to prifon. The child anfwered him, that his mother had taught him to forgive his enemies, but he would never forgive thofe who took his pappa away from him.

While they were difcourfing in this manner, they were interrupted by the arrival of Colonel James, who made a genteel apology for not having come fooner, becaufe he was, as he faid, engaged in bufinefs. He invited Mr. Booth and Dr. Harrifon to dine with him, and then he took his leave in the moft formal manner. As Amelia was invited at the fame time fhe was ftruck with furprize, but, recollecting herfelf, told her husband that fhe did not chufe to go into large companies, becaufe fhe could not enjoy any fort of mirth while her circumftances were in fuch a fluctuating ftate.

To this Mr. Booth anfwered, that had he known that it would have been in the leaft difagreeable to her, he would not have made the propofal; adding at the fame time that he was very well convinced that her objections arofe from the company of Mrs. James, who was to be there at the fame time. Amelia, who was one of the beft women in the world, endeavoured to conceal her real fentiments, and told her husband that fhe had nothing to fay againft Mrs. James, becaufe fhe had always behaved to her like a gentlewoman, and therefore fhe was

willing

willing to accompany her husband to any place he should desire. In a word, she resolved to go to the place according to her husband's desire, and for the present every thing was settled between them in the most amicable manner.

During the entertainment, Amelia behaved with the utmost decency, and, after it was over, she returned with her husband home to her children, and next morning Mr. Booth told his spouse that Colonel James had laid him under so many obligations, that he did not know in what manner to repay them. This news was not altogether agreeable to Amelia, in consequence of the suspicions that had been hinted to her by Mrs. Atkinson, but out of real compassion to her husband she dissembled her real sentiments, endeavouring to draw a veil over every thing that had been done by the colonel.

A short dispute arose concerning the merits of the colonel, and before it was decided, the doctor arrived, whose presence gave no small pleasure to Amelia, who wished for nothing so much as the company of so good a man. The doctor hearing the nature of their dispute, interfered between them, and delivered his opinion consistent with the nature of good sense, upon which both parties acquiesced, and the rest of the evening was spent in the most amicable manner.

Serjeant Atkinson was so much concerned for the happiness of Mr. Booth, that he could not help telling his wife what generous proffers Colonel James had made in his favour, and that he would in a short time be extricated out of all his difficulties. His wife, however, was not of the

the fame opinion, and having told her fufpicions to the ferjeant, he fell into a fort of fleep, and and dreamed that he faw the colonel ftanding by the bedfide of Amelia, with a drawn fword in his hand.

The thoughts of his beloved miftrefs being in danger, rouzed him fo much, that in the midft of his dream he got up, and catching his wife by the throat, declared that he would that moment punifh her as a murderer, for he believ- ed that fhe was the individual Colonel James, whom he imagined had attempted the chaftity of Amelia. His wife fcreamed out, which brought the ferjeant to himfelf, and Mr. Booth and his lady came up to their affiftance, in or- der to know what was the matter; but how great was their furprife, when they faw the bed all covered over, as if it had been fprinkled with blood.

Atkinfon, who doubted not but he had killed his wife, declared the whole truth, but upon en- quiry it was found, that there was no blood in the cafe, but only that a bottle of cherry brandy had been fpilt, which Mrs. Atkinfon always kept befide her, as an immediate cordial for a lownefs of fpirits, or any thing elfe. Here things being adjufted the parties' retired to reft, and nothing more important happened till next morning.

Mr. Booth, who was extremely uneafy, fent for the ferjeant after breakfaft, and afked him what he meant by making ufe of Colonel James's name, upon which Atkinfon told him, that he dreamt that he faw the colonel in his lady's

chamber

chamber, attempting to ravish her; and that had occafioned all the difturbance.

Mr. Booth, whofe paffions were all on flame, afked him if he heard of any thing done by the colonel that was of a difhonourable nature, and particularly whether he had attempted the chafti-ty of his wife. In anfwer to this, Atkinfon told him, that he had no great opinion of the colo-nel becaufe he had traduced the character of his wife, not knowing that they were married, and that if his ftation in the army had not fet him above him, he would have cut off both his ears. He then related to him the manner in which the colonel behaved, when he went to folicit him to be one of his bail; but infifted that he would not refent the injury. Booth promifed that he would not, and taking leave of each other, Booth returned to vifit his Amelia and the children. His lady received him in the moft complaifant manner; but her difcernment was fo great, that fhe could not help feeing that he was in a more than ordinary manner affected, but her good fenfe enabled her to humour him in the fame manner as every woman of good fenfe will al-ways do her husband.

Next morning Mrs. James came to pay them a vifit in her ufual gay manner, and told Mr. Booth that fhe would do any thing in her power in order to procure him a commiffion in a regi-ment on the Englifh eftablifhment. This fhe did, according to her own account, to oblige her dear friend Amelia, and, after feveral formalities fhe took her leave. Indeed Amelia had no great opinion of the profeffions made by Mrs. James, fhe began to confider her as no better than the colonel

colonel himfelf, and therefore fhe told her hufband not to place any confidence, in what fhe
faid.

The confufion and hurry had prevented Mr.
Booth and Amelia from waiting on their good
friend, Dr. Harrifon, according to appointment,
but at laft having recollected, they went to his
lodgings, and found him in clofe converfation
with a country gentlewoman and his fon. Booth
made feveral apologies for not meeting the doctor
fooner, but the good old gentleman interrupted
him by telling him that he would hear none of
his ftories.

Booth, who was all compliance, told the doctor that he would dine with him, and after dinner was over, the doctor told them that he would
take them to court, which was no other than St.
James's church, where they would hear the fervice of the church read, which was preferable to
all the gaities of this world.

From the church they proceede' to Vauxhall,
along with the children, and Dr. Harrifon did
every thing he could to make them as agreeable
as poffible. He treated the children with cakes,
and ordered ham and fowls to be brought for
Amelia; fo extenfive, fo benevolent, is goodnefs
when it happens to take a proper turn. It is
true, fome of the bloods who happened at that
time to be walking in the gardens, offered fome
indecencies to Amelia, but fhe took no further
notice of them, fave that of treating them with
the utmoft difdain. Dr. Harrifon faid fome few
words to fhew that they could not be gentlemen,
for no gentleman will ever treat a woman with
difrefpect, let her ftation be what it will.

When

When the entertainments were over, they returned home, and next day, while Dr. Harrifon
was difcourfing with a young gentleman, who
had lately entered into holy orders, he, received
a note from Amelia, telling him, that fomething of fo much importance had happened to
her, that fhe was under the neceffity of feeing
him as foon as poffible. As the doctor doubted
not but there was fome other writ in the cafe,
he made as handfome an apology as he could,
and then fet out to vifit Amelia, at her lodgings.
Ever compaffionate, he attended to the diftreffes
of his fellow-creatures, and by him imprudence
was never conftrued into a crime. He knew
the frailty of human nature, and as a man of
real benevolence, he refolved to do as he would
be done by, or, in other words, to vifit the afflicted, and give them all he could to comfort
them.

When the doctor arrived, he afked in the moft
tender and affectionate manner what Amelia
wanted with him, upon which fhe told him
that fhe had received two tickets for the mafquerade, but was determined not to go to it without his confent. The doctor was not long in
telling her his opinion, that he could not by any
means give his confent for her going there, becaufe it might injure her character, for in his
opinion, no modeft woman would be feen in
fuch places. In the mean time, while the doctor was converfing with Amelia Mrs. Atkinfon
came in ; a learned difpute enfued between her
and the doctor, concerning the merits of the
claffic authors, and the doctor was utterly fur-
prized to find a woman fo well acquainted with
the

the Greek and Latin languages. Both differed
in their opinions, and high words began to arife,
till Booth and his friend came in, and put an
end to the controverfy.

Amelia, notwithftanding the refpect fhe had
for the doctor, yet could not help complying
with her husband's requeft of going to the opera,
and, accordingly when the day came, they
arrived at the Hay-market, about eleven in the
evening.

They had not been long there when by the difference of their dreffes they foon loft each other,
and feveral commical fcenes enfued, while Booth
who was all impatience, went in queft of his
wife. The different farcafms that were thrown
out upon him are too ridiculous to be mentioned; but as nothing ferious happened, they all
returned home about five in the morning, an
hour when the virtuous are drowned in the
arms of balmy fleep, while the profligate is
fpending his time in riot and debauchery.

It has been already mentioned that Amelia
was at the mafquerade, but the truth is, fhe was
no farther than the door, and there gave her
ticket to Mrs. Atkinfon, who refembled her
both in ftature and voice. Booth, who had
taken particular notice of the drefs his wife had
on, followed Mrs. Atkinfon from one place to
another, and at laft faw her in converfation with
the noble lord already mentioned in the courfe
of thefe memoirs.

Booth was really jealous when, as he thought,
he faw his wife in company with a nobleman,
whofe character was none of the beft; and,
therefore returning home in a great rage, he
found

found his Amelia engaged in the nurfery with her children. She asked him to have fomething for fupper, but he told her he would not eat any, which grieved her fo much that fhe could not help asking him the reafon. He told her that he wifhed fhe had not gone to the mafquerade, upon which fhe affured him that fhe had not been there, and Mrs. Atkinfon coming in at the fame time, unravelled the whole myftery, by telling Mr. Booth that fhe had been fubftituted in the place of his wife.

Dr. Harrifon, with his ufual good nature, had projected this fcheme, and therefore he came next morning to enquire how the different parties had behaved. He asked for his child, for fo he called Amelia, and finding her well, embraced her with the utmoft tendernefs. He then told Booth that he hoped he would never more infift on her going to fuch places of diffipation, but fuffer her to remain at home to mind her own bufinefs, and take care of her family. Booth declared that he was very fenfible of his error, and that fo far from asking his wife to go to another mafquerade, he would never, as long as he lived, be feen at one himfelf.

The doctor highly approved of his refolution, and told him that while he perfevered in thefe fentiments, he would be fure to find him his fincere friend. After this converfation was over, the doctor took his leave, having promifed to fet out next day for the country, with his friend, who had a fon, for whom he had purchafed a living in the church.

Next day Mr. Booth took a walk to the park, where he met with major Bath, and asked him
feveral

feveral queftions concerning colonel James, for Booth was convinced that the colonel had fome defign on the chaftity of his wife. While he was in converfation with the major, Lieutenant Trent came up, and Booth, who had ferved along with him in the fame regiment, invited him home to his lodgings to fup with him. Trent, however, though his pockets were not over full of money, declined accepting of the invitation, and perhaps for this reafon, that he did not chufe to expofe his poverty.

Amelia, who had provided fome boiled mutton for her husbands fupper, waited for him with the utmoft impatience, but there being no appearance of him, fhe fat down with the children, and ordering the maid to wait for her mafter, went to bed, though fhe enjoyed no fleep.

About two o'clock in the morning Booth arrived, and, without fpeaking one word went to bed to his wife, and flept in her arms till next morning, and when he awoke, fhe could not help taking notice that fomething more than ordinary had happened to him. He told her it was true for he had loft his money at play, upon which fhe told him that the whole fhe had in her pocket was not worth the mentioning, and only begged that for the future, he would be more prudent. Booth was fo much overpowered by the goodnefs of his wife, that he embraced her a hundred times, and then told her that the doctor had informed him of a letter that had been fent to her by Colonel James, and that he was determined to have fatisfaction. Amelia was much frightened left any dangerous confequences fhould have enfued,

enfued, and therefore begged that he would take
no more notice of it.

Booth, who was eafily reconciled when favourable arguments were offered, foon became
more cool, and made his wife eafy, by telling
her, that he would not think any more of it;
and in the mean time, foon after breakfaft, his
old friend, Mr. Booth, came to call on him.
As Booth owed Trent fome money, the former
could not help thinking that the other had
come to demand it, and as he had it not in his
power to pay him, he was extremely uneafy.

After fome words they went to a tavern,
where they got once more to gaming, but as
Booth took care of his money, Trent confidered him as a filly fellow, who had no fpirit,
and the other began to confider him as a fcoundrel.

We will now return to Amelia, who, during the time that her husband was out, received
a letter from an unknown hand, containing profeffions of love, and the moft earneft folicitations
to fuffer him to vifit her, fhe had fcarce ftrength
to read to the end, when her trembling grew fo
violent, that fhe dropped the letter, and had probably dropped herfelf, had not Mrs. Atkinfon
come to her affiftance. Mrs. Atkinfon, in fome
furprize, asked her the meaning of her fright,
and being told that fhe had received a moft
odious letter; upon which Mrs. Atkinfon taking it up, and having read it, fell a dancing
about the room as if fhe had been mad.

Amelia could not tell what to make of her,
and asking her the reafon, was told, that the
letter was from the noble lord already mentioned,

tioned, and that it contained a commiſſion for her husband Serjeant Atkinſon. The fact was thus: while Mrs. Atkinſon was at the maſquerade, the noble lord, who took her for Amelia, came up to her, and ſhe embraced that opportunity of ſoliciting a commiſſion for the honeſt ſerjeant. His lordſhip, who would have ſooner ſeen the ſerjeant hanged than have granted him any ſuch favour, unleſs there had been a lady in the caſe, thought he had now a favourable opportunity of triumphing over the virtue of Amelia, and there-fore he went immediately to the miniſter and pro-cured the commiſſion.

Amelia was ſo much vexed at hearing that Mrs. Atkinſon had made uſe of her name, that ſhe could not help teſtifying her reſentment, upon which Mrs. Atkinſon flew into a moſt violent paſſion, and told Amelia, that her husband was now a gentleman, and ſhe did not value her.

She ſpoke theſe words with ſo loud a voice, that Atkinſon, who happened to be going up ſtairs, heard them, and being ſurpriſed at the angry tone of his wife's voice, he entered the room, and with a look of much aſtoniſhment, begged to know what was the matter. Mrs. Atkinſon told him that there was nothing more the matter, but only that ſhe had procured him a commiſſion, and Amelia was angry with her for doing ſo. It is certain Amelia did not deſerve ſuch uſage, but Mrs. Atkinſon, partly by drinking too much, and partly by the flurry of ſpirits ſhe was in, could ſet no bounds to her paſſion.

Mr. Booth, who had knocked gently at the door, leſt he ſhould diſturb his wife, came up

ſtairs

stairs just when the ladies were in the heat of the argument, and seeing Amelia in tears, demanded to know what was the matter.

Atkinson answered, " upon my honour, Sir, I know not what is the matter, but I am afraid some words have happened between madam and my wife, but I know no more of it than your honour." Booth having embraced his wife, demanded to know who had caused those tears to flow from her lovely eyes, wishing at the same time that as many drops of blood might be brought from their hearts. Amelia held him fast, and said all she could to pacify him, but Booth turning to the serjeant, ordered him to take the wretch, his wife, out of the house. The poor serjeant, who was extremely sorry for what had happened, and entirely innocent, was going to desire his wife to retire, but she saved him the trouble, and told him that she would never more acknowledge him for her husband. Mr. Booth and his lady sat down, and Amelia explained to him the whole affair, at the same time obtaining his promise, that he would not send a challenge to his lordship, but suffer the whole to sink into the utmost oblivion ; they then determined to remove from the house that same day, and accordingly took lodgings within a few doors of their worthy friend, Dr. Harrison.

Next day, after they had taken possession of their new lodgings, Mr. Booth took a walk into the park, where he met a brother officer who had served along with him at Gibraltar, but was then on half-pay with a wife and three children almost starving. He asked Booth to lend him half a crown, but poor Booth, who had not one penny,

in

in his pocket, told him if he would go home and dine with him, he would lend him double the sum out of his wife's pocket. The poor officer complied, and going home with Booth, received ten shillings, and went directly to purchase a joint of meat for his family.

Amelia, as soon as the officer was gone, asked her husband who he was, and was answered, that he had received an ensign's commission from the duke of Marlborough, but after thirty years service had retired on half-pay, because he had seen a vast number of boys preferred over him. The tender-hearted Amelia was so much affected, that she exclaimed, she did not believe our great men were human creatures. Booth answered, that he was much of the same opinion, but then he could not believe that there was any such thing in the world as virtue and vice. Amelia had for some time beheld with concern that her husband was, in consequence of his many afflictions, seduced from the belief of divine revelation, but she did not push on the subject, intending to get Dr. Harrison to talk to him.

Dr. Harrison, who never lost sight of the interests of poor Booth, went to a nobleman while he was in the country, and solicited his lordship's assistance for a commission on full pay for that unfortunate gentleman. His lordship was no stranger to the great merit of the worthy doctor, and therefore told him he would serve him to the utmost of his power, upon condition he would give him his assistance in the election of a mayor for a borough that lay in his parish. The doctor having enquired the name of the can-

M   didate

didate whom his lordſhip ſupported, told him in
the moſt honeſt blunt manner, that he could not
ſerve him, becauſe he had given his promiſe to
another, who was a gentleman of the ſtricteſt
integrity. His lordſhip; who did not think that
any man could deny him a favour, eſpecially
while ſoliciting for another, anſwered, that he
was ſorry he could not ſerve him. This anſwer
brought on a long diſſertation on the difference
between private and public virtue, the doctor
maintaining that they ſhould go hand in hand
together, while the peer inſiſted, that no miniſter
of ſtate was obliged either to keep his promiſe, or
pay the leaſt regard to moral honeſty. They
ſoon after parted, his lordſhip to attend the
election, and the doctor to enjoy what is worth a
thouſand places, namely, the ſmiles of a good
conſcience.

In the mean time Trent, the lieutenant, ſent
a letter to Mr. Booth, demanding a ſmall ſum of
money that he had lent him, but alas ! there was
no poſſibility of paying it ; though conſcious that
he had loſt the money at play, yet he would not
conceal his imprudence from his wife, but laid
the whole affair open to her. Amelia caſt a ſympathiſing look on her children, and dropped a tear
but turning to her husband, begged that he would
not make himſelf uneaſy, which laſt expreſſion
was ſo ſhocking to Booth, who was overcome
by her good nature, that he went out in order to
wait on a gentleman who belonged to the war-
office. Amelia having packed up all the valuable
things ſhe had left, called a coach, and ſet out
for the houſe of a uſurer, where ſhe procured the
ſum ſhe wanted, and then returned home.

Booth

Booth, though a tender father, and not infen-
fible of the mifery to which his conduct had reduced his children, yet was extremely glad that
he had it in his power to pay Trent, and accordingly fet out for his lodgings the fame night, but
did not find him at home. Refolving therefore
to return next morning, he took a walk to the
park, where he met with the old officer, to whom
he had lent ten fhillings, and both went to drink
a bottle of wine together. While they were over
the bottle, Booth informed his friend, that he
could procure a commiffion, upon condition that
he had fifty pounds to make a prefent of to a gentleman in the war-office, but although he had fo
much money in his pocket, yet it was not his
own, for he was obliged to pay it to Trent. His
friend, who had no more prudence than himfelf,
propofed by all means that he fhould make the
great man a prefent of the money, as it would
procure him a fubfiftence, adding, that there
was not the leaft doubt but Trent would wait for
it till he could pay him. Booth, overcome by
his arguments, returned home, refolving to comply with his friend's requeft next morning, contrary to prudence, and even common fenfe.

In the morning, Booth communicated his intentions to Amelia, asking her advice, but fhe
told him fhe would not advife him to any fuch
meafure, as he was much better acquainted with
thofe things than herfelf. While they were talking over the matter, the old officer came in, and
Booth fet out with him to the office, who received the money without the leaft hefitation.
Promifes went about in plenty, and Booth, on
his return home, found Mrs. James in company

with his wife. That lady had come to invite her to dinner, but Amelia frankly told her that she had been obliged to pawn the greatest part of her cloaths, and her servant maid moved off with the rest, so that she had no other shift besides the one that was on her back. Mrs. James hearing this, took her leave with great expressions of concern; but the truth is, all her concern was confined to words. Booth declared, that he would go that moment in quest of the girl, which he did, and in the mean time Mrs. Atkinson came in all pale and lifeless. Amelia was affected to see her in such a condition, and forgetting every thing that had happened, asked her what was the matter.

It seems Mr. Atkinson had been so much affected with the dispute that had happened between his wife and Amelia, that he went home and drank a whole bottle of brandy, which threw him into a violent fever, and he was given over by the physician who attended him. He begged to see Amelia, which request her good nature would not suffer her to deny, and therefore she went to his bed-chamber, where she found him seemingly in a dying condition. He told her he had stolen her picture when he was only eighteen years of age, but now he was ready to restore it, and begged leave to kiss her hand; Amelia indulged him, and shedding a tear took her leave in the most affectionate maner.

Booth had succeeded so far as to discover where the girl was who had stolen his wife's linen, but as he would not swear that it was worth forty shillings, the justice before whom she was taken, was obliged to discharge her; upon

upon which he returned home to his wife, who had received a letter from Mrs. Atkinson, intimating that her husband was, to all appearance, out of danger; a circumstance that gave Amelia no small pleasure. She had provided a genteel supper for him, in consequence of a present that she had received from an unknown hand; but poor Booth told her that he was obliged to go out a few hours.

Amelia, who was all condescension, made no objections to his proposal, but waited for him till the clock struck eleven, when a person brought a letter, informing her that he was at supper with Miss Matthews. She had scarce time to peruse the odious epistle, when a porter brought a letter to inform her, that he was once more in the spunging-house in Gray's Inn Lane.

It seems Miss Matthews had been at the bottom of all this, and poor Booth had been innocently led into the snare, but next morning he was visited by Amelia, who sympathized with him in the most tender manner. When she came to the spunging-house, the wife of the bailiff told her that she believed her to be a woman of the town; but Amelia telling her that her husband had been there before, and that as he was now a prisoner, so she was come to see him. She was suffered to go up stairs to speak with him. Booth, who was sensible of his wife's goodness, embraced her in the most tender manner, and told her of the unhappy connection he had had with Miss Matthews, while he was in prison, begging at the same time that she would forgive him. In answer to that she told him,

. M 3 . that

that she had forgiven him already, and pulling
a letter out of his pocket, presented it to him,
by which he was convinced that she was no
stranger to their amour, and then a very tender
scene ensued, for it was not in the nature of
Amelia to find fault with her husband.

Amelia, who heard that Dr. Harrison was to
be that day in town, set out for his lodgings,
but as good luck would have it, she first called
to see her children, and found the good doctor
along with them, for he had been directed to
her lodgings by Mrs. Atkinson. Seeing her in
confusion, the good man asked her, what was
the matter, upon which she told him that her
husband was once more arrested. The doctor
having asked her at whose suit, she told him,
at the suit of Captain Trent, for money lent at
a gaming table, which grieved the good man so
much, that he told her he would do no more
for him. The poor afflicted lady shed tears, but
the doctor looking at the children desired her to
make herself easy, as he would send them and
her down to his parsonage house, there to remain till he could see what could be done for
her husband. Amelia implored a thousand blessings on the worthy doctor, but told him at the
same time, that Colonel James had sent him a
challenge, and that she was afraid of the consequences that might happen.

The doctor desired her to make herself perfectly easy, as he would endeavour to make up all
differences between them, and taking his leave,
set out for the spunging-house, but in his way
thither called on Colonel James, whom he
found in company with Major Bath. A long
conversation

conversation enfued with refpect to the conduct of Colonel James, and the nature of duelling, but the good doctor fpoke in fuch a rational manner; that neither of the officers had one word, to fay, except fuch as came within the circle of abufe.

The doctor having fpent about an hour with them, fet out to the fpunging-houfe to vifit Booth, whom he found in much the fame condition as all others are, whofe misfortunes brings them into the fame unhappy circumftances. The doctor had actually not fo much money in town as would pay Booth's debt, and therefore he propofed giving bail, which could not be done without a fecond perfon, whom the attorney promifed to procure. While the attorney was gone, the bailiff came into the room, and told Dr. Harrifon, that there was a man above ftairs in a dying condition, who wanted to fpeak to him. The doctor did not hefitate one moment, but leaving Booth, went directly to the miferable place where the perfon was in bed. This perfon was one Robinfon, a man of a very loofe character, who had been arrefted for a fmall fum, and the bailiff's follower had wounded him in fuch a manner, while they were executing the writ, that there was not the leaft hopes of his recovery. He asked the doctor whether a death-bed repentance was in the leaft efficacious towards procuring acceptance with God, and being told that repentance never come too late, if it was fincere, he difcovered that one Murphy, an attorney, had employed him to be witnefs to a deed of conveyance, from one perfon to another, in a fraudulent manner, and that the injured

jured perſon was Amelia. He added that he
and one Carter, who was then dead, had received from Murphy two hundred pounds each,
but how much Murphy received he could not
ſay.

Before the doƈtor had time to ask Robinſon
any more queſtions, the ſurgeon arrived who
was to dreſs the patients wounds, and a dialogue enſued between him and the divine. The
reſult was, that Dr. Harriſon perceived him to be
a moſt ignorant fellow, no ways acquainted
with the nature of his profeſſion, but puffed up
with an opinion of his own ſelf-ſuperiority to
ſuch a degree, that he looked on all thoſe who
called his knowledge in queſtion with the utmoſt
contempt.

In the mean time Murphy, the attorney, arrived with the other perſon who was to-be bail
along with Dr. Harriſon, but hearing that the
doƈtor was up ſtairs along with Robinſon, he
took to his heels and ran out into the ſtreet,
Dr. Harriſon, who had heard his voice, ran after him, and called out ſtop thief, upon which
he was ſurrounded by a great mob of people,
who imagined that the purſuer was a bailiff.
The doƈtor, however ſoon undeceived them, by
telling them that the fellow had committed for-
gery, and in conſequence of that crime had ruined an innocent family.

He was then conduƈted before a juſtice, who
gave a warrant to ſearch his chambers, and in
them were found the whole title deeds of the eſtate, which had been left to Amelia by her mother. The juſtice immediately committed him
to

to prifon, where he remained till next feffions, when he was hanged ; and, upon the whole it appeared that the fifter of Amelia, affifted by Murphy, had acted in fuch a manner as to get a forged will, which was now fet afide.

Mifs Harris, the fifter of Amelia, abfconded, and Mrs. Booth took poffeffion of her fortune to the no fmall pleafure of the tenants, who loved Amelia, but hated her fifter. Robinfon, who was the only perfon who could give pofitive evidence againft Murphy feemed for fome time to think of reforming his life ; but he was too much habituated to the practice of vice ever to leave its dangerous paths. Accordingly, being difcarded by all thofe who had known him formerly, and at the fame time being reduced to neceffitous circumftances, he took to the highway, and was hanged for a robbery.

Colonel James, who had never lived on good terms with his lady, agreed to feperate from her, and took into keeping the celebrated Mifs Matthews, whofe adventures have made fuch a confiderable figure in this hiftory.

Mifs Harrifon, was obliged to go over to France, where fhe was fupported by the bounty of her compaffionate fifter, Amelia, to whom fhe had been fo inveterate an enemy. While Dr. Harrifon grew old in piety as well as years, and paid the debt of nature, beloved and lamented.

Mr. Atkinfon ftill lived on good terms with his wife, though her learning was fuch as often put him to the blufh, but at laft he rofe to high command in the army. As to Booth and Amelia, they lived together in all the happinefs that
could

could be imagined, the one to be an honour to his country, and the other an ornament to her sex. Amelia was a fine woman to the last, and her husband saw in her a thousand charms that he could not discover in any other. He was returned a member of parliament, and without regard to the ministry on one hand, or mock-patriotism on the other, he supported the dignity of his station and the interest of his country, so as to leave behind him a lasting memorial of his integrity.

THE END.